D0746477

Aiding the

(Stonefire Dragons #9)

Jessie Donovan

This book is a work of fiction. Names, characters, places, and incidents are either the product of the writer's imagination or are used fictitiously, and any resemblance to actual persons, living or dead, business establishments, events, or locales is entirely coincidental.

Aiding the Dragon
Copyright © 2017 Laura Hoak-Kagey
Mythical Lake Press, LLC
First Edition

All rights reserved. This book or any portion thereof may not be reproduced or used in any manner without the express written permission of the author except for the use of brief quotations in a book review.

Cover Art by Clarissa Yeo of Yocla Designs.

ISBN 13: 978-1942211525

Other Books by Jessie Donovan

Stonefire Dragons

Sacrificed to the Dragon
Seducing the Dragon
Revealing the Dragons
Healed by the Dragon
Reawakening the Dragon
Loved by the Dragon
Surrendering to the Dragon
Cured by the Dragon
Aiding the Dragon

Lochguard Highland Dragons

The Dragon's Dilemma
The Dragon Guardian
The Dragon's Heart
The Dragon Warrior

Kelderan Runic Warriors

The Conquest
The Barren (Aug 2017)

Asylums for Magical Threats

Blaze of Secrets
Frozen Desires
Shadow of Temptation
Flare of Promise

Cascade Shifters

Convincing the Cougar
Reclaiming the Wolf
Cougar's First Christmas
Resisting the Cougar

Chapter One

Aaron Caruso of Clan Stonefire stared at the old metal gate of Clan Glenlough's lands and resisted the urge to flip off the security camera watching him. He'd done the bloody ridiculous knock they'd asked of him. And yet, ten minutes later, he was still standing in the rain.

At least it was summer, so he wouldn't bloody freeze. Not that the Irish summer was any better than one back home, in the north of England.

His dragon spoke up. *Forget about the weather. We will see* her *soon.*

Not even dropping me in a vat of poisonous snakes will get me to kiss her, dragon. So, shut it.

This isn't Italy. Teagan is different.

Teagan O'Shea was the Irish leader of Clan Glenlough. *I learned my lesson about females. Maybe in ten years, I'll change my view. But for now, they're more trouble than they're worth.*

Try telling that to our mum.

Stop with the logic. Of course Mum is different.

The metal gate screeched as it opened slowly. In a few seconds, it revealed the form of a young male with red hair and the softness of late adolescence. Aaron added, *Great. They sent us a child. So much for a diplomatic welcome.*

The boy's lilting accent prevented his dragon from replying. "Sorry for the delay. Matters came up."

Aaron grunted. "Fine. Can we get out of the rain now?"

The boy raised an eyebrow. "They mentioned how cloudy weather made you tetchy. Odd, given where you're from."

Great to know the Irish clan was already talking about him. He forced his voice to be polite. "If you don't mind, I'd like to come inside and talk with your clan leader."

"Follow me, then."

As Aaron walked past the gate, he noticed few people walking about. The only other time he'd set foot on Glenlough, it had been night and pitch-black. Not even the cottages had had lights shining in the windows.

While he did spot movement behind the curtains of a few homes, he had the feeling everyone had retreated to merely watch what he would do. Aaron was starting to think he should've delayed his trip a few extra days to find a replacement for his usual Protector partner, Quinn Summers. Quinn's mate going into labor had been bad timing.

His beast sighed. *As if she had control over that.*

I'm starting to think she did. Vivian never wanted Quinn to go to Ireland for weeks on end.

Vivian is another good female example. You paint with too broad a brush.

Aaron mentally sighed. *Decent ones exist, but just not romantically for me. Accept it.*

It doesn't have to be romance. Just a kiss or two would be enough.

Not dignifying his dragon with a response, Aaron caught up to the boy. "Am I still not going to get a hint about why I'm here?"

The male shook his head. "It's not my place. Teagan will tell you."

At the name of Glenlough's female leader, his dragon perked up. *Good. So we will have a meeting with her.*

It's probably the only one, so don't get your hopes up.

I still say we should find ways to see her again. If you pushed aside your bitterness, you'd see what I see.

What? And have another female use me and toss me away like Nerina did?

She fooled you, not me. That's why you should listen this time.

Not wanting to deal with an arguing dragon, Aaron constructed a mental prison and tossed him inside. Aaron sighed in relief when his beast's roars weren't more than a murmur. Maybe now he could get some bloody work done.

Because no matter what his beast wanted, there was no fucking way Aaron was going to kiss Teagan O'Shea. Females were off the table for the next few years. His time was better spent eradicating threats and making his clan safe.

Or, as his current assignment dictated, ensuring the Irish clan's safety.

As they finally walked away from the area packed with cottages, the large, looming shape of an old castle came into view. From his previous visit, he knew it was their great hall. In daylight, he could better see the stones making up the walls as well as the turrets. "I wasn't aware my visit was going to be a clan-wide issue."

"It isn't," the teenager merely stated, a note of finality in his voice.

The male might be young, but he was dedicated. Aaron didn't think he'd spill any more information, so he merely followed the Irish bloke into the great hall and down a set of stairs. However, instead of turning down a corridor like his last visit, they went down a few more flights of stairs.

When they had to be fairly far underground, the male finally turned down a hallway and stopped at the door at the end. He rapped five times and then left the way he came without another word.

So much for Irish hospitality.

The door opened. Killian O'Shea's tall, dark-haired form filled the doorway. He was Glenlough's head Protector and in charge of clan security. He was also Teagan's younger, but overprotective brother.

Not to mention that since female leaders were viewed as weaker, Killian was the public face of the clan. To most of the world, Killian O'Shea was clan leader.

Killian grunted. "Come in quietly."

His curiosity piqued, Aaron complied. However, the room was empty except for him, Killian, and a table with chairs. There wasn't even a picture on the maroon walls. Aaron opened his mouth to ask what was going on, but Killian's glare silenced him.

Taking a seat, Aaron hoped his assignment with Glenlough was short. He wasn't sure how much longer he could prevent himself from saying what was really on his mind and that wouldn't do since Stonefire and Bram—Stonefire's clan leader—were counting on him to strengthen their alliance with the Irish clan.

He'd just have to focus on the end game of going home and protecting his mother. That would keep him in line, provided his dragon calmed the fuck down. As if to make a point, his beast pounded on the mental walls, but they held.

Aaron tapped his fingers against the table and waited for Teagan to arrive.

~~~

Teagan O'Shea laid a hand on the arm of the elderly female sitting next to her. "Are you sure she's not merely out for an adventure? Sadie has found herself in trouble before for sneaking away."

Eliza Kavanagh shook her head, her short, gray curls bouncing around her face. "My Sadie isn't one to be overly dramatic. If she said she's running away with that male in a note, she's done it."

"I believe you." Teagan kept her voice soft. "Why didn't you tell me of this earlier, right after you found the note?"

Eliza wrung her hands. "I know dalliances with Clan Northcastle are forbidden right now. I didn't want my granddaughter to get in trouble."

Clan Northcastle was the Northern Irish clan near Belfast. The two clans had been at odds for a number of years, and neither one liked matings between the clans because of it.

Teagan stared until the older female met her gaze again. "Eliza, you can always come to me, no matter what. Sadie isn't the first female to fall in love with someone she shouldn't."

Tears trailed down Eliza's face. "I know I should've come. I only hope my delay didn't make things worse. But I'm here now. Is there anything you can do to help my granddaughter?"

In fact, Sadie Kavanagh was the second member of Clan Glenlough to run away with a Northcastle member in the last year or so. While Teagan had been working toward mending relations, it hadn't been soon enough. Her failure had torn apart yet another family.

Her dragon huffed. *We can't fix everything.*
~~~

Perhaps, but this has been a long time coming. I promised our people that I would try to improve relations.

It's not our fault the Northcastle bastard leader is acting like a child, demanding everything without offering something in return.

Not wanting to get into that debate for the hundredth time, Teagan focused on Eliza. "I want you to go with Killian and tell him everything you know, down to the smallest detail. Also, take him to your cottage and help him sort through Sadie's things. There might be a clue somewhere that he can use to tighten the search. If there's a way to find her, my brother will do it."

Eliza sniffed and wiped away her tears. "Okay. Do you think there's a chance she'll come home to me? She's the only family I have left."

Teagan threaded confidence into her voice. "I'm going to do everything in my power to do so, even if it means inviting the Northcastle member to live with us. Don't worry, okay? Sadie is clever enough to stay under the Department of Dragon Affairs' radar."

The DDA was the Irish government's oversight agency for all dragon-shifters in Ireland. Their word was law, although their interference usually caused more headaches than anything else.

Eliza nodded. Teagan squeezed the elderly female's hand and stood as she said, "Stay here while I fetch Killian. Will you be all right by yourself for a minute or two? If not, I'll send someone to fetch him and wait with you."

"No, I'll be fine. I'll do whatever's necessary to ensure my granddaughter returns. Then I can hug her tightly while simultaneously giving her a dressing down."

Teagan chuckled. "Just bake up a batch of your famous whiskey cake, and it'll remind her of why she should stay."

"Bring her back to me, and I'll bake whatever you like as a thank-you and throw in some potato pancakes as well."

"You're making me hungry, Eliza. I'd better hurry up and set things in motion. I'm definitely going to remind you of your offer once Sadie's home again." Teagan moved to the door. "Contact me anytime if you need to. I'll go get Killian for you. He'll be here in just a second."

"Thank you, Teagan."

Satisfied that her clan member had at least stopped crying and was in slightly better spirits, Teagan took a deep breath and walked the short distance between the room with Eliza and the one where she knew Aaron Caruso should be waiting.

Her dragon spoke up. *He's not going to like that we kept him waiting. He's always impatient.*

Too bad. Eliza needed us. Only because Killian is watching him am I not going to let Aaron wait another half-hour so that he understands his place on Glenlough. His cockiness in the past, both in person and via video conferences, won't be tolerated on my home soil.

Her dragon sighed. *You shouldn't irritate him. That only makes him cranky. His reputation is one of joking and having a good time. I want to see that side of him.*

Even if I was interested in that side of him—which I'm not—a clan leader doesn't always get to do what they want. The clan comes first. Always.

Don't quote lines to me. A clan leader can do more than one thing at a time. To be honest, I don't know why you resist kissing him. I'm not only curious, but he might be a good match.

From the first time she'd met with Aaron Caruso, back when her clan needed help chasing away some dragon hunters, her dragon had constantly banged on about kissing the male.

Teagan answered, *No. You know what usually happens when a female leader finds a mate—she gives up her place as soon as she has a mating ceremony. I'm not about to do that.*

Her beast grunted. *I don't know why females have to do that when males don't. It's ridiculous.*

I agree, but let's focus on mending relations with Northcastle first. Then maybe we can worry about ourselves. Or, better yet, we can nudge Killian toward a female. I would be content as an aunt.

Good luck with that. He works all the time and rarely notices any of the females ogling him.

Well, that might change if we secure the alliance with Clan Stonefire and fix our standing with Northcastle. Killian will then have quite a bit of time on his hands if that happens. I can then nudge him toward a good female.

I doubt it'll work, but I'm open to trying. If he doesn't learn to relax a little, he'll die young. Just like Da.

Teagan paused a second before replying, *Da was different. We have no real battle warring. Yet.*

Another reason to be nice to Aaron. Stonefire will help secure a stable future, hopefully free of war.

I know my bloody job, she growled out to her beast.

As Teagan reached the door to the other room, her dragon fell silent. While her beast might harp on about things and voice strong opinions, she knew when to keep quiet. It was one of the many things Teagan admired about her dragon. Not every dragon-shifter was as fortunate, according to her grandmother and others.

Twisting the knob, Teagan entered the small room. Aaron's back was to her. While she appreciated his broad shoulders and his thick, dark hair, she smiled at how he was tapping his fingers. He always did that when it came to meeting with her, either in person or via a video conference. "Just make sure not to wear down my table with your nails."

Aaron's movements stopped. He turned and Teagan hid her surprise. The male had grown a close-cut beard since the last time she'd seen him. The dark whiskers made him look wiser.

And maybe a wee bit sexier. Not that she'd ever tell him that.

Then he frowned and she banished that thought. Grumpy wasn't what she needed, among many other things.

Aaron growled, "I wouldn't have to tap my fingers in the first place if you were on time."

Killian took a step toward Aaron, but Teagan put up a hand. "I'll deal with him. Eliza is waiting for you. Go with her and search Sadie's things. Update me on any developments."

Her brother nodded and exited the room. Like most males in her clan, he obeyed her orders without question.

Aaron, on the other hand, leaned back in his chair and propped his feet on the table. "Should I get comfortable whilst you use a power play to assert your dominance? Or are you actually going to tell me why I'm here?"

She walked up to his feet and pushed them off the table. "Keep your dirty bloody boots on the floor. Do that again, and I'll make sure you always have a bucket and rag to clean up after yourself."

His pupils flashed to slits and back, signaling he was talking to his dragon. "I'm not here to clean."

She shrugged. "The way I understand it, you're here to help me for the next few weeks. Bram didn't say cleaning was off-limits."

Aaron stood. His dark brown eyes met her green. They were exactly the same height, which was a nice change. Teagan was tall, even by female dragon-shifter standards.

She barely had time to note the flecks in his eyes when he spat out, "Cleaning is off-limits. As is babysitting or being assigned entry-level guard duty. I'm a trained Protector. If it's not related to my job, then I'll refuse to do it."

She raised an eyebrow. "And what? Disappoint your clan leader and destroy his hard work at trying to strengthen our alliance?"

"Bram would see it my way. Besides, you need this alliance more than we do. We already have Lochguard at our back. Who do you have?"

His words stung and her dragon stood at attention.

He was correct that she needed the alliance, but she wasn't about to put up with bullshit to achieve it. That was the wrong message to send to Stonefire.

She had dealt with many a male acting like Aaron Caruso. She knew what to do.

Fisting his shirt, she pulled him close. For a split second, her dragon reveled in his scent and the heat of his body so close to theirs, but Teagan quickly pushed her beast to the back of her mind. As Aaron's eyes flashed, she swept his legs with her own. Aaron lost his balance and Teagan guided him to the floor, face down. With his hands behind him and her knee in his lower back, she leaned down to his ear and whispered, "Just because I'm female doesn't mean you will treat me as any less of a clan leader, understood?"

He turned his head to meet her eyes. "I'm not doing it because you're female. I'm doing it because you're irritating."

Resisting the urge to press a talon against his throat, she replied, "That just earned you guard duty. Maybe twenty-four hours without sleep will teach you a lesson in etiquette."

She withdrew a key from her pocket and released Aaron. Before he could do more than rise to his hands and knees, she dashed out the sole door and locked it.

His voice was muffled through the door. "Let me out, bloody woman. This isn't how you treat a guest."

"Aye, you're right. It's how I treat a pest."

With that, Teagan strutted down the hall. She'd send one of her Protectors to deal with him soon enough, but thirty minutes alone might cool his temper.

In the meantime, she would have to contact Bram about a replacement. There was no bloody way she was working with such a disagreeable male. He would surely make things worse with Northcastle, not better.

Her dragon snorted. *You just want to make it easier for yourself.*

It took herculean effort, but Teagan kept Aaron's broad shoulders from flashing inside her mind again. *I see nothing wrong with that. Many a clan leader has fallen because of temptation. I'm not about to be one of them.*

CHAPTER TWO

After a few minutes, Aaron ceased pounding on the door. Teagan wasn't coming back.

He muttered a few choice words before he sat down in the chair and put his boots back on the table. It wasn't much in terms of defiance, but he would do whatever he could.

Just wait until Bram hears about this, he said to his dragon.

Bram will probably wonder what the hell happened to you. On Stonefire, you're usually teasing and smiling. If anything, he'll probably agree with the Irish leader about your behavior.

He can send someone else. I can't stay here.

Why? Because you keep remembering how her warm body felt on top of ours? Imagine if she were naked.

No, just stop. No kissing and no sex. You'll just have to live with it. When I risk giving a female a chance again, it's going to be with someone who treats me as an equal, not a subordinate who expects me to follow every order.

If you want that, then you first need to treat Teagan as the leader she is.

In truth, he'd forgotten she was the leader. *She ignited my temper. A good leader wouldn't do that.*

I don't have time to argue. Guard duty might help you figure out a few things.

His beast fell silent.

It seemed everyone was against him for the moment.

Still, the Protector side of him was curious about why Glenlough needed their help. If she'd only told him without treating him like a child, he could already be helping her.

Besides, if she were the strongest candidate to lead Glenlough, he had doubts about his clan forging an alliance. Dragon-shifter males had egos the size of the sun. A female leader would have to be aware of that and tread carefully.

His dragon spoke up again. *But why? She is leader. Dragon halves understand that.*

The human side of things isn't that simple.

It could be. Maybe you're more insecure than I thought.

I'm not bloody insecure. But should be respected as befits my role as Protector.

Then earn it instead of insulting her.

The lock clicked in the door and it prevented him from replying to his beast. Aaron stayed in place, not wanting to appear overly eager. However, when he saw the brown-haired form of Brenna Rossi—the Stonefire clan member who had been staying with the Irish dragons recently—he stood up. "Brenna. Are you here to rescue me?"

She frowned. "What did you do to piss off Teagan?"

He waved a hand in dismissal. "Nothing. She merely overreacted."

His dragon sighed, but Aaron ignored him. Brenna turned back toward the door. "I doubt that, but regardless, you're to come with me and I'll take you to one of Glenlough's senior Protectors."

"You're taking her side over mine?"

Brenna shrugged. "She's earned my loyalty. You, on the other hand, have a tendency to joke at inappropriate times and speak without thinking. I'm going to side with the saner, more levelheaded one."

He wondered if that was how people really saw him at home—a selfish bastard out to cause trouble.

Italy had changed him in many ways, and maybe some were not for the best.

Pushing aside that thought, he replied, "Just take me to the second-in-command. Maybe then I can call Bram."

"Not if you're on guard duty. There are more threats out here than back home, especially as this location is more remote. That means stricter rules about what you can and can't do whilst on duty. Distractions might cost lives, so no smartphones. Each guard has a simple mobile phone for emergencies that does nothing but make calls."

"Is this the Stone Ages?" he muttered. "Sitting and staring at nothing will distract me more than a phone."

She motioned with her head. "Stop your whining. No wonder Teagan locked you in here. Come on or we'll be late. I can answer more questions as we walk."

He followed Brenna. Ignoring her snide remarks, he took her up on her offer to get more information. "What are the threats to Glenlough? No one has told me much of anything about my post here."

Brenna glanced at him. "Teagan will tell you the details when it's pertinent to your duties. Just know that trouble is coming."

"That's all you're going to tell me? I can't do anything without information." he replied.

"Let's just say that you're not here to help smooth relations with Clan Northcastle. As I mentioned, when Teagan assigns you a related duty, you'll learn about what's going on."

He eyed the younger female. "How do you know so much? You haven't been here that long."

She shrugged. "Long enough. Unlike you, I respect Teagan and have earned her trust, so she includes me on clan matters. Try the same and you might learn a lot more about what happens here."

He frowned. "Be careful, Brenna, or they might kick you off their land for telling me anything."

She smiled. "I was told to brief you about this much, at least. If I hadn't, I wouldn't be talking."

It seemed Brenna was loyal to Glenlough. He had a feeling she might never come back to Stonefire to live again. "Their leader has rubbed off on you. I hope you're not treating her like a god."

Brenna looked at him with narrowed eyes. "Stop insulting her. She's right up there with Bram when it comes to caring for her people and doing anything to protect them. Give her a chance and you might see it the way I do."

Aaron doubted it.

His dragon spoke up. *Why are you so dead set against her? She bested us, yes. But I thought you'd like the challenge.*

Aaron didn't bother to reply. All females, except for a rare few, were trouble.

He merely picked up his pace. He'd count down the seconds until the end of his guard duty. Once it was over, his first priority would be contacting Bram to see what could be done about sending another Protector to take Aaron's place.

~~~
~~~

Teagan sat up straight when Bram Moore-Llewellyn's dark hair and blue eyes appeared on her computer screen. "That was quick."

Stonefire's clan leader replied, "Aye, well, you said it was important. And since I only sent you one Protector for the moment instead of two, I need to ensure things are going smoothly."

Their relationship wasn't as strong as she'd like, but she was comfortable enough to drawl, "Smoothly isn't the way I'd describe it."

Bram raised his dark brows. "What happened?"

"Let's just say that Aaron doesn't take kindly to following my orders."

Bram was quiet a second before he answered, "There's something you should know about him, O'Shea. He's capable, intelligent, and one of our best Protectors. However, his mother was attacked recently and not for the first time in his life. I think it shook him up a bit. While I'll send another of my clan soon, give Aaron another chance."

Teagan studied Bram's eyes, but they didn't reveal any emotion. She had heard about the attack on Aaron's mother, but hadn't really thought about it since. "If he's still shaken up from the attack, why did you send him?"

Bram shrugged. "He's been our liaison and knows more about your clan than anyone else here, apart from the one you've been holding hostage—Brenna."

"She's only here until you come to meet with me in person. Although, fair warning, I don't know if she wants to return to Stonefire."

The corner of Bram's mouth ticked up. "Is that your long-term plan? To entice my clan members one by one until you have enough to ensure my protection?"

Teagan blinked. None of the Irish leaders had a sense of humor. She wondered if it were more common in the UK.

Pushing aside the thought, she answered, "Not unless it becomes necessary. Aaron isn't one I want to convince to stay."

Bram snorted. "He may grow on you. Besides, he's worked with a few Northcastle clan members on a previous assignment, which may give you a foot in the door with their leader, Lorcan Todd. It would benefit us all for the dragons from Ireland and Northern Ireland to get along again."

The relations between the Irish and Northern Irish clans vacillated between friends and bitter enemies. Teagan believed the former was a necessity for survival in the future.

She answered, "I'll admit that Aaron having experience with some of their clan members will be useful, but it'll mean nothing if he doesn't shore up his behavior. I can punish and reprimand all day long, but if he's hell-bent on returning home, he'll try his best to irritate me so that I'll send him packing."

Bram replied, "I'll give you some advice: Put him to work and he'll focus. Keep him idle and he'll cause trouble." She paused to think of another way to persuade Bram to send someone else when Bram spoke up again. "I sense there's more than Aaron's behavior on your mind. You're keeping something from me. I can't help you if you don't tell me what's going on, lass."

Teagan paused. Given the possible threat looming over her head, trust was hard for her.

Her dragon spoke up. *Bram is honest. He has taken on the British Department of Dragon Affairs and won, and on more than one occasion. He also risked being discovered by the Irish DDA office by sending his clan members here to help us without first garnering a visitation pass. He wouldn't have done any of that if he didn't care about dragon-shifter kind in general.*

True, she'd heard a lot about Bram Moore-Llewellyn's reputation and deeds. The male had made human visitations to dragon-shifter land possible in the UK, provided they garnered permission from the DDA. He had even secured a special license so that his female clan member could mate a human male, which had previously been illegal in his country.

Still, it wasn't that easy for her to trust a male leader. *Remember the last time our clan trusted another leader so quickly? They attacked and we lost Da.*

That was many years ago. And that male never proved anywhere near Bram's level when it came to creating a better future for all dragon-shifters. His precedents may even help those of us in Ireland.

You sound like a politician.

So? Clan leaders are a type of politician. My influence will do you good.

Her dragon was correct. Platitudes and fake smiles had always been the hardest aspect of her job. If Teagan were male, she could be stoic and grunt a lot like her brother. But as a female, the standards were higher. She not only needed to lead, but she also needed to remind everyone that females could have strength, too. However, it had to be in just the right amount or she'd be labeled a bitch, or worse.

Thankfully the love of her clan and the desire to see them succeed kept her focused and sane so far.

After staring at Bram for a few more seconds, she sighed. "Is this line secure on your end?"

"Aye. Very few people can break into it. I would say no one, but there's always someone out there smarter who can find a way."

He's honest, her beast said. *I like him.*

She took a deep breath and decided to take a risk, or she might never succeed. Leaders who always played it safe rarely achieved great things. "Greenpeak, the clan in Killarney, has found out that I'm Glenlough's leader and has told everyone who would listen."

"And now males are going to knock at your door to challenge you."

She blinked. "Yes. How did you know?"

Bram waved a hand. "I understand males. Many of them are threatened by a female leader. Rather than watch their power and hold over females possibly diminish, they'll do whatever it takes to preserve the status quo in their clans." He raised an eyebrow. "Am I right?"

"Yes. Although I'm curious why you don't feel threatened."

The corner of Bram's mouth ticked up. "Let's just say my clan has been invaded by strong females and it's been for the better. I don't see them as a threat but rather an asset."

Her dragon stood tall. *See? I told you I liked him.*

Teagan ignored her beast. "Not everyone sees it as you do, though. And I can't risk reaching out to Northcastle until this is sorted, or they'll dismiss Glenlough as a liability instead of an asset. Having Aaron defy my every order is going to hinder any effort to show I'm strong enough to lead the clan when the other clan leaders start knocking at my gates."

Bram paused and finally said, "Tell Aaron he's not welcome home until your clan is safe again. If you agree, of course."

"I can keep him locked in a room…"

Bram grinned. "Under normal circumstances, I'd agree with your way of thinking." He sobered. "However, you need his help. Trust me. Once Aaron knows I'm serious about the assignment, he'll focus. Just make sure not to go overboard with asserting your dominance." She opened her mouth but he beat her to it. "It has nothing to do with you being female. You've kept your clan together for a few years. You clearly have skill. Aaron's father tried to use dominance to scare him and his mother into submission when he was a child. It still affects him today."

Her dragon spoke again. *That explains a lot.*

She ignored her beast. "He isn't going to like that you told me about his father."

"I'm trusting you with this, O'Shea. You've been dealing with males your whole life and are more than familiar with their egos than most, especially since assuming leadership. Handle Aaron as one of your own and everything will work out."

"I'll try. But you're still sending someone else?"

"Aye, Aaron's usual Protector partner is out for a bit since his mate just had a baby boy. I think I'll send Sebastian Randall. He's young, but determined and grounded. He's taken orders from a female before, so he shouldn't be a problem. He also knows Brenna well since they served in the army together. I'll let you know once Sebastian is on his way."

"Thank you. And I promise that once this is taken care of, I'll keep up my end of the bargain."

Bram wanted one of her clan members to pretend to defect and seek out the dragon-shifter traitors hiding out in the Scottish wilderness. That way they could infiltrate the group from the inside and take them down.

Bram replied, "That is a long-term plan, and your clan member would have to wait a few months anyway since we can't have too many dragons joining at a time or it'll make the rogue dragons suspicious."

"Then if there's nothing else, I need to prep my clan for the challenges and/or attacks I know are coming."

Bram nodded. "You'll succeed. Maybe once you do, we can finally meet in person, on an equal footing. Then I could convince Brenna to come home and maybe one or two of your clan members to foster on Stonefire."

"It's a possibility, but let's deal with all of the crap brewing here first. Besides, Brenna is in no rush to return. Not even your charm will change her mind, I think," Teagan replied.

Bram snorted. "I'm not surprised. There are too few female dragon-shifter role models. I hope you'll groom her into a fine female who might one day take over leadership here or even there."

She wanted to bottle up Bram's acceptance of a female leader and scatter it over Ireland, or even the world. However, that was impossible. Only hard work and strength would keep the others away and possibly change hearts and minds. "Thank you, Bram. I'll check with you in a few days. I hope my report on Aaron will be better then."

"I have faith in you, O'Shea. See you then."

Her screen went black and she leaned back in her chair.

She hoped Bram was right about Aaron. She had done her homework on him before he'd visited her clan the first time. He was capable, most everyone liked him, and he'd recently interacted with two of Northcastle's Protectors in Scotland. On paper, he should've been exactly what she needed to assist Glenlough with reaching out to Clan Northcastle.

The reality was proving quite different.

Knowing his past did help her understand him a little, even if Bram had been a bit vague. Maybe she could steer him toward being more involved and trusting her, all without revealing she knew about his father's actions in the first place.

Her beast grunted. *We'll do fine. He's not the first dragon-shifter to have a less than happy past. Once you fix him, you might see him as I do and want to kiss him.*

Just no. Both to the kissing and fixing him. All I need are his skills as a Protector and his former contact with Northcastle.

You can believe that if you wish.

Her dragon's hints told her more than she wanted to know about how Aaron Caruso could play into her future.

However, she would figure out how to deal with that later. For the moment, she needed to prepare for the attacks she knew would come. She only hoped another civil war amongst the Irish dragon-shifter clans wasn't brewing.

Chapter Three

Aaron sat in a chair outside a small jail cell used for minor offenses. Inside it was a sleeping twenty-something male. The younger dragon-shifter had apparently started a fight that had destroyed some property and was cooling off until morning.

All night Aaron had sat in the chair with nothing but coffee to keep him awake. He wasn't sure why they'd taken his mobile phone since there wasn't much of a threat in the small room that would require his attention and focus, but the long night had given him a lot of time to think, as well as plenty of chances to argue with his beast.

His dragon spoke up. *Do you agree with my line of thinking now?*

He paused and replied, *Maybe.*

His beast huffed. *Not everyone in a position of authority will use it for harm. You let your hatred of our father get in the way of treating Teagan fairly.*

Aaron tried not to think of his father, if possible. *Still, if only she'd treated me as an equal, then we wouldn't be having this conversation. I'm not entirely to blame.*

Then as I've said fifty times before, talk with her. Teagan is not our father. She won't belittle you or make you feel as if you've overstepped for merely making a suggestion.

For most of his life, Aaron had hidden his past with a smile or a joke to avoid probing questions. His father had verbally abused him during his childhood, and humor had helped to overcome the barbs and enjoy some aspects of life. His mother had taken the brunt of it, at least until Aaron was older and he'd directed the attention away from his mother and toward himself.

And yet, part of him was tired of the facade of always being happy and carefree. He thought he had finally found a female to share everything with, including his true self, back in Italy.

Of course Nerina had only used him to get to another male. If that wasn't enough, she'd tossed his past and trust back in his face, shaming him in front of the entire Italian clan.

Her voice rang inside his mind. *No one wants to hear you whine. All parents scold their children. You're a poor excuse for a male.*

Aaron clenched his fingers. Not every parent blamed their child for ruining their life and made sure they knew it every day.

His beast growled. *Enough. Nerina isn't worth our time. And Teagan is a clan leader. She won't throw information back in our face, and most certainly not in public.*

I'm sure as hell not going to talk about our dad with her.

You make things more difficult than they have to be.

His dragon turned his back on Aaron and plopped down for a nap. They had been going in circles for hours and Aaron had wanted nothing more than a little peace and quiet. Now that he had it, the eerie silence of nothingness beyond the faint snoring of the male in the jail cell rubbed the wrong way against his ears. It was as if the quiet was beckoning him to think about his past again—the yelling, the never being good enough, and the blame for everything going wrong in his father's life.

How everyone would be happier if Aaron had never been born.

He gritted his teeth. He wouldn't let his bastard father ruin any more of his life. Glenlough was a new clan, and he planned to take advantage of that fact.

Exercise would banish thoughts of his past. Standing, Aaron stretched his arms above his head before taking off his shirt and lowering to a plank position. Push-ups would keep him awake and occupied. His guard duty should be nearly over anyway.

As he used his muscles to lower his body and rise back up, he wondered what his life would've been like if Nerina hadn't betrayed him but had fallen in love with and mated Aaron instead of the other bloke. He'd still be in Italy and might even have a baby on the way.

He did want all that one day. However, he kept that thought tightly concealed from his dragon. As much as his beast might think he wanted Teagan, Aaron's home was on Stonefire. He trusted nearly everyone there. He also had his mother to think about. While his father was dead, she still needed him. Aaron never wanted her to be hurt again, especially after being targeted by the Dragon Knights recently.

Just remembering her unconscious on a hospital bed fueled his desire to return home to make sure she was safe. The doctors had ruled her healthy, but there was much they didn't know about the concoction used by the Dragon Knights. She could maybe experience a relapse, which meant her dragon would take complete control and go rogue.

As he finished his fiftieth push-up, the door to the room opened. It must be his relief watch. Aaron turned his head and nearly fell to the floor.

Teagan stood with a slight smile on her face and her hand on her hip. He'd caught her looking at his back, even if she had shifted her gaze quickly. Her long, dark hair billowed around her shoulders, and the faint scent of female drifted to his nose.

His dragon turned around. *Look at her eyes. She's interested. Take advantage.*

Ignoring his beast, Aaron turned to sit on his bum and propped his arm on his bent knee. "Like the view, oh great leader?"

Her smile faded. "I was just thinking that I could probably best you in a push-up contest. If we ever have a spare ten minutes, I'll show you."

He decided to just be honest and take the first step. "There's no need to prove yourself to me."

Her eyes widened, but quickly returned to normal. She cleared her throat and glanced at the cell. The Irish male was still asleep. "Come into the hall for a second."

It was on the tip of his tongue to point out that he would be abandoning his duty to leave the room, but he kept the remark in check. She'd never divulge information if all he did was piss her off.

His dragon huffed. *Good that you finally realize and admit that.*

Aaron stood and followed Teagan out of the room. He was careful to keep his gaze on the back of her head. If she caught him staring at her arse, he'd never hear the end of it. He might not want to kiss her, but any straight male with eyes would admit that her long, lean body curved in all the right places.

Once they were in the hall with the door to the holding cell room closed, Teagan propped her hands on her hips and tilted her head. "I think we need to start over."

"Pardon?"

She cocked one dark eyebrow. "Bram said you're clever. I hope he's not lying."

"Let's just say this isn't what I was expecting this morning," he drawled.

"When it comes to dealing with me, I'm full of surprises."

"Is that so? So does that mean I should prepare myself to see you skinny dipping in the nearby lake?"

The corner of her mouth ticked up. "That is part of my daily routine. So if you're trying to provoke me, you need to try another approach."

The image of Teagan's tall, lean, naked body gliding through the water flashed inside his mind, but he quickly pushed it away. "I'm sure you're a busy person. Shall we get back to the point?"

He swore disappointment flashed in her eyes, but it was gone before he could study further. "My first order of business is to share a message from Bram. He said you're to stay here until Glenlough is secure by my standards and your assignments are all completed to my satisfaction."

"Wait, what? Since when is there a danger?"

"Since the beginning. I would've shared the situation earlier if you hadn't disrespected me by putting your boots on the table and then challenging me." He opened his mouth to talk, but she put up a hand and cut him off. "This isn't the place to discuss the details of the threats or to hear another argument defending your behavior. As soon as your relief arrives, head to Killian's office upstairs. He'll fill you in."

His beast chimed in. *See? She's being honest.*

And bloody cryptic.

Aaron replied, "What's the next order of business? You said assignments, as in plural."

She searched his eyes. "I expected you to put up more of a fight about staying."

He shrugged. "I hope to talk with Bram myself, but if what you say is true, then I need to do my best to finish your tasks so I can go home as soon as possible."

She studied him a second before saying, "The second order of business is that once you're done with my brother, come to my office. We need to chat."

"Do I get any more information than that?"

"No," she stated.

He could tell she was assessing his reaction. If he defied her, he might never learn the truth.

And he needed all the information he could muster so he could go home to Stonefire.

He shrugged a shoulder. "Fine. Once someone comes to replace me, I'll find Killian and then you."

She opened her mouth to reply, but Aaron headed back into the holding cell room. Maybe he should've allowed her to end the conversation, but the longer he was in her presence, the greater the chance he would insult her. She might scold him later, but he could live with that.

Besides, once he discovered the mysterious danger, he would have a goal and could occupy his time with work. That way he wouldn't think of her toned body floating on the lake's surface. Or how her breasts would be pointing up, as if inviting him to lick one.

His dragon growled. *She could be ours.*

As much as I like your confidence, we've had this discussion.

The male in the jail cell stirred and Aaron sat back down in his chair. Within the next few hours, he'd finally learn what was going on and how he could tackle it.

~~~

Teagan walked toward her brother's office and tried to focus on her meeting with Killian.

Her dragon, however, had other ideas. A slow-motion video of Aaron pumping up and down with his broad back on display played on a loop inside her head.

She mentally growled. *Stop it.*

Why? It's just a memory. And one that you're enjoying.

It's just a reminder of what I can't have.

Not true. The rules apply to mating a male. But if you never mated him, then you could remain leader.

She missed a step but quickly recovered. *I'm not sure why you never mentioned that before.*

Because no male was worthy.

We don't even know Caruso.

There's something about him that tells me he could be. Any male who stands up to protect their mother from harm deserves a chance.

That's only a guess. We don't know for certain what he did.

Still, it's enough for me. Now, if you'll excuse me, I'm going to enjoy this memory a few more times before we have to talk with Killian.

Gritting her teeth, Teagan picked up her pace. She may not be able to stop her beast—she needed her too much to try to imprison her—but the quicker she arrived at Killian's office, the quicker her dragon would stop with the taunting.

Because, yes, she was attracted to Aaron. His broad back and defined muscles weren't anything unusual when it came to a dragon-shifter Protector. Still, she'd never wanted anyone to pull her close and hold her with said muscles before.
~~~

When he wasn't arguing or pissing her off, Aaron almost seemed nice.

Well, more than nice.

But her stealing away another Stonefire clan member wasn't an option, even if she'd joked about it with Bram. Not that she'd give in to her beast in the first place. Since she'd never bring a child into the world with a possible war brewing, having a family might never be in her future.

They arrived at Killian's door. She knocked and entered without waiting for an answer.

As usual, her younger brother sat in front of a laptop, frowning at something. "What now?" she asked.

His green eyes met her own. "When you have a second, you need to look at the bank accounts. Something is off."

"Off as in by a few cents or off as in thousands of euros?"

"Somewhere in between."

She waved a hand in the air. "And? What else can you tell me?"

"Let me look again, and you do the same. Then we can discuss it in detail."

Teagan should be used to his thoroughness. However, sometimes she wished he'd just make a guess and start from there.

"Okay." She parked her arse on the corner of his desk and changed topics. "I'm handing Caruso over to you."

He nodded. "We worked together once before. He's skilled."

"I don't want him idle, so push him. Maybe include some extra training exercises."

Killian raised his brows. "He's not a novice. Treating him as such might be unwise."

"I don't plan to treat him as a novice, but I just want to keep him busy. It'll help him get to know the clan better as well. It's been a long time since we've had two English dragon-shifters on our land as guests. However, if things go well with Bram, they might be a common sight. I need to dispel mistrust sooner rather than later."

"I will use him, but in strategic assignments and as a mentor. Revelin Collins could do with an older, firmer hand."

"Just be careful. Rev has a wee temper. I don't need a fistfight—or worse, a dragon fight—to break out."

Killian sat back in his chair. "I won't allow it to happen. Moving on, I have an update on Sadie Kavanagh."

Some might think her brother was arrogant, but Killian had proved himself many times over to Teagan. "Yes?"

"Sadie had scribbled some directions on a scrap of paper and tossed it into the rubbish bin. She's probably at the final destination with her Northcastle male, but I didn't want to send anyone to check until you approved the plan."

"Hold off confronting her for now, but maybe have someone discreetly watch the area. I want to give Eliza some peace, but not too much. Until Lorcan Todd and I work out our differences, I doubt he'll allow anyone from Northcastle to live here." Killian nodded. Teagan stood. "I'll take a look at the accounts and get back to you. Send Caruso to me once you're done debriefing him."

"How much do you want him to know?"

"Everything." Her brother raised his brows, and she added, "He has a mother waiting for him in England, who he wants to get back to. Caruso won't run off and spill secrets. Bram would punish him if he did, and if it was bad enough, maybe banish him. Aaron won't chance it."

Killian studied her eyes. No doubt her brother knew there was more to the story, but he didn't question her. "I'll talk with him."

"Good. Any other updates I should know?"

"The Killarney clan hasn't made a move yet, nor have the other two Irish clans. I have a team checking in with our contacts regularly, just in case they take action."

"Let's hope the others see reason and stay away. If any of the other clans attack us, the Irish DDA will probably punish all of us. Regardless of their views of female leaders, we all do better without the DDA's involvement." She moved to the door. "If you find anything specific or worrying about the bank records or have an update on the other clans, contact me immediately."

With a wave goodbye, Teagan left her brother and headed toward her own office. She had a full plate for the day and she hadn't even eaten breakfast yet. After four years as clan leader, she should be used to the busy workload, but every once in a while, she itched to stretch her wings and merely fly for hours in any direction. There was much of Ireland she had yet to explore.

Her dragon spoke up. *We can pop off for a bit at any time. I'm stealthy. No one will see.*

I know you are, love. But unless you can split us in two so that one set can manage the clan and the other can fly away, it's not going to happen.

If we had a partner in all ways, the male could help free up some time. It is possible.

Rather than answer her beast, Teagan entered her office and sat in front of her computer. She had work to do. The clan would always come first. And if she wished to keep taking care of them, she couldn't take a mate. The elder dragon-shifters would frown at living with a male but not mating him. And she refused to step down because of some ridiculous tradition.

So, Teagan logged into her computer and pushed aside thoughts of having a mate to lean on. She could handle things on her own, as she always had in the past.

CHAPTER FOUR

Aaron tried his best to hide his exhaustion as he walked toward Teagan's office. If he wasn't careful, he might yawn in Teagan's presence and he'd never hear the end of it.

His beast spoke up. *If you don't let one out, you will yawn.*

You're not helping.

I am. Yawn now and it'll be out of the way.

No. I'm not about to show weakness on my first full day on Glenlough.

His dragon huffed. To make things worse, his beast curled up and went to sleep. It wasn't the first time Aaron thought his inner dragon was more like an annoying sibling than a partner in life.

His beast opened one eye and promptly shut it. Aaron would probably pay for that thought later.

Taking a deep breath, Aaron closed his eyes a few seconds and opened them again. Killian had been straight to the point about debriefing him. The clan was waiting for a challenger to come and try to take over Glenlough. While Aaron appreciated the information, the lack of alternative solutions had grated. He could've told Killian his idea but had decided to save it for Teagan. That way he could watch the surprise in her eyes.

If he worked hard, he might be able to surprise her more than she could him.

His dragon shook his head and went back to feigning sleep. His beast must be exhausted to miss the chance at teasing him.

Aaron arrived at the old oak door at the very end of the hall. He knocked, and Teagan's muffled voice told him to enter.

Opening the door, he spotted Teagan frowning at her computer. His gaze then drifted to the multiple piles of paper stacked around her room—on her desk, table, bookcase, and even the small sofa. Before he could stop himself, he blurted, "How do you find anything in here?"

Teagan's frown deepened as she looked up at him. "I have a system. Shut the door."

He closed the door before asking, "Care to share that system? It looks like a rubbish heap to me."

"Ask me to find something."

He motioned around the room. "Where are last year's birth records?"

Teagan pointed to a stack on the table against a wall. "There. We had twelve babies born. I can list them by name and birth month, if you like."

He blinked at her quick response. "Er, no. That's okay."

Satisfaction glinted in her eyes. "If you're quite done criticizing me, then sit your arse down. We need to chat."

"I would take the sofa, but I don't want to disrupt your system. I'll have to settle for the hard wooden chair instead."

After he sat in one of two wooden chairs in front of her desk, she carried on as if he hadn't commented. "While Killian is in charge of your assignments whilst here, I want you to know that despite your tendency to irritate me, you can come talk with me at any time, provided we're not in the middle of a crisis. If someone is mistreating you, I want to know."

He hooked an arm over the back of his chair. "I can handle myself."

She shook her head. "That's not the point. Tensions are high as we wait and see if the other clans will attack. I can't afford a brawl to turn into something more. More than one male will probably have a penis-measuring contest with you as it is."

"Not literally, I hope. I don't fancy blokes myself."

"Caruso," she growled in warning.

Aaron decided to just be forthright and not continue to beat around the bush. Otherwise his gaze might linger on the adorable frown on her forehead. "Regarding high tensions about the possible threats, I have an idea."

"Pardon?"

The corner of his mouth ticked up. "There's more to me than muscles and brawn."

She cleared her throat. "Of course there is. You just changed subjects rather quickly. So what's this idea, Mister I-Just-Arrived-But-I-Already-Know-Better?"

He nearly plopped his feet on her desk for her snarky comment, but somehow resisted. If he angered her, she wouldn't listen to him, and that would only prolong his stay. "Invite the other Irish clan leaders to come here for an official challenge."

She motioned with a hand. "Explain."

He shrugged. "Instead of waiting around to see who comes knocking, just put out an invitation. The other Irish leaders are all male, aye? The invite will put them on the spot. If they truly believe you weak and incapable, they'll come. If not, they'll stay away. However, if any do come, it gives you the opportunity to prepare and ensure you can knock them on their arses."

He watched Teagan's face, but it remained neutral. For once, he willed himself to be patient. Rushing the female would be counterproductive.

She finally sighed. "What is it with males and wanting to beat the crap out of each other? You would think in the twenty-first century, we could simply talk and hash out details."

He tilted his head. "Is that doubt I sense? Have you let yourself go that much?"

She gave him the double-finger salute. "Not bloody likely. Winning Glenlough wasn't easy, yet I succeeded. I can do it again and take any southerners who come knocking."

He nearly said, "That's my girl," but caught himself in time. His dragon chuckled. *You'll see it my way soon enough.*

He ignored his beast. "So does that mean you'll use my plan?"

"That depends." She pointed a forefinger at him. "Are you going to lord it over me?"

He knew her question held a deeper meaning. "Not in public. I know how important appearances are for clan leaders. But in private? I will remind you often of my cunning and intelligence."

She rolled her eyes. "Why didn't Stonefire send me another female instead of a male?"

"Bram sent the best available. That would be me."

"You're pretty sure of yourself," she drawled.

"Are you any different? I can't imagine you belittling your skills."

"Fair point." She placed her hands on her desk. "I need time to think on this. I don't know what you usually do, but I don't rush into things when something important hangs in the balance, if I can help it."

"Just don't wait too long. If you issue the challenge once they're knocking on the front gate, it won't be as surprising. It'll be perceived as a panicked decision."

She frowned and he couldn't help but look at the cute creases again. The look really did diminish her badass appearance.

His dragon spoke up. *We all have many sides to share.*

Stop sounding like a bloody fortune cookie.

Teagan's voice prevented his beast from replying. "Judging from your eyes, your dragon has a few words to say. Care to share?"

His beast chuckled. *Tell her she's gorgeous and clever and that I'd like to strip her naked before I—*

No. Aaron focused back on Teagan. "He's hoping you use my plan."

"Is that so?" she drawled. "While I think you're lying, it's probably best I don't know the truth since I'm familiar with what male dragons often think about."

"Female dragons think the same, but just hide it better."

Teagan's pupils flashed. "Oh, believe me, you don't want to know what she's thinking."

His own dragon chimed in. *Invite her to shift, and we dragons can sort things out in dragon form.*

Not going to happen, mate. Aaron said, "Can we focus back on the plan? Are you going to use it? I rather think it's your best shot at putting the others in their places."

She put a hand on her chest and feigned surprise. "It almost sounds as if you want me to win and put the males in their place. That can't be right."

The O shape of her mouth made him think of what she could do with those soft lips.

His dragon spoke again. *Yes, like this.*

His beast flashed a naked image of Teagan as she swallowed his dick to the back of her throat.

It took everything he had to keep from choking, let alone keep his cock soft. Not wanting the distraction, he gave a warning. *Do it again and I'm going to lock you up.*

I only show what you try to hide.

Maybe he needed to find a female for a quick fuck to clear his head. A female like Teagan expected to be bedded and wooed, and he had no interest in the wooing.

Teagan's voice cut through his thoughts. "Your dragon is fairly chatty."

Aaron shrugged. "It happens. Now, with regards to wanting you to win, me and Bram already know who you are. Getting to know a new clan leader, especially one who might not want to form an alliance with Stonefire, would just make things difficult. I'm merely being practical."

Her own eyes flashed, but it was brief. She answered, "I'll talk with Killian and consider the pros and cons. For now, get some rest. Not only will you start your new duties this afternoon, but we're also having a welcoming dinner in the great hall this evening in your honor."

"Why are you saying that with a devious glint in your eyes?"

She tilted her head with a smile. "Oh, nothing. You'll find out."

He didn't like the tone of her voice but knew she wouldn't expand further. "Just know there's little you can do to embarrass me."

"Oh, is that so? I'll keep that in mind."

Aaron stood. "Clan leader or not, if you try to pull a prank on me or put me on the spot, I'm going to return the favor when you least expect it."

Teagan leaned forward and rested her forearms on the desk. He resisted looking at her breasts. "We shall see, Caruso. There's more to me than you think you know."

His dragon grunted. *I want to know all of it.*

He didn't dignify his beast with a reply. He moved toward the door. "Challenge accepted, Teagan O'Shea. There's plenty I can do without publicly challenging your leadership."

Before she could utter another word, he exited her office with a smile. Maybe his time on Glenlough wouldn't be completely tedious. He could even have a hand in strengthening the alliance. That would award him bonus points back home.

His beast sighed. *It wouldn't be tedious if you kissed her. She could help pass the time.*

Teasing her will be enough. I don't need the complication of a relationship, let alone a mate.

I never said she was our true mate.

He missed a step. *The way you're acting says otherwise.*

A dragon can want a female for many reasons.

And what does that mean?

You'll just have to find out for yourself. Kissing her won't start a frenzy, so your 'I don't want a mate' excuse is null and void. It'll be fun to see what you do next.

As his dragon fell silent, Aaron wondered if his beast was jesting him to see if he would kiss Teagan or not. In his experience, a dragon rarely wanted someone so strongly without a true mate pull.

Then he remembered how Stonefire's head Protector—and Aaron's boss—Kai Sutherland had mated a human female who wasn't his true mate. However, if anyone tried to take Jane Hartley from Kai's side, they would be on the ground and restrained within seconds, if not worse. Kai and Jane's bond appeared as strong as any of the true mate couples he'd seen. More so in some cases, such as when compared to that of his own parents who had been true mates.

He wondered if Kai's dragon had wanted Jane desperately, despite her not being his true mate.

Not like Aaron was going to ask him. Talking about females with Kai would be awkward since Kai wasn't chatty to begin with.

Aaron would just have to forget about his dragon messing with his mind. He had no intention of pursuing any female beyond a quick fuck in the near future.

Besides, there were more important matters to think about, such as if Teagan teased him, then he would be free to give payback, and he'd have to think of something good. No matter what his dragon may say or imply, Aaron wasn't going to miss his chance to embarrass Glenlough's leader in an officially approved capacity. Even though it meant donning a smile and charm for a few hours, he looked forward to the evening celebration.

~~~

As the light dimmed and the day turned into evening, Teagan watched as Colm MacDermot spoke with a fifteen-year-old boy named Emmet. Colm was a tall, fair-haired male who was a few years older than Teagan. He taught the older children how to fly and control their beasts, and did especially well with the difficult students.

While she tried her best not to listen, she couldn't block out Colm's words. "I know your parents always say that sneaking off the clan's territory is dangerous. But while I encourage exploration to a point, I agree with your parents right now. You
~~~

know other clans might attack at any moment, so explain to me why you thought it was okay to sneak off this morning."

Emmet raised his chin and tried to stand taller. However, he was still a foot shorter than Colm. Teagan bit back a smile, remembering her own bouts of trying to prove herself at fifteen. The boy said, "Gannon suggested I was scared and should go back to the younger class. I couldn't let him think lesser of me."

"Aye, and why is that?"

"Because," Emmet replied, "if I want to be a Protector, I need to be strong."

"Strength comes in many forms, son. Do you think if someone insinuated Killian was weak for not fighting a bear, that he'd go off and find one to wrestle?" Colm asked.

Emmet frowned. "Of course not. That's ridiculous."

"And so is letting one classmate get to you. A Protector focuses their energy on important matters. Accepting every dare isn't one of them. You'll lose focus and it'll consume you. Trust me, my cousin refused to believe he didn't need to prove himself to anyone who challenged him, and he died before he hit eighteen."

Emmet's posture slumped a fraction at Colm's words. "I forgot about that."

"Aye, well, you were a young child at the time. So when I say accepting dares and trying to prove yourself to everyone is a waste of time, I mean it. You only need to impress Killian and Teagan if you truly want to be a Protector. That means demonstrating restraint to show off your good judgment."

Teagan decided that was her cue to break her silence. She strode toward the pair as she said, "He's right, you know, Emmet. Improve your skills, demonstrate good judgment, and show you can obey orders. That will go a long way toward achieving your dream."

Emmet's cheeks flushed. "Of course, Teagan. I'll try better."

"Good. Then run home and start fresh tomorrow. If you show us you can change, then Mr. MacDermot and I may just forget to tell your parents about your little transgression." She looked to Colm. "Isn't that right?"

Colm nodded. "But I need to see a change of behavior straight away. I'm not going to give you chance after chance. If being a Protector is what you truly want, then you have to earn it. There are no second chances in a life or death situation."

"I understand," Emmet answered quickly.

With that, Emmet ran off and Teagan chuckled. "I sometimes forget how difficult that age can be. Between dragons trying to seize control at any moment and human hormones rushing through their bodies, I'm not sure how any teenager survives it."

Colm snorted. "I think you just don't want to remember how adventurous you were yourself."

She smiled. "Aye, I was a handful." She sobered. "But we'll have to save reminiscing for another day. I have a favor to ask."

Colm raised an eyebrow. "Which is?"

"Before I get to that, just know that I'm not trying to rub in winning the leadership trials, I promise. But your experience is what I need."

He rolled his eyes. "Unlike Hugh, I don't hold a grudge. You were the best, and you won, end of story."

Along with Colm, Hugh Burns had been one of her opponents during the clan leadership trials. "Good." She lowered her voice. "I'm going to hold another challenge, and I'm going to need your help with planning and running it."

Colm frowned. "Are you stepping down because of the arseholes who think you're too weak? You don't need to, Teagan. The clan has your back."

"I know, and I'm not stepping down anytime soon. However, if I invite Orin Daly from Killarney or any of the other leaders who wish to challenge me to a formal trial, then I can once and for all dispel the myth that females are too weak to be leaders."

Colm grinned. "Just thinking about Daly on his arse would make my day. Of course I'll help."

"Good. Then come to my office tomorrow during the midday break. I want to formally announce my intentions tonight, but I didn't want to do it without securing your help first. I can't do it on my own, and I'd like to have the second-place winner at my back."

"You always have my help, Teagan. If you doubt it again, I may have to challenge you myself."

He winked and she shoved him. "Fine, then I won't. Just remember to come, aye?" Colm nodded and she continued, "Then I should go change before the formal celebration. Unless there's anything else you want to talk about?"

"No, my students are doing fairly well overall. If Emmet truly tries to prove he's Protector material, most of the other lads should fall in line. He may not realize it yet, but they look up to him. He'll make a good Protector one day."

"Agreed." She turned away. "I'll see you tonight, hopefully. If not, then tomorrow."

Colm waved and Teagan walked briskly toward her cottage. Her dragon spoke up. *Are you sure you want to announce it so soon? It might be better to wait.*

Everyone is uneasy. If they know we have a plan, then they can breathe a sigh of relief and maybe even help prepare. I can't do this on my own.

You're assuming at least one of the other leaders will accept.

Orin Daly will. He has too much riding on this to back down. If he keeps quiet, it'll open up his own clan to challenge him.

Her beast grunted. *And he's too proud to let that happen.*

Yes. I've only met him the once, but that was enough. Using fear rather than trust, love, and respect to control a clan never ends well.

That's his problem and not ours. The pressing concern is making Aaron's jaw drop tonight.

Teagan rolled her eyes. *That is probably the least important item on my list.*

But admit it, seeing his eyes widen and him being speechless would be satisfying. You can use it to tease him more later.

I see what you're doing, dragon.

So? You still want to do it. You know as well as I that we can have fun with him and then forget him. There's no true mate pull.

Since when? You've been panting after Aaron since we met him.

He's a fine male. What's not to like? Besides, him not being our true mate means you have options. Most importantly, you won't be forced to have a child and give up your place.

She remembered Aaron's muscled back as he did push-ups. She'd peeked at his arse, too, and had no doubt the round globes were as firm as the rest of him.

Her dragon snorted. *I'm sure he's firm everywhere when he looks at us, too.*

Dick jokes are below you.

Considering I can't remember the last time we've seen one hard and jutting out from a trim body, I'll do whatever it takes to get you to think about them. Not just freestanding, but in your mouth, your pussy, and maybe even your arse.

Her dragon then imagined Aaron over them, his intense brown eyes full of heat.

She shivered and pushed the picture away. *I think you're just trying to get me to agree to making Aaron's jaw drop in lieu of jumping him.* Her beast sat silently, and Teagan mentally sighed. *Fine, but if I agree to dressing to the nines, then you promise not to flash images of him naked when we're in his presence.*

Maybe, maybe not. It depends on your effort. But you can't deny that a little sex would help you relax and release tension before the challenge.

Sex with our Stonefire liaison is a bad idea, as I've said many times before.

But why? If we pay attention to any males on Glenlough, the others will talk and plan. Hugh may even think you'll be stepping down. A foreigner is our only chance for some nonbinding fun.

Teagan sighed. *We can tease him and drive him mad, but no sex.*

What about a kiss?

The image of Aaron kissing her neck as his light beard rustled against her skin sent a shiver through her body. Her dragon chuckled, but Teagan ignored her. *Rather than argue about how far we're going before we even figure out how to surprise him is pointless. If you want to have some fun, then help me. It's been a while since I had to make anyone's jaw drop. At least when it didn't involve me kicking them in the balls.*

Her beast chuckled. *It was fun seeing Hugh go down holding himself during the trials.*

He tried to cop a feel. He deserved it.

Of course he did. But we should be a little nicer to Aaron. Despite his smiles and tendency to rile us up, I sense he's hurting inside. Maybe hold off punching or kicking him until he really upsets you.

Wait, what are you talking about?

Nothing. Just focus on getting ready for the celebration. Maybe you'll discover the rest yourself.

Teagan shook her head and jogged the remaining distance to her cottage. She missed her dragon's straightforwardness, which had seemed to disappear when it came to anything related to Aaron Caruso. Maybe once he returned to Stonefire, her beast would act normal again.

That wouldn't happen for quite some time, so Teagan focused on the evening ahead. Everyone would have questions, and she would have to make time for them. If she were lucky, she might not have to spend much time in Aaron's presence anyway.

CHAPTER FIVE

As Aaron strode toward Glenlough's castle slash great hall, he was grateful for the warmer than normal summer temperatures.

Formal celebrations required dragon-shifters to wear traditional-style clothing. The strip of fabric across his chest was attached to the kilt-like skirt wrapped around his hips. Since he wore Stonefire's dark red color, he stuck out amongst the sea of hunter green outfits. While the females had a bit more variety to the hues of green, the males all wore a single dark green color. And as he passed the Glenlough clan members, they studied him. Not with disgust or fear, but rather curiosity.

To be fair, it could be a lot worse.

Yet as he took in the observers, one face never appeared.

He hadn't spotted Teagan.

Not that he should be seeking her out. But she was a familiar face and one that would help him find his footing in the Irish clan.

His dragon spoke up. *We'll find her. I think you're as eager as me to see her in her traditional garb.*

I care little what she wears, as long as she's not naked.

So does that mean you admit you find her attractive? Otherwise, nakedness shouldn't matter.

Not going to answer that. Hush.

To distract himself, he glanced to Brenna Rossi at his side; she was in the same dark red color. "Given how much you love it here, I'm surprised you're not in green."

She glanced up at him. "Just because I respect Teagan and what she does, it doesn't mean I don't love my home. Even if I spend the rest of my days with Glenlough, I will always be a member of Stonefire at heart."

As Brenna waved hello to her tenth male in the time they'd walked from her cottage to the great hall, Aaron shook his head. "Methinks you'll be finding a mate soon enough."

Her eyes shuttered. "I doubt it."

Since Brenna was not only a distant cousin but also like a younger sister to him, Aaron wanted to press her further. However, a familiar female voice garnered his attention. "If you stand next to any of my clan members, people might start asking if we're celebrating Christmas early."

He looked in the direction of Teagan's voice and stopped in his tracks.

Her long, dark hair was piled atop her head with a few tendrils of curls dancing around her shoulders. Pale flowers were also tucked here and there on her scalp, a stark contrast to her dark hair. Her dress was the same one-shoulder, floor-length plain dress as every other female, but the green was more of an emerald. The same shade as her eyes, to be exact.

And even though the dress was only snug to the waist, it was the clearest view he'd had of her small breasts and trim ribcage. Both suited her tall stature.

However, despite the display of her female attributes, the defined muscles of her arms reminded him she had strength, too.

As he ogled Glenlough's leader, his dragon chuckled. *Are you still going to deny she's attractive?*

He mentally cleared his throat. *Of course she's bloody attractive. It doesn't mean I'm going to do anything about it.*

When the corner of Teagan's mouth ticked up, he focused back on the female and said, "Anyone who mentioned Christmas to a dragon-shifter would just show their ignorance since dragon-shifters in the UK and Ireland celebrate the Winter Solstice, not Christmas."

"You were speechless for almost ten seconds, and that's the comeback you came up with?" Teagan tsked. "You're going to have to work on your wit if you're to deal with me."

His beast grunted. *Forget the verbal sparring. Tell her she's beautiful.*

No.

But—

It's not up for discussion.

Aaron put his arm out for Brenna. With a puzzled look on her face, she obliged and threaded her arm through his. Aaron looked back to Teagan. "Now, if you'll excuse us, we should take our seats."

"I think you're trying to change the subject. I'll allow it for now. Come with me. You're the guest of honor, which means sitting on my right side, just like the kings and queens of old."

"So now you're a queen?" Aaron drawled.

"No, but there's nothing wrong with a little tradition now and then, as long as we keep the present in mind when following them and aren't afraid to adjust as needed."

Her response was odd, but Aaron decided to brush off his curiosity. "Then lead on, my lady. Royalty always leads the way."

Teagan held his gaze for another second before turning around and strutting toward the great hall's stone entrance.

Without her studying him, he allowed his eyes to wander to her swaying hips and bum.

Brenna whispered low enough that no one else should hear her. "If I mention you staring at her arse to Killian, he'll punch you and toss you into a jail cell until you cool off. Or, come to think of it, he may lock you away for the rest of your natural life."

He looked to Brenna and whispered back, "So now you're tattling to Killian?" He put a hand over his heart. "And here I thought you were like a sister to me. It's not good manners to wish your brother incarcerated."

"Forget the silliness. Teagan was looking at you too. She's unattached, you know. Maybe Glenlough is where you're supposed to end up after all."

He picked up his pace. "Definitely not. After my time in Italy, I'm more certain than ever before that Stonefire is where I belong. She can look all she wants, but she won't get these muscles to herself."

Brenna opened her mouth to reply, but they reached the throng of people filing inside the building and she promptly closed it. The female Protector still had sense. Of course, she'd probably bring it up again later.

His dragon stretched his wings out before folding them against his back again. *I'm not the only one who notices her interest. Make sure you ask Teagan to dance tonight.*

I'm not bloody dancing in front of a crowd of strangers. For all we know, they could do the traditional Irish dancing with all the fancy legwork and Teagan will 'accidentally' kick me in the balls.

His beast snorted. *It's amusing to see you so uncomfortable and cautious. I bet Bram would like this version of you. You would've caused a lot less trouble as a teen.*

I'm being bloody cautious because we're representing Stonefire. Remember, the clan is counting on us.

His dragon grunted but didn't respond. Thinking of the clan was one of the few ways to shut up his beast.

Aaron only hoped his dragon's silence lasted the entire evening. Because if his beast harped on about Teagan's appearance, especially if she issued a blasted dare, then he might do something foolish.

No. Aaron had let his guard down too quickly with Nerina in Italy, and his mother had been forced to return to England because of his irresponsible behavior. He wasn't going to let down anyone else because of his bloody dragon's demands or because he wanted to see a certain female naked and under him.

His dragon sat smugly at the back of his mind at that comment.

Behave, he mentally whispered to his beast. Approaching the stairs to the raised dais, he freed his face of any emotion. It was showtime.

~~~

Teagan was both glad and sad to have her back to Aaron. Glad because it gave her time to get over the shock of the deep red material against his olive-toned skin and his trim waist; sad because she couldn't stare at him for a few more seconds and drink in the male she would never be able to have.

Life had been simpler before becoming clan leader. Five years ago, if she saw a male she fancied, she could've slept with him and thought nothing of it. In the present, any attention she displayed would be scrutinized by the clan. Even if the male in
~~~

question didn't run away screaming, he might eventually grow tired of being second to a female in public.

It was simpler to just ignore males in general.

Her dragon huffed. *Let's see how the evening goes. You responded to the idea of kissing him earlier.*

That was a fancy, nothing more. There are more important things to worry about this evening.

Her beast paused a second. *Fine, but you might want to acknowledge Aaron's role in the plan to host a challenge with the other leaders. It will go a long way towards having a stronger alliance.*

I'm not a novice. Of course I'm going to acknowledge him, albeit not quite so directly.

I wasn't sure since it meant he could lord it over you in private.

She nearly told her beast that Teagan rather enjoyed teasing the male, but resisted as she reached the long table on the raised dais. Turning, she motioned to specific seats. "Aaron will sit next to me, and Brenna will sit next to Killian."

Brenna stiffened a second, but then smiled. "I'm sure my cousin will be honored."

Teagan looked between the pair. Apart from the same dark hair and olive skin tone, there were no other similarities. "You're cousins?"

Aaron nodded. "Aye, but distant ones."

When he said nothing else, Teagan cleared her throat. "We should take our seats. I'll be officially starting the event soon."

After Brenna and Aaron shared a glance, they parted. As Aaron walked toward her, his gaze never wavered.

Something about the determination and strength in his dark brown eyes nearly made her shiver.

Her beast snorted. *This will be fun to watch.*

Once Aaron sat next to her, she leaned over to murmur, "Before I say anything to the clan, I wanted to tell you that I'm going with your plan."

He leaned closer and it took everything Teagan had to focus on his words instead of the spicy male scent that filled her nose. "As you should. It's the only way forward, really."

His words cut through her appreciating his closeness and snapped her back into her role as clan leader. "There are several ways to handle the situation. I just look forward to one of the males challenging me so I can win and revel in the disbelief on his face."

Aaron raised his brows. "Maybe you should practice with me first, just to refresh your skills. After all, clan leaders tend to go a bit soft once they assume leadership."

She raised an eyebrow. "I can practice with Killian and the others, like I do on a regular basis, I might add."

He leaned a fraction closer and her heart rate ticked up at the heat radiating from his body. "You can, but it won't help you prepare properly. You already defeated the strongest members of your clan. What you need is a new challenger. I've never participated in a leadership trial myself because being leader involves too much diplomacy and paperwork, but I like to think I would have a fighting chance if I tried."

"You'll lose, of course. Can your ego handle losing to a female?"

He smiled slowly. "The bigger question is, can yours accept losing to a foreigner?"

She raised her brows. "That's rather presumptuous."

He shrugged. "I'm good at what I do, even if I'm a tad more impatient than my head Protector likes."

Her dragon chimed in. *Challenge him. It'll be brilliant to stand over him and have him admit defeat. Then we can claim our prize. One night of passion should do the trick.*

Aaron's voice prevented her from replying. "Care to tell me what your dragon is saying?"

Teagan pulled away and sat up straight. "No. We can discuss it later. My brother is signaling that it's time to begin."

To his credit, Aaron merely nodded and fell silent. It seemed he could follow orders when it came to important matters.

Once the doors to the great hall clicked closed, Teagan stood and walked to the front of the dais. Despite the fact an entire table of people would be staring at her from behind, she sensed Aaron's gaze on her arse. Her traitorous body warmed at the idea.

Pushing away what was only a response to a handsome male's attention, she raised her voice. "Everyone, welcome." The remaining chatter died and she continued, "Tonight we officially welcome Stonefire's representative and Protector, Aaron Caruso, to the clan. While most of you have already warmed up to Brenna from Stonefire, I hope you do the same with Aaron. He's here to learn and help when needed."

Someone shouted from the crowd, "We don't need outsiders to help us."

Teagan didn't miss a beat. "I know that we've lived isolated for many years out of necessity. However, me being clan leader has leaked. And I don't know about you, but I'm tired of living a lie and maintaining a ruse. Glenlough has a long tradition of female leaders and other clans should accept that. Having allies at our back will only help us in the long run." A murmur went through the crowd, and Teagan decided to just share the rest.

"But I do want to assure you that Killian, Aaron, and I have a plan of how to deal with the other Irish clans. I'm going to invite the other Irish leaders to a clan leader challenge."

Roars and shouting greeted her ears. Teagan held up a fist and waited until the room was mostly quiet again. "This is the best way to handle them. Otherwise, we'll be fighting with them for who knows how many years. Once that happens, Northcastle might pounce and take advantage of the chaos. I'd rather show the other leaders what I'm made of and then reach out to Northcastle as a potential strong ally."

A male shouted, "Northcastle is full of wankers. We don't need them."

Teagan answered without hesitation. "If that's true, then are we to sit back and watch as more and more of our clan run away with Northcastle mates? Allowing dragon-shifters to claim mates freely from anywhere in Ireland, North or South, is essential to our long-term survival. Many of us have distant relatives in Northcastle. It would be nice to see them, don't you think?"

A few people replied grudgingly in the affirmative, while others still protested. Teagan had known this part would be tricky. She raised a fist and waited for complete silence before she spoke up again. "However, doing anything with Northcastle is secondary to me fighting for my right to lead Glenlough. And not just for me, but for the future of other clans, too. Many of you remember my grandmother's time as clan leader. She helped us survive the human Troubles as well as strengthen our clan when the economy devastated many others in our country. Females have the right to be a leader as much as any male."

She paused as a roar of agreement echoed inside the hall. With everyone back on her side, she pushed toward the end. "But in order to prove how capable females can be, I'm going to need the support of my clan. Your cheers and faith in me will give me the extra strength I need to ensure no one perceives us as weaker ever again. Who's with me?"

For a split second, as silence stretched, Teagan wondered if she'd made a mistake. Then cheers and shouts rose in encouragement.

Her beast hummed. *Of course they support us or we would've had another challenge long before now.*

Logically, I know that. Still, I don't like to take our clan and their support for granted.

Raising her fist for the last time, the noise died down. "Right, then I have one more request. For the next few weeks, I need you all to only petition an audience with me if it's truly important. Killian will also assist with settling disputes until this is over so I can focus on the upcoming challenge. I have faith that Glenlough will have my back. Am I correct?" A resounding yes rolled through the crowd. "Then enjoy the celebrations tonight! If I have any say in the matter, we should be having another one before too much longer to celebrate showing the other clans that a female has as much right to lead as a male."

There were a few more cheers, and Teagan waved to certain members of the audience. As people sat down and started to dish out food from the serving platters that sat in the middle of the tables, she turned around and let out the breath she'd been holding. The first set of eyes she found were Aaron's dark brown ones. He gave an almost imperceptible nod, and she returned the gesture.

Not that she knew why she did it. Aaron's approval wasn't important in the grander scheme of things.

Before her dragon could go on about why it should matter, Teagan took her seat and reached for her glass of wine. She took a sip and Aaron leaned over to whisper, "I look forward to facing the strong female who just rallied her clan's support. Outsmarting you will be a worthwhile puzzle."

After swallowing the smooth red wine, she turned toward him. "Do my ears deceive me or was that almost a compliment?"

He winked. "Don't get used to it. But I'm big enough to admit when someone's doing a good job. I'll leave any greater compliments until I face you and see what you're made of."

Aaron's words should needle her ego, but instead, it made her anxious to get started. "And you shall. How about twenty minutes after dawn? Unless that's too early for you."

"That depends. Do I get coffee beforehand or not?"

"I'm tempted to say no, but I want you at your best for my win. So drink as much as you like. I love mornings, so I may fly a few laps whilst waiting."

He grunted. "Just tell me where and I'll be there."

She smiled and picked up her wineglass again. "I think I'll keep you in suspense for a little while longer. That way you'll have to stay and participate in your welcoming celebration."

Aaron's gaze swept the room. "I'm not one for small talk and diplomacy." He looked back to her. "Trust me, you should be urging me to leave as soon as possible before I start a war between our clans."

She shrugged. "I don't know about Stonefire, but this is Glenlough. We prefer honesty."

"I somehow doubt you lot always take honesty with a smile and nod."

"Of course not. But the ensuing consequences can be fun. The only real rules are to not permanently maim or kill anyone."

He raised his brows. "Those might be famous last words."

She waved a hand in dismissal. "All of that isn't important right now. What you should be worried about is that you're expected to dance tonight."

"If you think I'm going to flail my legs and look the fool, then I promise you I'll be kicking more than one person this evening."

She snorted. "We have a lot of the same traditional dragon-shifter dances you do, so stop moaning. I'll let you know when it's time for you to show everyone what you're made of. Once you do a few dances, then I'll tell you the location for tomorrow morning."

"You're devious."

She sipped her wine. "You say that as if it's a bad thing."

Aaron opened his mouth to reply, but one of her advisors called her name and Teagan went to the end of the table to talk with him.

Still, as she listened to the male, her eyes kept darting toward another. Aaron Caruso was starting to shatter her initial opinions of him. Maybe she'd see the carefree, teasing version of him yet.

And maybe she would take up her dragon's suggestion of a little fun while Aaron was there. She'd just need to make sure he understood it was temporary and that no matter what happened, he wouldn't sever the alliance because of it.

Her beast gloated, but Teagan ignored her to focus back on her advisor. Taking care of her clan would always be her top priority, even if it meant an isolated existence to carry out her duties.

CHAPTER SIX

Aaron watched Teagan from the corner of his eye as she conferred with one of her clan members. The older male had gray hair and smile lines around his mouth. His instinct sensed the male was more like a grandfather to Teagan than anything else. It gave Aaron the opportunity to merely watch her as she worked.

In contrast to Stonefire's leader, who used humor to comfort and calm, Teagan often touched a bicep, forearm, or shoulder as she talked. It was a much more female way to handle the situation, but that didn't make it wrong, just different.

His beast spoke up. *You're being too serious. This is a celebration. We should have some fun.*

There's nothing wrong with observing others, especially if we're to work closely with Glenlough in the future.

I think it's more a case of you wanting to defeat her tomorrow morning.

That, too. Knowing your opponent is never a bad thing.

Teagan caught his gaze and she tilted her head at him. Aaron didn't back down. He merely smiled.

She rolled her eyes and focused back on her clan member. Still, Teagan couldn't hide the faint blush on her cheeks that he bet wasn't because of the wine she'd drunk.

His beast spoke up again. *She finds us attractive. Take advantage of it. I bet she's a tiger between the sheets.*

Aaron shouldn't encourage his beast, but he couldn't help but reply, *I think you mean she's a dragon.*

That, too.

His gaze moved to the curve of her neck to where it met her shoulder. Some females were ticklish at that spot, and he wondered if running his bearded jaw against her skin would make her moan or giggle.

If only she weren't clan leader, Aaron would tumble her and leave the next morning without any regrets.

But Teagan *was* clan leader, and he wasn't about to fuck up his assignment to please his cock or his dragon.

His beast huffed. *I'll think of a way we can have it all.*

Not dignifying his dragon with a reply, Aaron watched her a little longer. When she finally leaned to stand and a tendril brushed her chest, he wished he could be the one not only touching but also cupping her soft breast.

Teagan met his gaze, and he refused to back down as she made her way back to him. Once she sat next to him again, she murmured, "Enjoying the view? You're supposed to win over the clan, not stare at me."

He turned a little toward her. "And exactly how am I supposed to win them over? You gave your rah-rah speech, but then quickly left."

The corner of her mouth ticked up. "Did someone miss me?"

"Don't be ridiculous," he answered. "Without you here, people were able to stare at me freely. You should be proud that I didn't start waving to everyone who caught my eye."

"Am I supposed to give you a cookie for not flipping them off instead?"

"Teagan," he growled.

She snorted. "You're so easy to provoke." She waved toward the floor below. "You can wander around the hall freely. Although, I warn you, a few of the younger clan members may accost you. If so, you're on your own."

"So you have rules about where guests need to sit, but you ignore the old tradition of clan leaders leading visitors out to greet the clan?"

She leaned toward him and Aaron resisted the wild, earthy smell that was Teagan to focus on her whispered words. "If you want me to lead you out, you must be asking me to dance."

His beast hummed. *Yes, then we can touch her skin and see how soft it is.*

He cleared his throat. "Don't be ridiculous. I'm merely trying to be polite."

"Oh, I think not." She stood again and offered her arm. "Come, Caruso. You can't refuse the invitation of a clan leader, now, can you?"

"I could, but who says I want to." Aaron stood and threaded his arm through hers. At the contact of her warm skin against his, his heart skipped a beat. He had no idea why the blasted female kept affecting him so, especially knowing she wasn't his true mate.

Pushing aside those thoughts, he was careful to keep his voice even as he added, "Whatever plan you have, I will one-up you on it. You've been warned."

Teagan blinked but quickly regained her composure. "We shall see. I look forward to you failing. It'll be a preview of what's going to happen tomorrow morning."

She moved, and Aaron had no choice but to follow. As he matched her strides, he noticed the people of Glenlough pointing and talking.

The whispers didn't faze Teagan. She kept her head high and her shoulders back as she made a beeline to a table at one side of the large room, where a variety of audio equipment sat. A male stood behind the table with a smile. Once they reached him, he asked, "You're that anxious for my skills, are you, Teagan?"

She laughed. "I just want to show our guest what he's missing. Start with my favorite. But first, I need the microphone."

As the unknown male picked one up, Aaron wondered what was Teagan's favorite.

Her voice blasted into the room. "I know some of you just started eating, but our guest from Stonefire is impatient to dance. So, he and I will kick things off, and then others can join when they're ready."

She handed the microphone back to the male and tugged Aaron toward the cleared area in the center. He frowned. "We're the only ones dancing to this song?"

Amusement danced in her eyes. "Is that a problem? I thought it was difficult to embarrass you."

"Oh, I'm not embarrassed, but if I don't know the dance, I don't want to look the fool so soon."

She grinned. "So you admit to looking the fool sometimes?"

He growled. "I didn't say that."

"I think you did." They reached the cleared area and she released his arm. Once she was a few steps across from him, she put her arms at her side. "And if you don't know this dance, then it's because you skipped class that day and it's your own fault."

Aaron opened his mouth, but the beginning notes of one of the oldest dragon-shifter dances filled the hall. He did know the dance and not just because of class. It was his mother's favorite, and Aaron had had to step up more than once to dance with her after his father's abandonment.

As he bowed, he whispered, "Let's see if you can keep up with me."

The music cut off Teagan's reply and Aaron took the first step.

~~~

Teagan's heart thumped inside her chest. Not because of all the eyes on her. She was used to that.

No, it was because of the devilish look in Aaron's eyes. She had a feeling he'd make her forget about everything but keeping up with him.

Her dragon spoke up. *That's a good thing. Once he knows our touch, he'll be begging to kiss us in a dark corner somewhere.*

Before she could state again that she wasn't going to kiss Aaron that evening, the music began. She and Aaron bowed to one another before circling each other left and then right.

His dark brown eyes were intense, but it was foolish to think he was focusing on her. The male was competitive and out to win. He was probably looking for any fault to take advantage of.

Too bad Teagan was determined to outshine him first. Just because she could take down a male who weighed several stone more than her didn't mean she couldn't be dainty and graceful in order to outdo a male on the dance floor, too.

She put out her right hand and Aaron his left. The instant their palms touched, a shot of electricity raced through her body. But she didn't have time to study Aaron and see if he felt the same pull of attraction as she.
~~~

True mate or not, she would admit he was a handsome male. And with his eyes and smiles, he'd probably danced with many females. Teagan wouldn't read into anything.

They twirled with their hands clasped and released at the right moment to spin around and face each other once more. Aaron reached out and placed a hand on her waist to pull her close. She sucked in a breath at the heat of his skin through the thin material of her dress.

Aaron's pupils flashed to slits and back before he took her hand and led her in the pattern of the dance. As their bodies moved in time to the music, she was content to allow him to lead.

Her dragon chuckled. *It's the first step to my grand plan. I look forward to him leading in other ways, such as when we're naked.*

Teagan concentrated on the steps of the dance before replying, *You're not helping. I don't want to stumble.*

Aaron increased his movements as the tempo picked up. She murmured, "You're better at this than I thought."

He tilted his head. "So are you ready to wax on about my dancing skills?"

She rolled her eyes. "One dance proves nothing. All I have to do is request an Irish one, and you'd be on the sidelines within seconds, nursing a twisted ankle or worse."

"Then it's a good thing I don't own a pair of the special shoes you need to make the tapping sounds. I can sit out from the beginning and merely watch your legs as they flail about."

As Aaron spun her, he pulled her tighter against his body. Only because the dance was ingrained into her being did she not miss a step. Aaron radiated an unimaginable amount of heat. A faint sheen of sweat probably covered her face from both dancing and being in Aaron's proximity.

Her beast spoke up. *We'd never be cold in bed again.*

Focusing on the male, she kept up with him. "We have plenty of those types of shoes to share. I'm sure one of my Protectors would lend you theirs."

"I might twist my ankle, and then I wouldn't be able to face you in the morning. Which would you rather have—me stumbling to prove you're a better dancer or having me available to brush up your skills to prepare for the upcoming challenge?" he asked.

"You're right. I think I'd rather pin you to the ground and have you cede to me. That'll be more satisfying."

Aaron put extra energy into his turn as he murmured, "I was just thinking the same thing."

As the song wound down, Aaron slowed his steps. When they stepped apart to face each other and bow at the final notes, Teagan resisted the urge to take his hand and perform another dance so that their bodies would touch again.

Her dragon huffed. *Invite him to the hallway and we can sneak away.*

As much as I'd love to act like a teenager with her first beau, the clan will have questions about my announcement. I need to make my rounds.

The clan is enjoying dinner and music. They can survive an hour without you.

An hour is being generous. Most males barely last five minutes.

Her dragon grunted. *I have plans. It's fun to tease and prolong the event. There's much we could do before sleeping with him.*

Aware that the music had stopped, Teagan put out her arm and Aaron threaded it through hers again. She quickly said to her beast, *Not tonight.*

Then you didn't say never.

Aaron's husky whispered filled her ear. "Is your dragon impressed with my dancing?"

"Wouldn't you like to know? If you win tomorrow, I'll tell you."

"That just gave me extra incentive. But if I get a boon, then you should have one, too. That will make the competition far more interesting."

You know what we want, her dragon answered.

Teagan knew she was on dangerous ground. Aaron was her link to Stonefire. She should keep her distance and merely use him as a tool to better help Glenlough.

However, before she could stop herself, she blurted, "You come to my cottage and make dinner for me."

He raised his brows a fraction. "How do you even know I can cook?"

"I did my research. I know you can."

He snorted. "That's not much of an ask."

"Ah, but I didn't finish. I want you to make dinners for as long as you're here. I hate cooking, and it'll free up so much time to do other things. Think of it as Stonefire assisting Glenlough. That's quite the important task."

Shaking his head, he replied, "Putting aside your ridiculous excuses, if I'm to agree, then I should get more than your dragon's answer about my dancing. You have to tell me what your dragon is thinking anytime I ask, provided it won't violate security protocols or risk someone's safety."

Her dragon's amused voice filled her head. *That could be fun.*

Teagan could make up excuses and bow out. She outranked Aaron. Soldier that he was, he'd have to accept that if he wished to complete his assignment on Glenlough.

Of course, that would put distance between them. And no matter how much she shouldn't want it, she already craved the ease of being herself in Aaron's presence.

For the first time in a long time, she didn't have to be a leader with someone. She could just be Teagan O'Shea. True, it was in small increments, but it was more than she'd had in years.

She stood a little taller. "Okay, but I'm not worried. I look forward to having a cook for a few weeks."

Aaron leaned over to her ear and murmured, "Since I understand how dragons think, I look forward to hearing what yours has to say. I'm sure your cheeks will go pink several times an hour."

Her dragon cackled, but Teagan ignored her. Since Teagan would win, she didn't worry about her dragon teaming up with Aaron to make her blush.

Her beast chimed in. *You've just issued a challenge to me as well. Maybe I should try to sabotage you and make you lose.*

They approached the table where her mother and grandmother sat. *Behave, or Gran will interrogate us to find out what's going on. Wine can only explain already flushed cheeks and not a sudden burst of pink.*

Fine, I'll save it for later. But just know that I'm not done thinking about him naked. And I really am going to have a think if it'll be more fun to help Aaron win or help you win.

Teagan wanted to shake her head, but she merely whispered to Aaron, "With our deal sealed and out of the way, you need to act like a representative again. My grandmother was once clan leader, and if you're not careful, she'll start thinking that there is something between us. Or worse, she'll play matchmaker, and she's one tenacious dragonwoman."

Aaron's muscles tensed under her fingers. "Can't have that, now, can we?"

His words were practical, but they stung. She only hoped Aaron didn't morph back into a formal, cold Protector. She'd lose her rare chances to be herself again for who knew how long, especially if she never took a mate.

Thankfully Teagan was good at keeping a smile pasted on her face and doing what was necessary in the moment.

Her dragon spoke up. *You could always go to another table first, to better prepare for a meeting with Gran.*

That will only make Gran suspicious. You know that.

Aaron's words prevented her from replying. "That must be her. Let's get this party started. I have a way with charming older females, especially when it comes to strangers."

Teagan barely resisted rolling her eyes. Only because her grandmother had spotted her heading in her direction did Teagan keep her face neutral. While her gran would never berate or question her publicly, she wasn't shy about doing so in private. And she certainly didn't want an interrogation to add to her plate.

Teagan smiled wider and stopped in front of her mother. "Grandmother, Mam, I'd like to introduce Aaron Caruso, from Clan Stonefire. Aaron, this is my grandmother, Orla Kelly, and my mother, Caitlin O'Shea."

Her mum smiled, her blue eyes crinkling at the corners. "It's good to see more Stonefire members on our land. First Bennett Moore-Llewellyn coming with his mate to look after his mother-in-law, then Brenna Rossi, and now you. Before long, it may be like my childhood when we went back and forth without blinking an eye."

Her grandmother frowned. "It wasn't exactly like that, Caitlin. I'm the old biddy who's supposed to romanticize the past." Orla turned her gaze to Aaron and studied him a second. "You're a bit young, son."

Teagan bit the inside of her cheek to keep from laughing. Her grandmother wouldn't be easy to charm, and she looked forward to seeing Aaron try to do so.

~~~

Aaron knew the older, silver-haired dragonwoman was trying to bait him, but she wasn't the first gray-haired dragon to do so. He smiled. "We're all young at heart, which is all that matters."

Orla waved a hand. "I do know a few males in their sixties who act like children. Or even worse, those in their forties who rely on their females to function because they're simply lazy. Irresponsibility is one of the worst faults. There's such a thing as being too young at heart."

"There's also the right amount," Aaron replied. "I'm sure over time I can convince you that I have that balance."

"You're a bit cocky," Orla stated.

"There's cocky and then there's knowing yourself. False modesty tends to delay everything in my opinion. I like optimizing my time. I think you like efficiency, aye?"

The older female studied him before she replied, "That was the right answer. Always be direct with me, Aaron Caruso. I'm too old to beat around the bush."

Teagan's mother, Caitlin, frowned. "Mam, be nice. He's our guest after all."

"If he was a male who required fancy words, I wouldn't still be talking to him. He can handle it, can't you, lad?" Orla asked.

Aaron felt Teagan's eyes on him, but he kept his focus on Orla. "I wouldn't be a Protector if I couldn't."
~~~

Orla chuckled. "Honesty as well." She raised her cane to point it at him. "Still, I'll be watching you. I didn't keep this clan together during my time to see things fall apart now. Undermine my granddaughter and I won't hold back."

Teagan spoke up. "Gran, I can take care of myself."

"Of course you can. But you're still my granddaughter. If I don't look out for you, then who will?"

"Mother, I'm sitting right here," Caitlin answered.

"You're too kindhearted," Orla said with a sigh. "Gracious knows you take after your father's side of the family in that regard."

Sensing a reoccurring argument, Aaron spoke up. "If either one of you cares to dance later, I'd love to claim one. We can get to know each other better."

"Why? Are you planning to court me? I'm not sure you can handle me," Orla stated.

Aaron grinned. "Dancing is all about handling your partner, but I'll be a gentleman and resist your flirtation to do so."

Teagan choked next to him, but Aaron kept his focus on Orla. He sensed he was passing a test and damned if he'd fail.

Amusement danced in Orla's eyes. "I rarely dance these days, but if I can lean on you, then I just might. I'll signal you when I'm ready."

Teagan cleared her throat and Aaron looked over at her. Only because he was standing next to her did he notice the tightness in her jaw.

His dragon laughed. *It seems even clan leaders have to deal with eccentric family members.*

Aaron turned to Teagan's mother. "My offer extends to you as well."

Caitlin smiled warmly. "No, thank you. My son usually wears me out after a few dances."

Orla shook her head. "That boy is too protective of you."

When all three females remained quiet, he sensed there was more to the story.

However, he wasn't going to prod and ruin the mood. Family secrets sometimes needed to be kept that way. "We should be going since Teagan mentioned that I have a lot of people to meet. Until later, Mrs. Kelly. I'll be waiting for our dance."

Orla looked to Teagan. "Just don't wear him ragged before I claim that dance. It's been a long time since a handsome fellow unrelated to me has asked to twirl these old bones around the great hall."

"He'll be more than ready for you, Gran," Teagan answered flatly.

"Good." Orla moved her gaze back to Aaron. "Then I'll see you soon, Mr. Caruso."

After Aaron murmured his goodbyes, they walked toward another table. Once out of earshot of her relatives, Teagan let out a long sigh. Aaron squeezed her arm in his. "I think I managed that well."

"We can discuss you flirting with my grandmother later. For now, I need to ferry you around the room before my gran wants to dance. Keep her waiting and you'll never hear the end of it."

"So, she's a normal grandparent, then?"

Teagan smiled. "Yes, but don't tell anyone else that. She's a former leader first and foremost. She doesn't want to appear soft."

"Well, I like her. She has fire."

Teagan glanced at him for a few seconds before steering him toward a specific table. "Just don't try to poach her for your own clan. Orla Kelly lives and breathes Glenlough."

"I didn't say anything about stealing her. Bram would kill me for bringing a strong-willed, older female for one. But it's nice to have allies whilst living on foreign soil."

"Why do you need her as an ally? So that you can gang up on me?"

"Well, if by some small chance I lose tomorrow morning, then I'll make sure to invite her to dinner most nights. That way it'll be two against one."

He winked and Teagan's pupils flashed. Not for the first time Aaron wondered if her dragon was on his side or against him.

His beast spoke up. *I think she's on our side. Teagan usually blushes when her eyes flash. I may use that later to coax a kiss or more.*

Are you still harping on about sleeping with her?

Why not? She obviously wants us, too.

Before he could think of yet another excuse of why that was a bad idea, Teagan stopped at one of the tables and introduced him to more clan members. His exchange with Orla had lightened his mood, so it was easy to wink and charm.

It also helped distract him from thinking about his challenge with Teagan the next morning.

Chapter Seven

The following morning, as the early rays of sun broke through the clouds, Teagan stood at the edge of a clearing nestled between the hills, with the lake to her right. She hated sharing the location of one of her secret spots with Aaron, but the fewer clan members who knew about her practice with the Stonefire male, the better.

Who knew what her grandmother would do if she found out? Aaron had managed to charm Orla, which was no easy feat. Just remembering her gran trying to dance with him the night before made her want to simultaneously smile and groan. If he kept it up, Orla would try to find ways for the Stonefire male to stay. Orla liked to be entertained, and Aaron was her latest diversion.

Her dragon spoke up. *So? He will be our diversion soon enough.*

Speaking of the devil, Aaron's large green dragon form came into view. As his powerful wing muscles moved and flapped, she had to admit he was a fine specimen.

Her beast huffed. *We are better.*

So now you're on my side?

I'm on my own side.

Aaron maneuvered his dragon down and gently landed about ten feet away. As his body began to shrink, her heart rate kicked up. She was finally going to see his nude body.

Not that she should care. All males, especially when it came to Protectors, had the same parts—muscled chests, broad shoulders, toned abs, and powerful thighs. Yet as Aaron's human form took shape, she studied his nice but not a rug amount of chest hair, chiseled abs, and the defined V of his hip bones that made all females drool. When she finally reached his groin, her dragon hummed. *He'll do nicely.*

Teagan tried her best not to flush, but knowing her traitorous pale skin, it would still show.

Aaron strode toward her with a smile. "Glad that you like what you see, darling."

She raised an eyebrow. "My name isn't 'darling.' And I was merely assessing my opponent. Isn't that what you said you were doing last night?"

He grinned wide. "Tell yourself that's all it is, if it helps." He reached where she stood and the faint breezed ruffled his hair. Teagan nearly reached out to put a stray lock back into place, but Aaron's voice prevented her from doing so. He continued, "But I know your time is valuable, so state the rules and let's begin."

She paused a second at his words, somewhat surprised he realized her time was short, and finally replied, "The rules are simple. There will be two rounds in dragon form. You'll be the first to hide. I'll then have to find you and, in order to win, I have to get you to admit defeat. You can also win the round by making me cede. For the second round, I'll hide, and again the winner has to get the other to admit to losing. If we each win one round, then we'll have a final tussle in human form. The only restriction to any of the rounds is not killing or permanently maiming each other. Questions?"

"Tussle, aye? Since I didn't bring any clothes, I'll have to be careful. Although it almost seems an advantage to be wearing your loose dress to protect all your lady bits."

Teagan resisted the urge to smooth the purple and blue patterned material. "If it comes to a tie-breaker, then I'll take off my dress. After all, it would only hinder my movement, and I want to pin you as soon as possible."

"If you can at all."

"Well, cocky lad, it's your turn to hide first. I'm counting to a hundred and going after you."

She began her countdown and Aaron dashed far enough away to shift. She watched his body grow into a large dragon.

Her beast spoke up. *I want to feel his hide. I see at least one scar running down his side. There's a story there. Maybe even a brave one.*

Or a stupid one. The point of this morning isn't to feel his skin in either form. Focus, dragon, so we can win. Then he'll be over every evening. That should please you.

Her beast snorted. *I knew you wanted more than cooked meals. With him over, then we can kiss him whenever we like without the clan knowing. If anyone asks, all we'll have to do is mention he lost a bet, so that's why he's at our cottage.*

I'm more interested in having a chef. You can ogle him and get the Stonefire male out of your system.

You'll see it my way soon enough. Him being around will give me time to convince you. I already know you like spending time with him.

Her earlier confidence about Aaron not being her true mate slipped a fraction. *Are you hiding something from me?*

No. But sometimes a true mate isn't the best option for all involved.

Her beast fell silent. Rather than think about her dragon's cryptic message, Teagan continued to count as Aaron flew into the distance.

Most of the hills in Glenveagh National Park, which was where Clan Glenlough was located, weren't high enough to hide a dragon unless they crouched down. And a dragon hunched with their wings folded against their back had little room to jump into the air on short notice. All she had to do was eliminate the hills shorter than Aaron's dragon form, and it would narrow her list of possible hiding spots.

When she finally counted to one hundred, Teagan tugged the dress over her head and imagined her arms and legs growing, her nose elongating into a snout, and wings sprouting from her back. The second she stood in her gold dragon form, she leaped into the air and quickly surveyed the land.

Aaron wasn't behind any of the hills in her immediate area. Neither could she scent him, which meant he was either positioned downwind or far enough away that she couldn't pinpoint his location. Combining her knowledge of the area and the wind's current direction, Teagan took off toward the south.

As she scanned the land below, she wanted to laugh at fate making Aaron a green dragon. Ireland in summer was bright green, especially this year with the amount of rain they'd had, which made him harder to spot.

Teagan approached one of her favorite hiding spots as a child, nestled between two hills. One of the bushes moved in the opposite direction of the wind, signaling that something alive was there. She folded her wings against her back and dove down.

The next instant Aaron jumped into the air and used the combination of the wind and his powerful muscles to fly away. Male dragons had slightly larger wingspans than most females, but females were lighter. Teagan embraced her beast and beat her wings as hard as she could.

Aaron dove toward the lake, but rather than pull up, he went into the water. Teagan hovered in the air above and waited for him to surface. As long as she was in the air, she had the advantage.

When Aaron didn't come up for air, she wondered if he'd hit his head on one of the large rocky outcroppings beneath the water's surface. Many parts of the lake were deep, but the shallower areas had caused more than a few injuries to young dragon-shifters in the past who had acted before assessing anything.

Her beast spoke up. *Give him another minute. Otherwise, he might be playing on our concern for others.*

She wanted to argue that concern shouldn't be seen as a negative trait, but her dragon was right. When it came to a challenge, a good Protector would use whatever tools they had at their disposal.

A green dragon head popped out of the lake close to the shore, followed by the rest of his upper body as he stood upright in the shallow water. Snapping his wings, water droplets danced in the air before Aaron jumped into the sky once more.

Teagan swooped toward him and managed to collide with his large green body. Opening her wings to slow their descent, they hit the ground softly enough to not do any damage. As they rolled on the ground, Teagan noticed Aaron had a harder time gaining control from the left side. So she changed her movements to keep forcing him to move to the left. She nearly had him pinned, but Aaron finally managed to use his heavier weight to flip them over. Before he could pin her shoulders, she smacked her tail against his testicles. Aaron roared, and Teagan rolled out from under him and jumped onto his back. Wrapping her forelimb around his throat, she applied enough pressure to make his breathing ragged, but not enough to suffocate him.

Aaron tried to knock her off with his tail, but Teagan ignored the sharp stings with each slap. She growled in question—Would he cede?

For good measure, she placed the talons of her free hand at the major artery running down Aaron's neck and pressed gently.

Aaron's entire body went limp, and he gave a low roar.

Teagan had won.

Jumping back, she waited for Aaron to shift. His wings melded into his back, his stature shrunk, and his green hide faded into the olive complexion of his human form. Once the shift was complete, he glared at her. "What the fuck was that? You slapping me in the balls is against every rule I've ever seen in a dragon competition."

Teagan shrugged a golden shoulder. In her experience, major challenges like those for a clan leadership never followed all the rules. She also had stated earlier the only restrictions were to not kill or permanently maim. Stinging balls was certainly within that purview.

Not that she was going to shift and explain it to Aaron. Teagan crouched down and jumped into the air. It was her turn to hide.

As she flew away from Aaron, she just made out his "Bloody hell." Smiling as much as a dragon could smile, she flapped her wings harder. One round down, another to go.

~~~

Aaron watched Teagan's golden form disappear into the horizon. He'd lost and rather easily, too.
~~~

His pride might be hurt, but his defeat only fueled him to defeat her. There literally didn't seem to be any rules beyond don't kill. He wasn't going to hold back any longer.

His dragon growled. *I told you not to go easy on her just because she's female.*

Believe me, I'm not going to do so any longer. She wants a challenge, and I'm going to try to give it to her.

He envisioned his body changing shape again and once complete, he jumped into the air.

Since Teagan was a gold dragon, she would need to be more creative with her hiding spot. There wasn't much gold or brown to hide her in the summertime.

Aaron might not know the area, but that didn't mean much to a Protector. Enemies often didn't show up in one's neighborhood, but they still needed to be defeated. With her limited options, she either had to hide in a lake or in a big enough copse of trees.

His dragon chimed in. *Or in a cave, or even a large hole.*

I know, dragon.

His beast huffed. *Just making sure. If you don't give her a decent showing, then I may have to take control. Otherwise, we're not really helping her prepare for any possible challengers.*

Until this round ends, she's the enemy and nothing more.

You just want to impress her.

No, I just want to win.

Losing wouldn't be so bad, his dragon said. *After all, we can see her every night.*

Aaron was careful to keep his thoughts focused on the task and not what could happen if he saw her every evening. *If she sees us as weak, then she might send us home. Italy made us softer than I realized.*

We're not soft. Now stop chatting and let's win this round.

Aaron would usually point out his dragon had started the conversation, but instead, he embraced his dragon's senses. There was no sweet female scent in the air and no gold hide glinting in the weak sunlight. While the densest woods were near the former human castle, Aaron didn't think Teagan would go near them just in case any humans were around; two dragons fighting, even near a dragon clan's lands, would probably earn a reprimand or even a punishment from the Irish DDA.

And considering Aaron was in Ireland without an official visitation pass, he might end up in jail.

Looking farther afield, he also spotted a small island in the middle of the lake covered in trees, but that would severely limit her escape options.

However, there was a denser field of trees a mile or so ahead, away from the castle grounds.

Careful to remain downwind as much as possible, he made his way toward them. Teagan may have shifted back to her human form despite her rules, but Aaron was going to remain a dragon. That would give him the advantage, even if he had to crash through the trees and possibly break a bone or two to capture her.

His dragon grunted. *No breaking bones. We'll be no good to her then.*

If it means we win one round, then it'll be worth it.

Why do you care so much about her approval?

Can we talk about this later? I have a female to find.

His beast fell silent, and Aaron looked for any broken trees or unusual movement beneath him.

On closer inspection, many of the trees were too short to hide a full-grown dragon. But some of the ones slanted on a hill could be deceiving. The curve of their trunks could possibly create a big enough space for Teagan to lay in wait.

He hovered above a large hill, using the wind currents when possible to conserve his energy. The scent of female hit his nose and he moved a fraction lower to the treetops. The smell intensified from the area directly below him.

The scent marking could be a trap, but as it continued to invade Aaron's senses, she had to be below him or the scent would have dissipated already. It wasn't as if she were carrying around a sack of worn clothing to mislead him.

Spying his best opening, Aaron folded his wings and dropped down between the trees. One crashed into his right side, but he paid it no attention. His eyes adjusted to the dimmer light, but he didn't spot any sign of golden hide. *Fuck.* Just as he looked up to find his best way out, Teagan's naked human form jumped out. She caught his neck with her arms and slid around to his back. In a split second, she had a talon extended and against his artery once more, but fuck if he'd lose again.

He imagined his form shrinking down to a human. As his form changed shape, Teagan landed with an oomph next to him, facedown; she'd probably had the wind knocked out of her.

He didn't waste any time, and the second he stood in his human form again, he lunged to cover her body with his. With adrenaline pumping through his body, he didn't pay attention to her naked back and arse against him.

Wrapping an elbow around her neck and grabbing a fistful of hair, he gently tugged her head back. "You lose. Cede to me."

With a growl, she rocked her head back and hit his chin. He loosened his grip at the quick, sharp pain and Teagan managed to roll them both over. She quickly moved to straddle his neck between her thighs and reached back to grab his thumbs. As she pulled his thumbs farther back in the wrong direction, he grunted. She was going to fucking break his fingers.

Yet between her flashing pupils and her heaving chest above him, Aaron almost wanted to lose if it meant he could stare at Teagan's supple body a minute longer.

Then his beast roared inside his head. *No. We win this time.*

The words snapped Aaron back to reality. He swung his legs up and around Teagan's neck before pulling her down. She released her grip and Aaron flipped until he had her belly to the ground. He tugged her wrists behind her and dug his knee into her back. For good measure, he tugged her arms a little more until she grunted. He growled, "I win this round. Cede."

For a few beats, only the sound of their labored breathing filled the air. Then Aaron leaned a bit more of his weight into Teagan's back. She cried out, and his every instinct wanted to release her and examine her to ensure she wasn't hurt.

But giving up wouldn't help her prepare for a possible challenge. The other Irish clan leaders sure as hell wouldn't stop to check for injuries.

He gripped her wrists tighter and yanked a little more. "Admit defeat and we go to the tie-breaker round. Me observing you in action will only help you in the long run."

Teagan relaxed under his body. "Fine, then you win this one."

Aaron released her and stood. As she rolled over, he offered a hand, and she took it.

Pulling her up, she tripped and stumbled against his body. Aaron held her close to keep her from falling, but her nipples were hard points against his chest, and his cock took notice.

If he leaned down to take one of the tempting points into his mouth, he wondered if Teagan would tell him to stop or thread her fingers through his hair and beg for more.

He moved a hand down her spine, but before he could reach the indent of her lower back, Teagan raised her head to meet his eyes. Her pupils were slitted. Maybe her dragon wanted the same thing.

Or she might tell him to stop.

No, his dragon purred. *You can smell her arousal as much as me.*

Her husky voice interrupted his thoughts. "I think you're happy to see me, Caruso."

She leaned her body back a fraction. Before he could growl and pull her back, she lightly ran her hand down his chest. The movements of her fingers made his skin burn and yearn for the light scratch of her nails.

As she inched downward, Aaron held his breath. His cock was hard and heavy against his belly, and it pulsed for Teagan's light touch.

She brushed his sensitive tip and lightly teased his swollen flesh with her nails. He groaned, and she moved her finger from his tip to the side of his shaft.

Without thinking, he whispered, "Fuck, don't stop."

Teagan chuckled and wrapped her fingers around his cock. She squeezed gently, and Aaron dared to move a hand to her breast. If he was going to lose his mind, then so was she.

He tweaked her nipple, and Teagan hissed between her teeth. As he continued to pinch and roll the hard bud, she increased the pressure of her grip on his cock. Between her touch, her feminine scent invading his nose, and the heat of her body so close to his, Aaron said screw it. One kiss couldn't hurt. They could both use a little post-battle release.

He leaned down, but when he was a fraction away from making contact with her lips, something sharp poked against his balls.

Teagan's husky voice filled his ears. "I win this round and thus overall."

He blinked. "So all of this was a ruse?"

"Oh, I enjoyed making you moan. But this is a contest, and I'll do whatever it takes to win."

The sharp pressure against his balls, which had to be her fucking talons, increased. He growled. "You wouldn't."

"Oh, believe me, I would. The choice of becoming a eunuch or not is yours. Do you cede?"

He pushed aside the sting of falling for her trap. Blasted females always seemed to use him for something. "I think you're bluffing," he bit out.

She raised her brows. "You obviously haven't experienced a true clan leader challenge. Beyond not killing or permanently maiming an opponent, there are no rules." She pushed her talon harder against him. "Although sometimes the no maiming requirement gets a bit fuzzy."

"In other words, you cheat."

She shrugged. "Do you always play by the rules when it comes to missions or protecting the clan?"

He grudgingly muttered, "Fair point."

She tilted her head as she tapped one of her talons against his bollocks. "Now, admit defeat and maybe I'll suggest another competition in the future. Then you can give me an actual challenge."

It was on the tip of his tongue to make a pithy retort, but his dragon spoke up. *Just do it. Not only will we see her every evening and can better assess her weaknesses, but we can propose another bet and win next time. Maybe then we can claim more than knowing her thoughts or how she hisses when we play with her nipples. I want to explore her body with our tongue.*

For all we know, she faked everything to trap us.

She did it to win a competition. It has nothing to do with toying with your heart.

Fuck, dragon, you make me sound like a sentimental fool.

His beast sniffed. *Sometimes you are. Give Teagan a real chance.*

As Teagan stared at him, waiting for an answer, he wondered if he'd feel the same way if a male had cheated to best him. Granted, a dragonman wouldn't turn him on with delicate fingers and pert breasts, but there were always other ways to startle and/or disarm an opponent. Teagan had merely used the tools available to her.

In other words, she was clever.

On top of that, while Aaron should feel used, after his brief encounter with Teagan's fingers on his cock and his hands on her breasts, he wanted more. He had no desire to form a long-term attachment, but taking her to bed a time or two would do.

He cleared his throat. "I will admit defeat on one condition—that we have a rematch soon. Now that I know there aren't any rules, I plan to do whatever it takes to win, no holds barred."

Teagan raised her brows. "In real life, there aren't always second chances. But since I'm curious to see what Aaron Caruso looks like without holding back, I'll consider it. However, I want to have a personal chef for a few nights at least before I risk giving it up."

He searched her gaze. "So you think I can win?"

She shrugged. "A leader who thinks they're invincible is bound to fail sooner rather than later."

Aaron's opinion of Teagan went up a notch. "All right, then I cede and look forward to our next rematch."

The pressure of talons against Aaron's balls disappeared and she patted him twice, sending a jolt up through his body. "Good. I'd rather not damage your goods." She glanced down and back up. "They are fairly impressive."

His beast spoke up. *She wants us.*

As they stared into one another's eyes, Aaron waited for Teagan to move away, but she didn't budge. She merely tilted her head once more. "Like what you see, Caruso? Or has being bested by a female turned you sour?"

The curiosity in her green eyes was genuine.

There were a hundred reasons why Aaron should make a crack and walk away. The disaster with Nerina being the biggest one. He also knew that battles always made him hard and ready for sex. But as her hot breath tickled his chin, he didn't think of the alliance, his past, or why he needed to get back to Stonefire. He itched to fist Teagan's hair and taste her sweet lips. Something about the female called to his baser urges.

His dragon growled. *Just kiss her before she changes her mind.*

He placed a hand on her bare hip and lightly brushed her skin. Some males might be intimidated by the toned flesh under his fingers, but Aaron only saw strength and dedication. Teagan did what was necessary to protect her clan.

Her flashing pupils gave him the courage to murmur, "I'm the opposite of sour. I'm impressed. And I'm going to prove it to you."

Leaning down, Aaron kissed her.

~~~
~~~

Being surrounded by trees in an isolated area had emboldened Teagan. First with nearly giving Aaron a hand job and then prodding him with words.

Her plan to distract him had nearly backfired, though. Just the light brush of his fingers had almost made her knees give out. His skin was rough, yet warm. Aaron was a male who wasn't afraid to work with his hands. She'd always had a weakness for strong, rough hands.

Her dragon hummed. *Yes, yes, I want to feel them everywhere.*

She ignored her beast and studied Aaron's eyes. As soon as he admitted defeat, she could've easily walked away and gone back to Glenlough. The sting to Aaron's pride would've sent him packing and given her one less distraction to worry about.

But as her heart thumped in her chest and the flesh between her thighs pulsed, she admitted that she wanted at least one taste of his lips. She couldn't even remember the last time she'd kissed a male.

Her dragon huffed. *That is your own fault.*

And risk another incident like with Bard? I don't need a male boasting to the entire clan of kissing me and then saying how mediocre I am.

Pshaw. He was the sloppy kisser. I feel sorry for whatever female ends up with him.

Aaron lowered his head toward hers and Teagan decided she had a few minutes to spare for herself, without thinking of the clan. Anything to ease tension would help in her quest to fend off challengers to her role, so it wasn't completely selfish.

Aaron's warm lips brushed hers before taking the bottom lip between his teeth. As he worried the tender flesh, Teagan wrapped her arms around his neck and opened her mouth to welcome his tongue. There was no mate-claim frenzy spreading through her body, driving her to fuck Aaron until she carried his child, but as his tongue stroked hers, she groaned and leaned against him.

He was no sloppy kisser.

As he tangled his tongue with hers, she met him stroke for stroke. Teagan wasn't the type of female to give up easily, and it was best Aaron understood that now.

Her dragon hummed. *And why is that?*

She ignored her beast to rub her nipples against Aaron's chest. The light dusting of chest hair rubbed against her own tender skin, and she increased the strokes of her tongue.

She had a feeling Aaron was the type of male to meet her head-on in bed.

Aaron moved a hand to cup one arse cheek and lightly squeezed. Each whisper of his fingers caused heat to flare and shoot straight between her thighs.

Her dragon growled. *Yes, yes. Maybe he'll take us right here. I like sex in the open.*

As if reading her dragon's mind, Aaron swung her around until her back pressed against a tree. She broke the kiss at the swift movement, but Aaron beat her to speaking first. His flashing eyes told her his dragon was close to the surface. "Tell me what you want, Teagan," he whispered. "I don't want to disappoint Glenlough's leader."

At the mention of "leader," it was as if ice doused her body.

Aaron was just like all the other males who'd pursued her since becoming clan leader and saw her role first and the individual second. She was just a notch to add to his belt. Once he returned home, he could brag about fucking her.

She pushed hard against his chest, and Aaron stepped back with a puzzled expression. "What?"

She shook her head. "This never should've happened." Teagan took a deep breath and added, "Killian will be expecting you. And don't forget, you're cooking me dinner. Make sure you're fully clothed when you show up, or I'll have a special set of clothes waiting for you. Ones that will make you think twice about disobeying my orders."

"Teagan—"

She ignored him and strode toward the edge of the trees. She needed to put distance between them.

Her beast growled. *Why did you stop?*

If you have to ask that question, then you don't know me at all.

Her beast sighed. *He doesn't want us simply because we're leader.*

And you know this how?

I sense it.

Too bad. I allowed a hot body and my own desire to cloud my judgment before. Any male who kisses me and wants another one does so because he wants me for me. My position shouldn't be the first factor.

But—

No. I've let you convince me with too many males in the past, and they all saw me as something to be conquered. And then I had to quell the questions about my judgment and ability to lead. Never again, especially when I have challenges coming from other clans. I can't afford a challenge from within Glenlough itself.

Not wanting to argue with her dragon on the subject, Teagan tossed her beast into a mental prison.

Smoothing her hair, Teagan picked up her pace but kept to the trees. She had several secret clothing stashes around the national park. With humans often visiting, she wasn't going to risk being stranded.

As the underbrush and lower branches tickled her skin, Teagan took a deep breath and clenched her fingers into fists at her sides. If she were male, things would be easier. She could sleep with whomever she wished, and the clan would joke about trying out the clan to find the right partner.

However, she was female. And despite Glenlough's rare tradition of mostly female leaders, the old views on sex and mates still prevailed. She was expected to have one male and only one; sleeping around marked her as indecisive. Bloody hell, in her grandmother's time, they often had expected the females to remain virgins until they mated, but not the males. And some of the elder clan members probably expected the same of Teagan.

During her first year as leader, she'd given those beliefs the finger and slept with whomever took her fancy. It hadn't taken long for it to bite her in the arse. She'd come dangerously close to a leadership challenge because of rumors spread by a disgruntled former lover.

Well, fuck that. Raising her head high, reason returned to her brain. She'd just have to swear off all males until either she found a partner who'd help her challenge tradition or Teagan eventually gave up her role as leader to have a family.

Regardless, she wouldn't be used as another male's power play. And most certainly not by an English dragonman. She'd just have to show him his place and not waver from it.

Chapter Eight

As Aaron reached the cottage where he was staying on Glenlough, he slammed the door shut behind him and stomped up the stairs.

He hadn't expected Teagan to lead him on and then walk away.

His beast spoke up. *It's not fair to assume she led us on or used us. That was Nerina's way.*

Then what the fuck happened? I was even being charming.

There's much we don't know about Teagan. Maybe if we spend some time with Orla, we'll find out.

And why should I care? We kissed her and there's no true mate pull. Most dragons would move on and look to the next female.

His beast huffed. *She is interesting. I want to know her better.*

Since when are you going against your instinct?

This isn't the Middle Ages. If there's an intriguing female, we can pursue her. I'd rather have someone keep us on our toes than merely find a female to have a baby.

Aaron drawled, *That's pretty forward-thinking for a dragon.*

Stop insulting me or I'll replay the kiss with Teagan when you least expect it.

Don't even think about it.

Just watch me.

His dragon turned his back and ignored Aaron, which was bloody hard to do considering it was inside their shared mind.

Still, he'd let his beast cool down. Aaron needed to calm down himself and shower before meeting with Killian. Teagan's scent covered his body, and he didn't need the questions.

He gathered some clothes and hopped into the shower. As the hot water cascaded over his body, the heat eased his muscles and bruised ribs. He had just stepped out to dry off when someone pounded on his front door. Quickly wiping his body, Aaron wrapped the towel around his waist and went downstairs. He opened the door to a stoic Killian.

Aaron raised an eyebrow. "I didn't expect a social call from you."

Killian grunted and pushed his way into the cottage. Once the front door was closed, Killian spoke up. "Where did you go this morning with my sister?"

"That's her business. Ask her."

"I trust her, but I'm on the fence about you."

"You trusted me to help with tracking down those dragon hunters not that long ago." Killian took two steps closer to him, but Aaron didn't so much as bat an eyelash. He continued, "Look, I'm going to make this easy on you. I have no interest in your sister that way. I'm here to hold up my end of the bargain and go home. But if you persist in harassing me about this, then I may just mention to Teagan how her brother is being overprotective. That can't be good for her image."

Killian clenched his jaw and his pupils flashed. After a few beats, he replied, "Watch yourself, Caruso. If you hurt anyone in my family, be it my sister or my grandmother, I will personally hand out your punishment. Your cheekiness and swagger won't help you there."

It was on the tip of Aaron's tongue to make a snide comment, but he forced himself to be civil. Fighting with Killian would cause an unnecessary headache for Teagan, and she didn't need that with possible trials hanging over her head. "Understood. Is there any other reason why you trekked all this way?"

"Yes. The invite was put out this morning, and two clan leaders have confirmed that they're going to challenge Teagan for the leadership. As an outsider, you're going to be in charge of security for some of the judges, who will all be from other clans."

"So you don't trust me to meet with your sister, but you trust me to do this?" he drawled.

Killian grunted. "You know the Scottish clan well and they trust you. That makes my job easier if they accept the invitation."

"Wait, what? Who is coming from where? I can't do my job if I don't know what is going on."

Killian crossed his arms over his chest. "The other leaders agreed to the challenge provided that unaffiliated parties conduct the judging. Each clan nominates a pair from their list of allies. Since none of them will have direct ties to Ireland, it will help with lessening bias."

"Except for the part where they're allies," he murmured.

"All judges must come to a consensus. The differing viewpoints will have to convince each other of the best choice."

Aaron had to admit that was a clever idea. "So who's coming from Clan Lochguard in Scotland to judge?"

Killian answered, "Teagan is asking for Lochguard's head Protector, Grant McFarland, and his co-leader, Faye MacKenzie."

A female judge would definitely help rein in the bias against Teagan. "And the others?"

"Wildheath has people coming from Snowridge in Wales, and Greenpeak has people coming from Normandy in France."

Aaron tilted his head. "As in Clan PerleForet?"

Killian nodded. "Yes. The French clan has long been an ally of the Killarney dragon-shifters."

"And the Irish DDA is just going to allow the French to waltz into Ireland?" he asked.

"As long as no more than four dragon-shifters come from a particular clan, and the total for all visitors remains under twenty, they will allow it."

Aaron doubted the British DDA would be that understanding, let alone grant permission so quickly. There must be a history in Ireland he wasn't aware of. "So when does this take place and when will McFarland and MacKenzie arrive, provided they agree to judge?"

"The judges will arrive in two weeks, the day before the competition. As for the trials, Teagan has fifteen days to put it together."

"That's a rather specific number." When Killian didn't expand, Aaron sighed. "Fine, I'll find the meaning on my own. Is there anything else that can't wait? I'd rather have clothes on before I start my next duty."

"Considering my grandmother has requested your presence, you had better be dressed. I'll wait here. We'll leave as soon as you're done."

Aaron wanted to say he didn't need a bloody escort, but since he hadn't received a formal tour of Glenlough, he didn't actually know where Orla Kelly lived.

He took the stairs two at a time. Inside his room, he dressed and wondered what the elderly dragonwoman wanted with him. It had to be important if his visit took precedence over arranging security for Faye and Grant.

~~~

Teagan glanced at her computer screen for the tenth time. She didn't know Finlay Stewart—the Scottish leader of Clan Lochguard—that well beyond rumors, but she needed his help. The question was whether he'd answer her sudden request for a video conference or not.

She went back to the stack of DDA paperwork on her desk. A few more minutes ticked by, but her screen remained blank.

Maybe she'd have to reach out to Clan Stonefire first and ask their leader to reach out to Finn. Sure, it had to be a surprise for Lochguard to learn that Glenlough's leader was a female and that Killian was merely used as a ruse. But from what she knew, Finn would be open to that more than most given his own troubles with his clan accepting him because of his nontraditional views on dealing with humans.

On top of that, he was around her age. Usually that helped with being treated as an equal compared to dealing with the elderly.

Just as she moved a completed form off her paperwork stack, her video conference app rang. She cleared her throat, squared her shoulders, and hit Receive. The blond-haired, tired-but-smiling face of Finn Stewart filled her screen. He spoke first. "I'll admit I was surprised to learn that Glenlough's leader was actually a female, let alone that you wanted to talk with me, but I'm always open to expanding my list of allies. What did you need, O'Shea?"
~~~

While she wanted to ask why he accepted a female in charge so easily, Teagan focused on what was important. "I actually need a favor."

"Oh, aye? And what type of favor are we asking for?" She explained the challenge and upcoming trials. Before she could ask her favor, Finn frowned and said, "Don't those bastards have more important things to take care of than to worry about what set of genitals a leader has?"

She smiled. "You would think so, but they aren't as secure in their manhood as you are." She waved to the pink baby blanket sitting on his shoulder.

Finn shrugged. "I have a daughter, and her mother hates pink, so of course I have to use it as often as possible. If that makes me a bad leader, then maybe the person thinking so shouldn't be part of my clan."

She raised her brows. "Wait, you irritate your mate on purpose? Despite the fact she recently birthed three babies?"

"Aye, it's what we do. It's part of the deal with loving me. But that's not what this call is about. Ask me directly what you want, or I'll end the call. I have three bairns that'll be waking up soon."

Teagan didn't so much as blink an eye at the steel in Finn's voice. She wanted to point out that he had derailed the conversation, but restrained herself until she knew him better to fully speak her mind. "Each participating leader needs to invite two judges from a non-Irish clan. I was hoping you could give me two of your Protectors. Your coheads, McFarland and MacKenzie, would be my top choices."

Finn studied her a second. "If I do this, then I want to start talks about an alliance. That way Bram can't lord it over me at every opportunity."

She tilted her head. "Despite barely knowing me, you seem fairly confident I'll win."

He shrugged. "You care enough for your clan to put up with this bullshit challenge. Add asking me for a favor out of the blue, and I admire your guts."

Her beast chimed in. *I like him. He will make a good ally.*

Rather than argue about how her dragon could be so certain already, Teagan answered Finn. "We'll start talks of alliance as soon as the trial is over."

"Good. And no more being polite with me either, O'Shea. I can sense you holding back. If you ever make it to Lochguard, you'll see that isn't admired here." She nodded and wondered if she'd ever have a chance to see his clan. Finn continued, "Then I'll send you my dual head Protectors, Grant and Faye."

"Good. I was hoping at least Faye could come. Female Protectors are rare in Ireland."

The corner of Finn's mouth ticked up. "Aye, you aren't the only one challenging tradition, lass."

A few minutes ago, she would've let the term slip, but Finn wanted honesty. "I'm not a 'lass.'"

"Right you are, O'Shea. You passed the test. I'll send Faye and Grant's information after I chat with them." A baby cried in the background. "The song has started. I'll reach out to you later."

The screen went black.

Exiting the video conference app, Teagan swiveled her chair to the other side of her desk. She spoke to her dragon. *That went better than expected. I'm sure the other leaders are going to be upset with me for including a female judge.*

Too bad. We might not know Faye MacKenzie, but she will help keep the judges from turning against you simply because you're female. They must all agree for a winner to be announced.

And who knows, the French clan may have a female judge as well. Our clans have never been close, so I know so little about them.

Her dragon merely grunted to end the conversation, and Teagan focused back on her paperwork. Every form had to be filled out in duplicate and sent to the DDA office by the end of the day if she wanted to hold the trial at all.

Paperwork was definitely her least favorite activity, but it kept her mind busy. An hour had soared by before there was a knock on the door. "Come in."

Colm MacDermot walked into her study. With his warm smile and gift of handling the younger dragon-shifters, not to mention being born and bred on Glenlough, he was exactly the type of male she should want at her side.

But his friendly gaze did nothing for her, unlike Aaron Caruso's heated looks. All Aaron had to do was stare into her eyes and her heart rate would tick up.

She wondered if she'd ever find a good compromise within her own clan.

Her dragon huffed. *I want more than a compromise.*

Ignoring her beast, she smiled at Colm. "Is it time for the midafternoon break already?"

Colm looked around her office. "I still say you should have some help dealing with all of this. Most clan leaders have assistants."

"Well, let's just say that between dispelling rumors, facing challenges, and now coordinating a leadership trial, I don't have a lot of time to vet possible assistants."

Colm sat in the chair in front of her desk. "Once this is over, you need to make time or I might mention to your mother how tired you look."

Teagan sighed. "Please don't. Mam will probably come here herself to help ease the burden. Considering she runs the clan's daycare, she doesn't have the time to spare." She sat up straight in her chair. "But enough about that. As I mentioned yesterday, I need your help."

He smiled warmly. "Name what you need, Teagan."

"I need for you to comb through the records from previous leadership trials. I want this one to be unique, and unlike any other they've faced."

"A bit of surprise to throw their way?"

"Aye, I hope so. I know you're busy with classes, but can I count on you? If you need a helper or two, Aaron Caruso and Brenna Rossi can do it."

Colm paused a second before stating, "Your dance with Caruso last night seemed a bit intense. You want to talk about that?"

Since many years ago, Colm had fancied Teagan. She wasn't about to hurt him unnecessarily by talking about another male. "Definitely not. We're both competitive, end of story."

Colm studied her and shrugged. "I won't pry. But if you need a listening ear, I'm here."

Her beast chimed in. *Please don't encourage him. He's nice, but boring.*

He would make an excellent partner to challenge tradition.

Right, and he'd be afraid to push you like you need. Compare how you feel now—calm, rational, and collected—to when you see Aaron tonight.

Her dragon sent a rush of images of Aaron's naked body, both standing in front of them and on top of her. *Damn you, dragon.*

Her beast merely chuckled. Teagan pushed aside the images and focused back on Colm. "Thanks, Colm. Let's meet every other day, but you can come anytime if you find something important."

Colm nodded and stood. "I'll probably reach out to Caruso for help. It'll give me a better chance to assess him myself."

She didn't know if it was to protect the clan in general or her specifically. "I already have one overprotective brother. I don't need another."

Hurt flashed in Colm's eyes but disappeared before she could blink. "You carry a lot on your shoulders, Teagan. There's nothing wrong with the clan looking after you, too. I'd do it even if you were male."

"Colm, I'm sorry—"

He put up a hand. "Don't worry about it. You're under a lot of stress." He glanced at the clock on the wall. "I need to get back to my students. Their other class is nearly over."

Before she could say anything else, Colm exited the room.

Teagan laid her head on her desk. She'd unintentionally hurt one of her greatest supporters. She would have to be more careful of what she said.

Her beast spoke up. *It's stress and denying what you truly want.*

If you say something about sex, then so help me, I will keep you locked up all day.

You said it, not me.

Her dragon turned her back and ignored her. Teagan let out a long breath and then sat up again. Maybe having Caruso come over to cook her dinner had been a bad suggestion.

Regardless, she wasn't going to run away now. The evening would give her the chance to clear the air between them and regain her focus. She couldn't afford to snap at any more of her clan members, especially when they merely tried to help her.

Chapter Nine

Aaron sat inside Orla's cottage on an old, worn sofa covered in faded flowers. It seemed all the Glenlough leaders, both former and current, liked to keep him waiting.

His dragon spoke up. *She is elderly. If she doesn't arrive soon, we should check on her.*

As Aaron debated whether to listen to his dragon or not, Orla thumped down the hall and into the room. Using her cane, she maneuvered herself into a pale blue armchair. Once her arse made contact with the cushion, she gripped the top of her cane with both hands and leaned forward. "I know you left with my granddaughter this morning. Tell me why."

Bloody hell, not her, too. Aaron raised his brows. "That is between Teagan and I. Killian asked the same. It seems your family thinks it's okay to ask around behind Teagan's back instead of confronting her directly."

Orla thumped her cane against the floor. "My concern is with you, not her. Tell me."

"No."

Silence stretched for nearly a minute before Orla nodded. "You know how to keep your trap shut, which is a good sign."

He resisted rubbing his brow. "Is there a reason I'm here? Because if it's just to pass some bloody test, then I'm going to leave."

"Hold your horses, boyo. I have a job for you."

"Since when are you handing out assignments?"

She tilted her head. "Since when am I not?"

Aaron sighed. "And here I thought coming to Glenlough would be an easy assignment."

Orla thumped her cane once more. "Oh, hush. In my time, we had feuds going on, plus the nonsense the humans call The Troubles. Being close to Derry is both a good and bad thing."

"Shouldn't you say 'Londonderry slash Derry' to play it safe."

Orla frowned. "I'm too old to be politically correct. If I said that every time I talked about the city, I'd never get anything done. Derry is merely a timesaver for me."

Aaron resisted snorting at the old female's remark. "Then if you're worried about time passing, why don't you tell me why I'm here? You've lost precious minutes off your remaining lifespan already."

"Cheeky bastard," Orla murmured before she smiled. "That's why I like you and want you to relieve some of my Teagan's stress."

"If this involves me being naked, then I'm going to run right out the front door. Talking about sex with a grandma isn't high on my list of enjoyable events."

Orla tsked. "Someone's mind goes to the gutter fairly easily."

Aaron gripped the arm of the sofa and managed to get out, "How did you want me to help?"

Orla rocked her cane one way and then the other. "Sneak Teagan out of the clan every few days and force her to fly. Her dragon might fancy hunting as well."

"I'm not here to be a babysitter," he gritted out.

"And you won't be. My granddaughter works harder than anyone I've ever met, including myself. You seem to have a way of getting her to do things she wouldn't normally do. Otherwise, she never would've snuck off with you this morning." Aaron opened his mouth, but Orla beat him to it. "I don't care what you did. Females have more freedom these days to sleep with males before marriage, even if it's still scrutinized. Good for them. All I ask is to get her away from the bloody desk sometimes and into the fresh air. If she doesn't learn balance, she'll come to hate her position, and everyone will suffer in the long run. An overworked clan leader is never a good thing."

He studied the older female. "Are you speaking from experience?"

"Perhaps. I think it's why I accepted my beau's proposal to be mates so easily. In retrospect, I should've fought the bloody ridiculous rules about females stepping down once they find a mate. But I was tired and lonely, so I capitulated."

Since Stonefire hadn't had a female leader in centuries, Aaron had never heard of the rule. "Let me guess, Teagan wants to challenge the rules."

Orla waved a hand. "I don't know if she ever thinks about it. She works all the time and doesn't accept help easily."

"She actually sounds like my clan leader before he found his mate."

Her pupils flashed. "Wouldn't that be something, if my granddaughter found hers?"

Aaron cleared his throat. "I wasn't sent here to be a stud, and I doubt Teagan would like your suggestions."

"Aye, I know, although it's fun to watch you squirm. All I care about is my granddaughter's health. Are you going to help with that?"

"And if I refuse?"

Orla pointed her cane at him. "Don't push me, lad. This old biddy still has a few tricks up her sleeves."

Aaron couldn't help but smile. "If things ever calm down, I'd love to see you challenge a male your age. We might have to pad each of you to keep from breaking a hip, but it would be entertaining."

"You are a rascal, Aaron Caruso. But I reckon a loyal one, judging by everything I've read about you so far. I'm going to assume your answer is yes?" Aaron couldn't think of a reason big enough as to why he should refuse, especially given how Orla had asked him instead of ordering him to do it. Not even his dragon had piped up. So he nodded and Orla motioned with her hand. "Good, with that settled, you can go. As much as I want to be entertained, I'm sure you're needed elsewhere."

He stood and bowed at the waist. "Until I'm summoned again, my lady."

Orla snorted and Aaron exited her cottage. The elderly dragonwoman reminded him a bit of his own grandmother. She had died when he was a boy, but her sarcasm had rubbed off on Aaron. No matter what else happened, he hoped to spend more time with the old woman. She hid it well, but she missed being busy and involved in everything. He could at least help alleviate her boredom once in a while.

His dragon spoke up. *If you have time for that, then you have time to look after Teagan, too.*

I doubt 'look after' is the right phrase, but I'm going to see what I can do. Bram used to be a workaholic, too, until Evie and the babies came along.

Evie became Bram's mate. Are you planning to do the same with Teagan?

You, too? Stop being ridiculous. Aaron picked up his pace toward the Protectors' main building. *I just want her to win.*

If you say so.

Aaron arrived at the Protectors' central command and went inside. The sooner he found out his next task, the sooner he could complete it and plan Teagan's dinner for the evening. Because even though he had no intention of ever bedding Teagan, let alone trying to woo her, he prided himself on his cooking abilities. It might make more sense to do a horrible job so she would order him to never cook again, but if he could aid Teagan in some small way to help her keep control of her clan, he would. There was no bloody way he wanted to start over negotiations or even lose an alliance if one of the other bastards won. He wasn't going to return to Stonefire as a failure. Keeping the Glenlough leader fed was the first step to success.

~~~

The sky was nearly dark when Teagan finally entered her cottage. Even though she wasn't finished for the day, she would complete her remaining work in her pajamas, complete with a nice cup of tea with biscuits for dinner.

However, as she laid down her stack of papers on the table in the entrance, she instantly froze at the faint clanging sound of dishes coming from the kitchen. The place should be empty, especially since she'd texted Aaron to postpone their first supper.

Her beast spoke up. *He is stubborn and might have let himself in any way.*

If so, then I might have to kick his arse. This is my private space.

True, the piles of crap she needed to put away covered most raised, hard surfaces. And her decorations consisted mainly
~~~

of donated pictures of flowers and birds from her grandmother, so it was far from glamorous. But it was the one place she could shrug off most of her responsibilities and merely relax.

Anyone who trespassed would think twice before doing it again.

Teagan inched toward the kitchen, careful to avoid the two squeaky floorboards along the way. Just as she popped her head into the doorway, Aaron's voice rang out. "You might have been stealthy down the hall, but a child could've heard you opening the front door."

She entered the kitchen and frowned. "What the bloody hell are you doing here?"

He didn't turn away from the cooker. "Do you always ask questions you could answer by merely opening your eyes?"

Teagan tossed her bag on one of the counters and stormed up to Aaron. "You're on dangerous ground, Caruso."

He glanced over his shoulder. "Is that so? And here I thought I was merely fulfilling my end of the bargain."

"I told you I would be late and to not worry about it."

He met her gaze. "Have you eaten?"

"No, but that's beside the point."

"Even considering you're a dragon-shifter leader who needs to be in good shape, you're too thin. Sit your arse down and I'll feed you."

She clenched the fingers of one hand. "I'm this close to punching you in the jaw, stripping you, and leaving you in the middle of the clan's high street tied to a pole for all to see."

He shrugged. "I'm sure more than a few are curious to see an English dragon-shifter and what he's made of."

She opened her mouth and shut it. Aaron was bringing out the worst in her. She needed to calm the fuck down and take a different approached.

Her beast chuckled. *Why? This is fun.*

She ignored her dragon and crossed her arms over her chest. “Look, I’m tired, cranky, and hungry. Just leave and promise not to enter without my permission again and I’ll let you off with a warning.”

“And if I don’t leave?”

“You’re under my command whilst here. You’ll suffer the same punishment for disobeying an outright order as anyone else.”

“As much as I’d rather not spend a few nights in a jail cell, you need to try this first.”

In the blink of an eye, Aaron stuffed a piece of chicken between her lips. She had no choice but to chew, but as the meat melted in her mouth, she nearly moaned.

The bastard could cook.

Smugness filled Aaron’s eyes as he said, “So you can either punish me and go hungry or sit down and eat dinner. It’d be a shame to toss all this into the rubbish bin.”

Teagan was about to tell him to fuck off when her stomach rumbled. Her dragon sighed. *Just have dinner.*

And let him think it’s okay to disobey my orders?

Set some ground rules. This is our sanctuary. Here he is just a male and you are just a female. Outside, he is our soldier to command. Set that in stone with him.

You just want to ogle his body and persuade me to sleep with him.

Yes and no. For tonight, just eat. Good food will help you unwind.

She hesitated. Apart from her family, Teagan rarely invited people inside her cottage. If too many of her clan members treated her as a friend rather than a leader, order would soon slip and fall apart.

It was one of the things her gran had drilled into her before Teagan had put her name into the last leadership challenge. Leaders had to make tough decisions and people needed to be willing to follow a command with few, if any, questions during emergency situations.

Aaron opened a cupboard and took out two plates. The action snapped her out of her head. "If you know where the dishes are kept, then you snooped around, too, it seems."

He flashed a grin, and Teagan's heart skipped a beat at how his eyes crinkled at the corners. "Of course. Although I left your bedroom alone. For now."

She sighed. "Look, I appreciate the food and will eat it. However, only on one condition. Outside of this kitchen and dining area, you are one of my soldiers. There will be no ordering me around, no taking advantage of me, and sure as hell no disobeying my orders whenever you feel like it."

"You forgot about our practice sessions. I can't give you a true challenge if you punish me for bending the rules."

She raised an eyebrow. "There's only one more challenge. I never said anything about regular practices."

He placed the plates on the counter, turned around, and leaned against it. "You need to be in fine form. Given what I've heard today of how much time you spend in your office, you need the exercise."

"Did you just imply that I'm out of shape?"

He waved a hand in dismissal. "Stop with the niceties. I once broke my leg and spent weeks sitting mostly on my bum. It took a lot of work to get back to full fighting force. I think you need to do that yourself, if you'll let me help."

"Did you actually just ask my permission?" she drawled. "Maybe I should note the date and time for posterity."

"Be serious for a minute, woman, and think about it. I'm not a member of your clan and so me discovering any weaknesses won't jeopardize your standing. I've also gone through recovery myself and know what needs to be done, even if you're in much better shape than I was back then. Give me free rein to push you to your limits, and you'll be badder and stronger than ever."

Teagan studied Aaron's face. His pupils flashed once, but that was the only sign of emotion. "First tell me why you're offering to do this. It wasn't why you were sent to Glenlough. And you were making a big show about being assigned guard duty early. Helping someone exercise isn't exactly a normal Protector duty."

He smiled. "Let's just say I made a promise to an old woman and I intend to keep it."

Her gran and her blasted meddling. Teagan would talk with her later.

For the moment, Teagan merely studied Aaron. She could deny his words, but then she'd be lying. An extra training session or two a week wouldn't hurt. She had already planned to increase her exercise regimes, but having someone to remind her to do it and really push her to her limits would help greatly. After all, Teagan had never served in the army like Aaron, and no doubt he had a few tricks to teach her.

Placing one hand on her hip, she pointed at him with her free hand. "Before I agree to anything, I need to extract some promises and state conditions. Will you keep them or do I need to draw up a contract for you to sign in case I need to prove you're out of line later?"

He rolled his eyes. "You've clearly been dealing with the DDA too long if paperwork is your answer."

She closed the distance between them and poked his chest. "Unless you really want to push a hungry, cranky dragonwoman, then you'd better hurry up and answer."

The corner of his mouth ticked up. "I'm tempted to try just to see what happens."

"Aaron," she growled.

He chuckled. "Fine. I know one of your conditions is following your orders everywhere but the kitchen, dining room, and during our practice sessions. So my defiance is actually keeping to that condition since we're in the kitchen. You should be proud of me."

Teagan resisted rubbing the bridge of her nose with her fingers. "Remember that bit about me being hungry and cranky? I'm about ready to unleash my dragon on you."

Her beast huffed. *Don't bring me into this. I'm having fun watching.*

Aaron tilted his head. "I'll deal with her soon enough. But I won't question your orders elsewhere, unless they truly merit it, and then I'll do so in private. What else am I supposed to agree to?"

"No more breaking into my house. If I don't let you in or give you a key to enter, then you stay out."

"I can do that. Although if you miss too many meals, I'll bring something to you, no matter where you are at the time."

Part of her wanted Aaron's words to be actual concern, but she quickly brushed that aside. "Good. Then can I sit and eat already?"

Aaron pointed to the two plates. "One is for me." She opened her mouth to protest, but he beat her to it. "I'm hungry as well, so don't even think of tossing me out of the kitchen to order me around."

She moved to stand close to him and hopefully throw Aaron off, but he took her shoulders and put her at arm's length. "I've learned my lesson about letting you near my balls. Sit and I'll bring your food."

For a second, neither one of them moved. His warm, strong hands on her shoulders sent a tingle through her body. Up close she finally noticed the flecks of gold in Aaron's brown eyes. There was also a small scar near the corner of his mouth.

His lips parted a fraction, and Teagan quickly looked away. If he thought she was interested and then leaned in to kiss her, she might allow it to taste his soft lips once more. For all his sarcasm and sass, his lips were inviting and bloody well knew how to kiss a female properly.

Her beast chuckled. *His kiss can be our appetizer.*

Did you really just say that?

Her dragon hummed. *He would taste good.*

Aaron leaned forward and Teagan noted his slitted pupils. With his breath against her cheek, heat flooded her face as she remembered the last time they'd kissed.

Her dissuasion tactics weren't working as well as she'd hoped.

Her beast sighed. *And a good thing, too. Why wait for him? Kiss him already.*

She tried to remember the reasons why she should walk away. But as Teagan focused her gaze on Aaron's lips and the small scar at the corner of his mouth, she toyed with the idea of kissing the former injury before gently biting her way down his neck. After all, there was no one watching.

However, before she could decide to give in to her hormones or not, Aaron quickly released her shoulders and stepped away.

He cleared his throat. "The food will get cold. Take a seat and I'll serve you."

Teagan quickly turned toward the table and barely resisted placing her hands over her surely-pink cheeks. Of all the males in the world, why did Aaron have to be the one who stirred her body and her beast? With the trials coming up, she didn't have time to deal with any male, let alone one from another clan who liked to drive her mad.

And who might still only want her because she was a clan leader.

She'd just have to eat as quickly as possible and send him on his way. She could then fortify herself against his touch and strategize how to resist his lips in the future.

Her dragon sighed. *We can do more than one thing at a time. He is good for us.*

You say that, and yet he's not our true mate. We know so little about him.

Then ask him questions. It's not like I'm proposing to mate him and have babies. A little sex would be nice.

Right, because the clan will treat that as casually as you, especially if he starts boasting to his fellow Protectors.

Oh, stop it. He went to the trouble of breaking in to cook you dinner. That's a lot of work for a one-night conquest.

He is male after all.

Her beast huffed. *Talk to him and give him a chance. Besides, if he's here, no one will know about the dinner or more. Use the time to get to know the foreign visitor. That's part of your duty as clan leader.*

Teagan knew her dragon was prodding her on purpose. But as Teagan watched Aaron's broad back move under his shirt as he dished out supper, she itched to trace his muscles and maybe have those huge arms hold her close as she found her release. While she loved her clan, every once in a while, she yearned to have a night or two where she was merely a female.

Placing her hands on her cheeks, she willed the heat in them to cool. She needed to be the distant clan leader for the meal. If Aaron understood how his touch affected her, he'd surely lord it over her. Or worse, he might kiss her and who knew what mess would result.

Taking a deep breath, she thought about all the paperwork sitting on her desk. Remembering her hand cramp from writing tiny letters in impossibly short boxes, her heart rate slowed a little.

Good. She should be able to handle Aaron professionally now.

Her dragon laughed, but Teagan ignored her.

~~~

Aaron turned his back on Teagan and took a deep breath. Resisting the female was exhausting.

His dragon spoke up. *Stop lying. It's fun. You're just upset that you nearly pulled her close and kissed her.*

You might fall for her pretty eyes and wit, but I have no interest in becoming a eunuch. I imagine she would be the one doing the kissing on her terms, or else sharp talons would skewer my balls.

Did you not see her flushed cheeks and flashing eyes?

He finished dishing out the chicken, potatoes, and veg. *Just let me handle and survive this meal without too much commentary. Can you do that?*
~~~

To Aaron's surprise, his dragon fell silent.

Schooling his face into a neutral position, he carried the plates to the table and laid them down. Sliding into the seat across from Teagan, he motioned toward the food. "I assure you it's not poisoned."

She raised an eyebrow. "That thought hadn't crossed my mind until now. Maybe I should be worried."

"Oh, for fuck's sake." He picked up a fork, took a bit of everything from her plate, and stuffed it into his mouth. Once he swallowed, he held up his hands. "Ta-da."

She smiled, and his gaze was drawn to the dimple on one cheek. At her voice, he quickly looked back to her eyes as she said, "That was easy. I expected more arguing before you wanted to prove everything was fine."

The amusement in her eyes, combined with her bloody perfect smile, made him want to poke her temper again. He felt more in control when she argued. It was easier to resist the desire to taste her lips when she was threatening various parts of his body.

His dragon chuckled. Aaron ignored him and dug into his meal. A minute ticked by in silence as they both ate. Teagan was first to break the silence. "The food is really good. Where did you learn to cook?"

Rather than make a quip, he decided to answer truthfully. Maybe then Teagan wouldn't tempt him with another grin. "My mum. She said all males should know how to cook."

"She's a smart female."

He smiled. "Aye, she is."

When he didn't elaborate, Teagan asked, "What else did she teach you?"

He couldn't tell if Teagan was merely being polite or truly interested.

His dragon spoke up. *Just tell her. It wouldn't hurt to get on her good side.*

At the curiosity in Teagan's green eyes, the words spilled from his lips. "Everything, really. My father wasn't big on being a parent in the first place."

Fuck. He rarely talked about his father with anyone. What the hell was wrong with him?

His dragon chimed in. *She's a leader and you know she won't share the information.*

Teagan swallowed her latest bite and looked at him again. "Was your mother a sacrifice?"

Aaron decided what the hell. "No, I was born a few years before the program started on Stonefire. My parents were true mates that somehow went wrong."

"Care to tell me why or is that in the 'no fucking way' column?"

He liked that she didn't try to tame her language. "There's not a whole lot to tell. My father was a bastard who liked to make my mum and me feel small and worthless through words. When I was old enough to stand up to him and threatened to fight him, he left and went to America to be with some of his distant relatives. We never saw him again and he eventually died there."

He waited for pity to shine in Teagan's eyes, but she merely tilted her head. "Well, at least you and your mother are free from him for good."

"Yes, but I still worry about my mum after all these years. Most of her family lives in Italy, and she would be happier there. Caruso is her surname, not my father's."

As soon as the words slipped from his lips, Aaron wanted to take them back. She would probably ask why his mother wasn't there, and he didn't want to spoil the night talking about Nerina and his own fuckup.

It had to be the clan leader in Teagan that brought out his secrets.

His beast spoke up. *Or maybe you fancy her and want her to know all of you.*

Thankfully Teagan's voice prevented Aaron from replying to his dragon. "Your look turned guarded just now. Should I prod or is that a conversation for another dinner?"

"So you admit that you want me back?"

She shrugged. "Maybe. It depends what's next on the menu."

"I'll keep you in suspense, and maybe the wondering will keep you from working past suppertime. Then I won't have to talk with your gran and have her track down your whereabouts for me."

She swallowed her latest bite. "Do I want to know why my grandmother is already your ally? She should be on my side, not yours."

Aaron grinned. "She likes me and that's enough."

Teagan sighed. "Her taking a shine to you is both a blessing and curse. Although if she focuses her time on you, then maybe she'll leave me alone for a while."

"Leave you alone about what?" Teagan remained silent, so he added, "I poured my heart out about my father. You can surely answer one question honestly."

She pointed a fork at him. "Telling me he dashed off to America and died is hardly pouring your heart out."

"Are you sure you're a clan leader? Because I don't think you understand male dragon-shifters. That was major breakthrough territory." She rolled her eyes and he continued, "So tell me—what does your gran go on about?"

She searched his eyes and Aaron kept his face neutral. As persistent as he could be when he wanted, there were some things people needed to explain on their own terms. Maybe this was one of those for Teagan.

His dragon snorted. *Since when are you patient about anything?*

Shut it, dragon.

Teagan brushed her hair over a shoulder, and his eyes moved to the graceful curve of her neck. If she wore her hair up, every male in sight would itch to trace the elegant lines. Under the table, his fingers flexed, yearning for the same.

Then reach over and try it, his beast murmured.

His hand moved a few inches before he clenched his fingers into a fist. He met her gaze again, but not before he noticed the flush on her cheeks. Blood rushed to his cock at the sight. For all her tough talk, she was extremely feminine and innocent in private moments.

The contrast made him want to kiss her all the more.

Teagan's eyes flashed. Her voice was low as she said, "Maybe you should go."

He leaned forward a few inches. His voice was husky to his own ears. "What did I do now?"

Her skin turned a darker shade of pink as she moved what remained of her supper around on the plate. "Your eyes keep flashing as you stare at various parts of my body."

"Is that a bad thing?"

He reached out and took her free hand in his. At the contact, electricity raced through his body.

He should release her fingers, excuse himself, and return to his own cottage. But as Teagan's hand tightened around his own, he met her eyes and growled at the desire shining there. Teagan's voice caressed his skin as she whispered, "My gran wants me to settle down and find a mate. But that's not what I want right now."

He lightly brushed the back of her hand with his thumb. Each stroke of soft skin only made him want to kiss her more and see if she was just as soft everywhere else.

His beast hummed. *Yes, yes, kiss her. No strings attached. She'll like the idea of fucking once and walking away.*

"That's not what I'm looking for, either," he answered. Aaron leaned over and kissed Teagan's soft wrist. So close to her skin, he reveled in her feminine scent.

As he lightly caressed her skin with his tongue, Teagan drew in a breath. Her voice was strangled as she asked, "What are you doing, Caruso?"

He moved his lips to one of her fingers and kissed the tip of it. "I think calling me Aaron is better suited to this situation." He flicked his tongue against another finger pad. "And I think we both need a little release without strings attached."

He waited to see if he'd misread the situation. If he weren't drunk on the taste and scent of Teagan's skin, he might've been able to see sense and walk away.

But after tasting the female, he wanted more. Since she was clan leader and he was only on Glenlough for a short time, they could enjoy each other without forming attachments. They each had responsibilities to follow through. Hearts wouldn't need to get involved. He wouldn't be doomed to repeat his past. He could finish his assignment and return to Stonefire on time.

His dragon growled. *Don't be so sure. I think you'll soon be singing a different tune.*

Aaron barely noted his dragon's words as he brought Teagan's hand to his cheek and lightly rubbed it against his jaw. It was time to see if she was on the same page as him.

Chapter Ten

Teagan's heart pounded as Aaron's short whiskers tickled her skin. Just the feel of his lips on her wrist had made her wetter than she'd ever been in her life. She could just imagine what it'd be like to have him naked and over her. Hell, behind her, below her, and anyway she could think of.

Her dragon grunted. *We can have him. It's always best to try them out anyway.*

Aaron moved her palm to his lips and flicked her skin with his tongue. She sucked in a breath at the hot, wet sensation. "Aaron."

"Is that a 'Yes, Aaron' or 'No, Aaron?'"

Her gaze trailed over his jaw, his broad shoulders, and his muscled arms. For the first time in years, she was going to do something spontaneous for herself.

She met his eyes again. "As long as what happens between us stays in this house and no one else finds out, then it's a yes."

In response, he took one of her fingers between his lips. He flicked and swirled her digit. Teagan moaned, and all too soon Aaron released her. His gravelly voice went straight between her thighs as he said, "So that means your entire cottage is now part of our deal."

"Are you really—"

Aaron stood, tugged her up and against his chest. "I want to take you anywhere I can tonight. Inside this cottage, you're not clan leader and I'm not one of your Protectors. Agree before anything happens. I won't be ordered about in this arena."

She moved her hands to his back and slowly moved them down until she could grip his arse cheeks. "You'd better make it worthwhile, Caruso." She pressed her breasts against his chest and loved how his pupils slitted. "So, my answer is yes, but for tonight only."

With a growl, he took her lips in a rough kiss. In the next second, he nipped her bottom lip and she opened. As his tongue entered and stroked the inside of her mouth, she pulled his lower body tighter against hers and rocked her hips. Aaron groaned into her mouth, and the sound made desire pound harder between her legs.

She broke the kiss and pushed him away. Confusion flashed in his eyes, but as she tugged her top off and tossed it to the side, his eyes moved to her bra. Aaron licked his lips and her already tight nipples hardened further.

Undoing the clasp on her back, she also removed her bra. In the next second, Aaron closed the distance between them and kissed her neck, the base of her throat, and then the top of her breasts. Her nipples pulsed in anticipation. He'd better not be in a teasing mood or she might just chance ordering him around to get what she wanted.

As Aaron's hot mouth took one of her nipples, she threaded her fingers through his hair and arched her back. Each swirl, nip, and suckle made her knees a little weaker. She wrapped her other arm around his neck to keep from falling.

He finally released one and moved to the other. He bit slightly harder, and she cried out at the mixture of pleasure and pain. He soothed the sting with his tongue before nibbling again.

The pressure built and she wondered if she'd come without Aaron ever touching her clit. She closed her eyes and focused on the pleasure, but before she could fall over the edge, he pulled away.

Teagan opened her eyes and demanded, "Why did you stop?"

He kissed one corner of her mouth and then the other before whispering, "I want to have all of you at my mercy." His hands went to the top of her trousers. He ran his fingers just inside the waistband. The roughness of his skin against her eased her irritation and made her belly flip.

Aaron looked up. He never broke her gaze as he undid the top button. The zipper opened bit by bit, the sound filling the room and making her heart pound. Most males ripped off clothes to get to the deed as soon as possible, but not Aaron. And oddly, his patience made her hotter.

He placed his hand on her abdomen and ran it gently around to the top of her bum, the whisper of his fingers leaving a trail of heat in their wake. She could just imagine what he could do with those fingers if she were completely naked.

When all he did was slowly rub her skin above her panties for a full thirty seconds, warming her skin and nearly making Teagan squirm, her patience morphed into something else. She frowned. "What the bloody hell are you waiting for?"

He smiled slowly and a predatory look filled his eyes. "Anticipation makes things that much sweeter. You should know this as leader."

Well, two could play that game.

She placed her hand over his jean-clad cock and gripped his hardness. She squeezed and Aaron bit his lip to keep from groaning. Teagan chuckled. "Then maybe it's my turn to remind you of what anticipation feels like."

It may have been two years since her last sexual encounter, but with Aaron, the long stretch meant nothing. With confidence, she moved her hand toward the base of his dick and tightened her grip. In response, Aaron slid his hands inside her panties and cupped her bum. One hand moved further between her legs and lightly caressed her folds, and she sucked in a breath.

His husky voice made her shiver. "You seem to forget that you're the one mostly undressed, which means I can make you scream sooner than you could me."

Her beast hissed. *Yes, let him try.*

I'm not giving up that easily.

She was about to undo the fly of his jeans to even the playing field when he tugged down her trousers and panties, and they both fell to the ground around her ankles. Aaron's gaze zeroed in on the juncture of her thighs, and her heart pounded harder.

He took her hands in his and nodded toward the floor. "Step out of your shoes and clothes."

In other areas of her life, Teagan would never take an order from someone lower down in the hierarchy. But as she stood mostly naked in front of Aaron, she knew this was different. Inside this cottage, she was just a female and he a male. Clan politics didn't matter.

Still, she hesitated. She'd trusted before and been burned.

Aaron's voice filled the room again. "What happens here stays here, Teagan. I vow it."

Her dragon spoke up. *I hear the truth in his voice.*

Taking a deep breath, Teagan bobbed her head. "I hope so."

His pupils flashed, but she focused on the moment. Otherwise, she might talk herself out of it.

Teagan complied and kicked her clothes out of the way. Aaron held her arms out to the side and raked her body from head to toe with his eyes, complete with a growl. "Fucking beautiful."

Her entire body warmed as her pussy pulsed. There was something strangely erotic about being naked and perused by Aaron while he stood fully clothed.

She expected her dragon to demand skin or equal footing, but her beast remained eerily silent.

Before Teagan could think too hard about it, Aaron met her eyes again. She barely noted the flashing pupils as he ordered, "Sit in the chair and spread your legs." He released a hand and lightly caressed her cheek. "I want you open and willing for me."

~~~

Aaron wasn't sure if Teagan would respond to his order. While he had no trouble following a command while on duty, he enjoyed being in charge when a female was naked with him.

The question was whether Teagan wanted it too or not.

After another second, she turned, and he watched her curved hips sway as she moved to the nearest dining chair, moved it further away from the table, and turned to sit down with her legs closed. Before he could remind her to open her thighs, Teagan widened them. At the sight of pink, swollen flesh, he licked his lips. "I want to taste you." He looked up. "But if I kneel, you have to keep still until I say so."
~~~

She hesitated before answering, "I'll try, unless you do something I don't like."

"I'll just have to make sure you're too far out of your mind to notice anything but the feel of my tongue."

Her lovely pale skin flushed, and he drank in the sight of Teagan's pert breasts, the swell of her hips, and her long legs. He would save the image of her for future showers. For all the reasons he could never have her, she was clever and gorgeous, and he wanted to remember her.

He approached Teagan and leaned down to her right ear. "Place your hands on the sides of the chair and scoot that fine arse a little further toward the edge of your seat."

Her ragged breath made him smile.

His dragon grunted. *You should undress first. I want her hands on our skin and maybe even her nails in our back.*

No. I want to focus solely on her first. After everything she does for her clan, she deserves some attention.

He nipped her earlobe. After caressing the soft skin with his tongue, he moved to his knees. At the sight of her hands gripping the seat and her pussy even more on display, he met Teagan's lovely green eyes again and growled. "Mine."

Her eyes flashed, but instead of reprimanding him, she merely tilted her head back as she shook her hair and jutted her breasts forward. "Either prove your skills or leave. I will only wait so long."

It seemed the female had a bit of bite, even when vulnerable. Aaron would remember that for later.

Tracing the side of her neck down to her collarbone, he murmured, "One last thing—don't remove your hands from the chair until you come or I'll stop."

"Fine. But if you hurt me, all bets are off."

Lightly circling one of her nipples, he grunted. "I will never willingly hurt you, Teagan. If I ever do something you don't like, then feel free to skewer my balls." He moved to her other nipple. "Although a little pain can bring a lot of pleasure in the right circumstances."

Before she could reply, he gently pinched her nipple, and Teagan's legs opened wider. "There's my girl." He twisted a little harder, and Teagan moaned as her head fell to one side.

With her dark hair cascading over one shoulder and flushed skin, she was the most beautiful female he'd ever seen.

And for some reason, he wanted to know her better.

His dragon roared. *Then hurry up. I want to know what she tastes like.*

Ignoring his beast, he focused solely on Teagan. "Don't try to hold back or temper your moans. Your reactions are like instructions. Most males tend to ignore them, but not me. I plan on using them to make you scream harder than you ever have before."

She was halfway to panting, which made both man and beast smug. Teagan whispered, "Just hurry up, already."

Taking both of her breasts in his hands, he moved his head to kiss her lips. "If nothing else, trust me in this."

He leaned back to watch her eyes. She searched his for a few seconds before nodding. "You only get one chance, though."

He grinned. "That's all I need."

Running his hand down from her breasts to her waist, he rubbed her soft skin a few minutes before moving to her thighs.

He couldn't resist her pale, toned leg and leaned down to run his whiskered cheek back and forth against her most tender spot, on the inside of her thigh. He repeated the movement on the other side, and Teagan's muscles relaxed further under his touch. "Now, let's see how wet you are for me."

Aaron lowered his head and stared a few seconds at her swollen flesh. She was already glistening for him.

He flicked his tongue between her folds and reveled in the earthy, womanly scent that was Teagan O'Shea.

His dragon finally spoke up. *More, I want much more.*

Patience—

No. Fuck her with our tongue.

As his dragon paced inside his mind, Aaron could tell his beast might try to take control and ruin all his hard work if he didn't do something fast.

Gripping Teagan's thighs, Aaron moved in to taste her once more. With each lick, swirl, and thrust of his tongue, her breath increased.

Opening his eyes, he glanced up to watch Teagan's face as he devoured her pussy. With her head thrown back and breasts thrust forward, she was close.

Aaron stopped and moved a few inches away.

Teagan's eyes opened and she moved to look down at him. Her pupils flashed. "Don't even think of stopping."

"Watch me devour you, Teagan. It'll make you come that much harder."

She hesitated a second and Aaron wondered about the males before him. He bet most of them never took her needs into account. Hell, they probably had thought of their own conquest and nothing else.

His beast roared. *Don't think of them. Only her.*

"Trust me, love. You'll like it."

She nodded, and he never broke eye contact as he ran his tongue up her slit to circle her hard nub. He increased the pressure on her clit and Teagan's muscles tensed under his hands.

As her pupils remained slitted, he sucked her clit between his teeth and bit gently. Her breathing became more ragged. He bit harder and she murmured, "Again."

Aaron repeated the action before soothing the tender flesh with his tongue. As he continued to alternate nibbling and licking, Teagan's face flushed a brighter shade of pink. She finally cried out, and Aaron quickly thrust his tongue inside her. As he moved in and out, he reveled in the grip and release of her muscles. When he could finally taste her orgasm, he focused at licking and branding her taste into his memory.

Teagan's hands lightly brushed his hair and he reluctantly moved away from her pussy, only to be greeted by Teagan's satisfied look.

He inched his torso forward until her thighs bracketed his waist. He threaded his fingers through her hair and asked, "So, did you like it?"

"Are you really going to make me answer that?" she replied in a sated tone.

"Well, I can't make you orgasm even harder next time if I don't know what you like."

She moved her hand from his hair to his chest. She lightly ran her nails back and forth against his chest there. "Why are you so intent on my pleasure? In my experience, males are accustomed to getting their cocks inside me as quick as possible."

"Those males were bastards."

She tilted her head. "You're full of surprises, Aaron Caruso."

He gently tugged her hair. "And so are you, Teagan O'Shea."

As they smiled at one another, Aaron wondered if this was what happy couples experienced after an orgasm. Usually after he'd made Nerina come, she'd smiled and feigned exhaustion, leaving him hard and hurting more often than not.

No. He wouldn't let Nerina ruin this moment.

Teagan frowned. "What were you just thinking of?"

"You must not be that relaxed if you're still so observant."

Her brows knitted closer together. "I mean it, Aaron. Your face shuttered. Tell me why."

"I thought this was a space where you couldn't order me around."

"I'm not ordering, I'm asking. And considering I'm naked and you still have my taste on your tongue, it's a reasonable question at that."

He rubbed a hand up and down her back. "I thought this was supposed to be a no strings attached encounter."

"Then that's all the more reason for you to confide in me. I can't make you come harder than you ever have before if you're holding back. You should feel free tonight as well."

Aaron debated what he should do. His dragon spoke up. *Just tell her. Otherwise, you'll keep thinking about the other one when I want to enjoy Teagan's touch.*

Sharing my story will bring closeness and that's not what I need.

You often don't know what you need.

What the hell are you talking about?

You know.

His beast fell silent, and Aaron tried to figure out what the bloody hell he was going on about.

Teagan opened her mouth, but a fast-paced pop song echoed inside the room, and she sighed. "That would be Killian. I need to take the call."

Grateful for the distraction, Aaron retreated and stood. "A group of human females singing isn't what I'd first think of for your brother."

Teagan rolled her eyes as she walked to her mobile phone and picked it up. "Hello."

As her gaze turned serious, Aaron knew their night together was over. His hard cock was disappointed, but Aaron was almost glad since it meant not talking about his past and keeping Teagan at a distance.

His dragon growled. *Coward.*

Teagan hung up and looked back at him. He raised his brows in question and she answered, "One of the Protectors found a spy in the nearby forest."

He scooped up her clothes and handed them over. "Who?"

She took the clothes. "A Protector from Clan Wildheath. I'm sorry, but I need to check in and probably interrogate him."

He shrugged. "Don't apologize. Clan comes first, always."

Confusion flashed in her eyes, but quickly vanished. "Yes. And while I wish I could invite you to help, you should probably go to your own cottage. Otherwise, my brother might take notice of us. For all that it's a night of no strings attached, there's no denying things will always be slightly different between us." She pointed toward his crotch. "And, of course, there's that."

Her gaze zeroed in on his straining cock, punching against his jeans. If she kept looking at his dick, he would never be able to tame the bastard. Aaron cleared his throat. "I'd suggest a quick wash as well. We can finish this tomorrow evening, after supper."

Her brows furrowed. "Tomorrow?"

"We didn't get a full night as promised. We have some hours to make up for. Besides, I can't wait to see you on all fours with your arse up in the air, hips wiggling in anticipation for my cock." He paused and added, "Unless you truly don't want it. I'll never force you to do something you don't want when we're alone, Teagan. I hold a different opinion when it comes to making you eat or take a break, though."

She stared a few seconds and Aaron's heart rate kicked up. He'd deny it to anyone who asked, but he wanted to sleep with Teagan more than he even wanted to admit to himself. Tasting her once wasn't enough.

Bloody hell, he was in trouble.

His dragon huffed. *Why such the big deal about wanting to see her again? She's strong, loyal, pretty, and intelligent. Any male would want her.*

That's not what I'm afraid of, and you know it.

Your fear is blinding you to what you might need.

She walked up to him and touched his cheek, banishing everything but her touch and words. "I still want to see your gorgeous, naked body. But only for tomorrow evening and no more."

Rather than answer, he kissed her. He lingered another few seconds before he released her sweet lips. "I look forward to hearing you scream my name."

With a wink, he turned and gathered his belongings. He probably wouldn't sleep much during the night, but it gave him time to plan what to do to Teagan the following day. If he only had one night, he was going to make it count.

His beast huffed. *I doubt one night will be enough.*

Too bad. It's going to have to be.

CHAPTER ELEVEN

Teagan had expected Aaron to curse and act like a spoiled child when she mentioned needing to attend to the clan's safety. Any other male she'd been with who'd brought her to orgasm but didn't find his own would've done so, complete with grumpy, stilted responses.

Yet as she closed the distance to the Protectors' main building, she remembered Aaron's quick acceptance and promise of another go the next day.

He kept destroying her assumptions about him. Maybe there was a reason from his past as to why he'd been grumpy every time she'd talked with him before his recent arrival on Glenlough.

Not that she should care. He wasn't part of her clan and he'd return to Stonefire soon enough.

Her dragon spoke up. *Do you want him, too?*

What kind of question is that?

We both enjoyed relinquishing control for a short while. It would be nice to go home to that every night.

He's not even our true mate.

So? He doesn't have to be.

What game are you playing?

No game. I'm a better judge of what's good for us than a random act of fate.

She arrived at the back entrance to central command. *I need to focus, so hush.*

Used to being pushed to the side for clan business, her dragon didn't fuss. Of course, that didn't mean she wouldn't badger Teagan later to think about Aaron again. Maybe by then, Teagan would have some more worthwhile excuses about why opening up to him was a bad idea.

Yet despite her best efforts to forget the evening, Aaron's words came rushing back to her. *"Sit in the chair and spread your legs. I want you open and willing for me."* Teagan shivered. Deep down, she wanted to experience his husky commands again.

Not that she could have it again if she didn't finish her current task and protect against any oncoming threats. She took a few deep breaths to clear her mind.

Arriving at Killian's office, Teagan entered and shut the door behind her. "Care to fill me in?"

Killian stood and handed her a sheet with a picture at the top of a middle-aged man with dark hair and key details on the bottom of the paper. Her brother answered, "That man, Roarke Bell, is with Clan Wildheath. He was setting up a tent and campfire in the forest when one of our patrols found him."

She raised an eyebrow and met her brother's eyes. "He's not clever, then. Why would the Wildheath leader bother sending him at all if he's that inept?"

"Their leader, Padraig O'Leary, is older and showing it. The only way for him to win over someone twenty-odd years his junior is to cheat. No doubt Roarke Bell was sent here to watch you train, scout out the surrounding areas, and to find out what he could about Glenlough by watching our activities."

"Has Bell mentioned anything about a contact inside Glenlough?" Teagan asked.

Killian shook his head. "No. We haven't been able to get much out of him. You should visit Bell and see what you can find out."

"I will. Afterward, I need to think if contacting Wildheath's leader sooner or much later will be better in the long run. If I outright disqualify him for cheating, the other leaders will say I did it because I'm afraid I can't win."

Killian grunted. "They're insecure arseholes."

She snorted. "I won't disagree, but if I offend their delicate male egos too quickly, then we could face years of challenges. Since I have no desire to be forced out through constant attacks, we'll have to somewhat put up with their crap in the interim, at least until the trials are over."

"Or we could just buy you a fake dick and you can wave it about when they arrive, since that's all that matters to them."

Her brother rarely made a wisecrack, but when he did, it was golden. She grinned. "I might save the dildo waving until I beat their arses."

"Make it a silver-colored one."

"Yes, that glints in the sun." She sobered. "But I can't do any of that if I don't deal with our current prisoner and plan my response." She handed back the sheet of paper. "I'll let you know what I find out. And make sure to do extra patrols from now until the leadership challenge. I don't want any spies to succeed in taking home an advantage."

"Of course. The prisoner is in interrogation room one."

Teagan turned and exited Killian's office. She made it to the correct room but entered the viewing booth to one side of it first. One of the older Protectors, Lyall O'Dwyer, sat in a chair behind the desk overlooking the room. Through the two-way mirror,

Teagan spied the stranger sitting in a chair. She looked to Lyall. "Anything new to tell me?"

"Not really, Teagan. He's been sitting there fairly still, staring at a fixed point on the wall. If he hadn't been found so easily, I would say he's readying himself for your interrogation," Lyall answered. "But that contradicts with his actions thus far.

Teagan studied the prisoner through the glass. He didn't fidget, nor did anything show in his eyes. "Unless he wanted to be captured and brought inside the clan's lands."

"Aye, that could be it, too. Are you still going to talk with him?"

"Doing so might give away a bit more about me, but I don't really have a choice." She waved toward the small television screen, which showed the prisoner inside the room. "Just make sure to record our session. I may need to use it when talking with his clan leader later."

"Got it."

Teagan exited the observation booth and entered the interrogation room via the hall. At her presence, the male shifted his focus from the wall to her.

The picture Killian had shown her hadn't captured the pure disdain shining in the man's eyes. So much for him being controlled.

Or he hated the thought of a female leader that much.

Her beast growled. *He probably uses fear to control females back home.*

Perhaps, perhaps not. Now hush.

Thankfully Teagan had dealt with her fair share of arrogant arseholes. She pulled out a chair to a safe distance and flipped it around. Sitting down, she raised her brows. "If you have a mate, then she must either have unlimited patience or has a thing for jerks."

"She follows tradition, unlike your self-absorbed arse."

She propped her chin on her hands, which rested on the back of the chair. "You're such a charmer. Too bad we don't have time to share tea."

The male narrowed his eyes. "I can't wait for one of the males to beat you in the leadership trials and take control of your clan. Only a weak female leader would invite English dragon-shifters to her land, considering their betrayals over the centuries."

Rolling her eyes, Teagan sat up. A traditionalist and a long-term grudge holder. "Yes, yes. I'm an abomination. I'm a traitor to all males. I'm only interested in myself. Blah, blah, blah. Anything else I forgot? I want to get all of the crap out of the way so I can learn why you're here."

"If you think flashing me a pretty smile is going to make me talk, then you're even stupider than I'd guessed."

Teagan extended a talon, stood, and closed the distance between them to press the sharp point against the male's throat. "I was giving you a chance to talk without threats. Your clan leader would never know it, but sometimes violence isn't necessary to solve a problem." She pressed a little harder and the male visibly swallowed. "However, I'm not against using it to protect what's mine. You trespassing on my land gives me the right to do as I see fit. Not even the DDA will interfere."

He opened his mouth to say something but promptly closed it. Teagan smiled. "It seems you're learning. Now, this stupid female already guessed you're here to spy on me. Padraig O'Leary is getting on in age and can only win through cheating. I want to know what your purpose was for coming here. What, exactly, did he want to know?"

Silence stretched, so Teagan pressed hard enough to prick his skin. A few drops of blood rolled down his throat. She ran a finger to catch one and held it up to his face. "This is my last warning before I hand you over to someone who is a lot less polite about interrogations than me. Is there anything you want to share?"

The male stared at the blood on her fingers for a few seconds before he answered, "No. Killing me will only drive the other leaders harder to defeat you. If my death means preserving tradition, it will be worthwhile."

Fucking patriarchal maniac, she murmured to her dragon.

In this one instance, I wish we followed old traditions. Then this male would be executed with pomp and circumstance.

As much as I'd like to see that, we can't. The humans will never become our allies if we return to fear and violence to rule.

Her dragon huffed. *I suppose.*

Teagan focused back on the male. "It looks like we're going to have to move you to someplace cozy, with a new flatmate. I'm sure he'll be much quicker to extend a talon than me."

Hatred flashed in his eyes. "Weak bitch. You will know your place soon enough."

Not rising to the bait, Teagan turned and exited the room. Her dragon growled. *If we were male, we'd be called strong and leader-like. But because we're female, we're a bitch.*

Don't let him get to you.

Are you sure I can't drop him from a great height?

Not at the moment. But I never rule out all possibilities so early.

As she made her way back toward Killian's office, Teagan resisted running a hand through her hair. She didn't want to have her best interrogator work on the male and probably cause harm, but there was little choice.

Until some of the old traditions were shattered for good, she would have to follow some of the same tactics as the other clans to get her point across.

Bloody pointless violence. She needed to make the trials as challenging as ever to truly prove her worth. There was no fucking way she was going to repeat the process year after year, just to appease old-fashioned male egos.

She picked up her pace. There was much to do and Teagan didn't give up easily. She would change Ireland for the better, even if it killed her.

And given that some of the clan leaders weren't above killing her to get what they wanted, it just might.

~~~

As the sun sank low in the sky, Aaron headed toward Killian's office. Every available Protector had done double duty, spending part of the day patrolling the areas surrounding the clan to look for trespassers. Since many humans came and went every day to visit Glenveagh National Park, where Glenlough was situated, it made the task that much more difficult, especially if a female human mate from one of the other clans had been sent to spy on them. It would be bloody difficult to spot her, if she existed.

His beast spoke up. *Bloody stubborn arses. At this rate, we'll never have time to help Teagan train.*

She never promised to do it today, anyway.

Still, I want to race her in dragon form.

We'll see her naked tonight. That should count for something.
~~~

Maybe.

He snorted at his dragon's tone. *Priorities, dragon, priorities.*

You seem to think about her a lot.

It was one of the reasons Aaron had been glad of the extra duties; he could forget Teagan while he was distracted with work.

However, her smiling face flashed inside his mind for the hundredth time. He shouldn't care, but he kept wondering what she had done for the day. Maybe he could help her with something.

His beast huffed. *We will find out soon enough. Besides, we need to make sure she eats properly.*

Of course we will.

Thankfully he reached Killian's office so Aaron's beast couldn't reply. Aaron knocked on the door, and Killian's muffled voice said, "Come in."

Aaron entered to find Killian sitting at his desk and an unfamiliar male sitting across from him. Killian motioned toward the fair-haired male who was probably a few years older than Aaron. "This is Colm MacDermot. He's helping with planning the leadership challenges."

Colm smiled. "Nice to meet you, Aaron." He looked to Killian. "I should be going anyway. I still have lessons to prep for tomorrow."

Colm took his leave. When they were alone, Killian spoke up again. "Did your team find anything?"

"No, but there must be another reason you wanted to see me since we already reported our findings, or lack thereof, not that long ago."

"There is." Killian leaned back in his chair and placed his hands on the armrests. "Why did you leave my sister's house late last night?"

Shit. He'd been seen. "She's a grown woman. It's none of your business."

"As her brother and head Protector, it is most definitely my business. She can't afford to be distracted right now."

Aaron decided to screw it and be forthright. "Everyone in your family keeps claiming to be protecting Teagan, yet you do so behind her back. Why don't you fucking sit down and talk with her? You might learn something that way."

Killian rose and closed the distance between them. "You being here is a privilege. I can send you back to Stonefire tomorrow."

A few days ago, Aaron would've jumped at the chance to return to England. But he wasn't ready to go back just yet. "Try it and I'll appeal to Teagan. She can then decide my fate."

Teagan's voice filled the room. "Why do I need to decide anything? You two look about ready to go a few rounds. Maybe we should schedule some training time together. Male bonding and all that. Beating each other to a pulp should make you best friends."

Aaron turned to look at Teagan, and it took everything he had not to rush up to her and kiss her. With her hair dancing around her shoulders and amusement dancing in her eyes, she was so fucking beautiful.

She cocked an eyebrow and Aaron focused back on the situation. He motioned toward Killian and then to her. "Ask your brother. Maybe he won't chicken out and will actually talk with you."

Teagan met her brother's gaze. "What's going on, Killian? I leave for a few minutes and all hell breaks loose."

Killian grunted. "I'm just trying to protect both you and the clan."

"What's going on?" she demanded.

Killian waved toward Aaron. "I saw him leave your cottage late last night. I was trying to figure out why."

She shrugged. "He lost a few challenges and now is paying up his debt by cooking me supper. He'll be at my cottage fairly often."

His dragon perked up at that remark, but Aaron focused on the conversation at hand. Killian sighed. "Are you sure that's a good idea? I know you want the alliance with Stonefire to work out, but we know little about him."

"I'm standing right here," Aaron drawled.

Killian met his gaze. "I'm aware."

The urge to punch Killian coursed through his body, but Teagan's voice prevented him from doing something stupid. "Now, now, boys. I think you are going to train together tomorrow. I can't afford any in-fighting for the next few weeks."

Aaron felt about ten years old. Teagan was trying to keep her clan together, and he was throwing a fit. "There's no need for special training. I'll be nice if he is."

Killian looked between Teagan and Aaron. "Is there something going on between you two? Because if so, I need to know so I can prepare for the repercussions."

Teagan rolled her eyes. "If me having Aaron in my cottage to cook for me causes a scandal, I'll handle it. Speaking of which"—she took out a key and tossed it at Aaron—"get started on supper whilst I finish up here."

Killian scowled. "Teagan—"

"Just stop, Killian. I need my head Protector right now, not my brother."

Before coming to Glenlough, Aaron would've made a crack and flipped off Killian. But not wanting to create unnecessary work for Teagan, he merely headed for the door. "Don't be too late because I'm going to eat with or without you."

"Then let's hope another spy doesn't show up at our front gates or you might have to start a delivery service. Killian might need some food, too. You wouldn't want us to starve and lose focus, now would you?"

He could feel Killian's eyes on him, but Aaron ignored him. "That wasn't part of our terms. If you want an extra portion, then it's going to cost extra."

Her pupils flashed. He wondered if her dragon was thinking of ways to tip him.

Killian's deep voice garnered his attention. "I'm fine. We have lots to discuss, Teagan. Send your cook on his way."

Aaron did meet Killian's gaze then. Unfortunately the bastard's expression was neutral so he couldn't tell if Killian was planning how to murder him or not.

Teagan waved toward the door. "I'll update you if I'm going to be late."

Not giving Killian a chance to speak again, Aaron exited the room and strode briskly down the hall. His dragon spoke up. *Make something light. I want to spend most of the time naked and inside her.*

Patience, dragon. I'd rather she unload her day and come to bed relaxed and curious.

His beast huffed. *But it's our turn. I want her hands and mouth on our cock.*

The image of Teagan's hot lips brushing the tip of his dick flashed into his mind. *Stop it. I'm not about to spend the next two or three hours with a hard-on.*

It'll motivate you to see things my way.

His response was to toss his beast into a mental prison. While his dragon thumped and attempted to escape, it held.

Maybe this way he could actually talk with Teagan over dinner. If he focused on her, then he wouldn't have to talk about himself. He'd revealed more than enough the night before.

Besides, he'd noticed the tightness around her eyes. Something had happened and he wanted to know what.

CHAPTER TWELVE

A little over an hour later, Teagan smiled and answered questions from every clan member she passed on the way home. For good reason, everyone was concerned and full of questions about her announcement the other night.

So when her cottage's glowing windows finally came into view, she let out a sigh of relief. A few more steps and she'd be inside her sanctuary.

Her dragon spoke up. *And what about Aaron? He will be waiting, too.*

Before Teagan could wonder what Aaron might do to her once she was naked again, the voice of Colm MacDermot boomed behind her. "Teagan, there you are. I was wondering if I'd catch you on your way home."

So close and yet so far.

Pasting a smile on her face and standing up taller, she turned. "What did you need, Colm?"

"I was hoping we could discuss some of the historical documents I found about the leadership challenges." He raised his arm holding a cloth bag. "I figured we could make it a working dinner date."

Her dragon grunted. *No. Aaron is making dinner and waiting for us to jump him.*

This is more important.

Are you sure?

Look, I wanted a night of kinky sex too. But if it costs us the clan, then what?

Her beast sighed. *I suppose.*

Teagan motioned with her head toward the door. "I just need to let my visitor know the change of plans, and then we can work in one of the conference rooms inside the Protectors' central command."

"If your gran is here, we can do it tomorrow morning. I'm not about to put Orla Kelly out. She'll make sure I never forget it, and I don't need the trouble."

"No, it's not her. Just give me a second."

Teagan put a hand on the door, but Colm's voice prevented her from entering. "We could just work here to save time."

She looked back at Colm's green eyes but couldn't read them. She didn't think he had an ulterior motive of wanting to woo her, but with dragonmen, it was hard to tell. "It's messy, and it's safer for all if we use one of the conference rooms."

He smiled. "I live alone. Believe me, my place is worse. If your place is worse than mine, I'll owe you twenty euro."

Teagan hesitated. She didn't like bringing work into her home, at least work that involved others. Yet she needed Colm's support and help. Turning him away might make him distant, especially since they'd known each other their whole lives and had always gotten along.

He winked. "It can't be that bad."

"All right. But I still need to let my guest know of the change. Come in." She entered and waved toward the mostly clean sofa. "You can wait in there."

Colm raised an eyebrow. "Who's this guest of yours? And why the secretive nature?"

Aaron's voice echoed down the hall. "Yes, why?"

Aaron appeared a foot away from her and she met his gaze. While to most he'd appear nonchalant, she noticed the tightness of his jaw.

Her dragon chuckled. *Good. He'll work harder to impress us later.*

Teagan acted as if her beast hadn't spoken. "Colm MacDermot, this is Aaron Caruso. Aaron, this is Colm. He's helping me plan the leadership trials."

Aaron studied Colm a second before saying, "We met earlier. It's a good thing I made extra. Come on, let's eat."

Aaron turned before Teagan could say a word. Colm spoke, his voice full of amusement. "I thought he was a Protector."

"He is. He's just helping me out."

Her dragon chimed in again. *So, you're not going to mention the bet? I wonder why.*

It's between Aaron and me. I don't need Colm thinking Aaron is weak.

Look who's defending who.

Teagan motioned a hand toward the kitchen. "Come. I don't know about you, but I'm starving."

As she made her way into the kitchen, Teagan only hoped Aaron wouldn't act possessive and try to undermine her authority. She hoped he understood that when others were inside the house, their agreement of being equals was on hold.

Her dragon huffed. *He's intelligent. Give him some credit.*

I don't have a brilliant track record with males.

Aaron is different. Wait and see.

Teagan hoped so. She might want some sex to relieve stress, but she wasn't about to suffer alpha male bullshit to achieve it.

It was time to see if Aaron passed the test.

And why is that important? her dragon asked.

Ignoring her beast, Teagan entered the kitchen.

~~~

Aaron shouldn't care that Teagan had brought someone home with her. After all, it was her house and not his. Not to mention he had zero claim on her.

Still, seeing the smiling, handsome man he'd spotted earlier in Killian's office at Teagan's heels had made him clench his fingers into a fist.

His dragon spoke up. *You should just admit that you want her as much as I do.*

You want a relationship. I just want sex.

Tell yourself that. We'll see if you feel the same way once dinner is over.

Aaron busied himself with dishing out the shepherd's pie he'd baked. He heard Teagan and Colm sit down at the table, but he focused on his task. The rhythmic motion of dishing out food, in tandem with measured breaths, helped to ease his irritation.

Once he could paste a smile on his face, he picked up two plates and turned toward Teagan and Colm. He walked over and laid their food down. "It's nothing fancy since I didn't have a lot of time today."

Teagan smiled. "It's better than a sandwich or reheated stew for supper."

Since he'd laid cutlery on the plates, the two took their first bites. Aaron quickly retrieved his own supper and sat down. He accidentally brushed Teagan's thigh with his own as he settled. Electricity raced up his skin and her gaze shot to his.
~~~

She must've felt it, too.

What was wrong with him? She wasn't his true mate and merely brushing a thigh shouldn't set him on edge.

Besides, if he pulled her to his lap and kissed her in front of the other male, Teagan might never forgive him. The clan watched her like a hawk and she couldn't afford gossip right now.

He held her eyes for a few seconds more before he looked to Colm. The dragonman studied Aaron but spoke up with a smile. "So, Caruso, how did you end up cooking for our fine leader?"

Teagan opened her mouth, but Aaron beat him to it. "My own clan leader told me to do whatever was necessary to help. Teagan asked, and I agreed. It also means free food for me since Teagan buys the groceries."

"And males do love their food," Teagan muttered.

Colm grinned. "That we do." He asked Aaron, "So are you helping with the planning, too? I heard you were assigned to guard the judges but didn't know if you'd be doing anything else."

Aaron looked to Teagan for permission. She swallowed and answered, "Aaron is helping in other ways. But we should start going over what you found in the records now so that we're not here all night." Colm hesitated, and Teagan added, "Caruso can be trusted."

Her words stoked his ego and his dragon said, *She's as eager as us to get this bloke out of here.*

Or she could just be thinking of her clan and doing her job.

I like my reason better.

Colm's voice prevented Aaron from replying. "Well, let's start with the differences. Whilst most trials today focus on stamina, strength, and getting out of tough situations, the ones of old were more like quests."

"What do you mean by 'quests'?" Aaron asked.

Colm took a folder out of the cloth bag at his feet and opened it on the table. He took out a document, scanned it, and then read from it. "The finding of the golden dragon egg proved my most strenuous task to date. I nearly drowned finding one of the clues and singed my hair trying to heat another clue hot enough to make it glow with the final destination."

Teagan interrupted Colm. "He or she didn't actually find it, did they? I think the clan would know if they had the mythical necklace stored somewhere."

Aaron frowned. "I must've missed that day at school. What, exactly, is this mythical dragon egg?"

Teagan answered, "Only the treasured necklace from the supposed first dragon-shifter to ever set foot in Britain."

"But we're in Ireland," Aaron drawled.

"As much as I hate to admit it, Irish dragon-shifters and British ones are descended from the same first settlers," Teagan stated.

Colm spoke up. "The legend goes that the first female dragon-shifter who set foot in what is modern England produced three dozen dragon eggs all whilst wearing the legendary necklace. In a way, it represents the beginning of all of our clans."

Aaron sighed. "But it's all rubbish. Dragons don't lay eggs, for one. And even if we did, a female still requires a male to help spawn the babies."

Teagan rolled her eyes. "Leave it to you to take the miracle of childbirth and lower it down to 'spawning.'"

Aaron smiled. "Technically, it would be dropping eggs."

Teagan forced her gaze to Colm. "Ignore him. Tell me about this leader and the overview of the quest."

"I bet it involved knights, swords, and sorcery," Aaron drawled.

Teagan shot him a look, her eyes full of warning, and he focused on his food. It was easy to forget he and Teagan weren't alone.

His beast snorted. *Be glad, or she wouldn't be so polite. You're being a tad irritating.*

She's the one talking about bloody myths and dragon eggs.

Just listen to what the other male has to say. We can't help Teagan if we don't know what she might be planning.

Agreeing with his dragon, Aaron took a bite of pie and motioned for Colm to continue.

Colm tapped the paper in front of him. "Her name was Orlaith."

All Aaron heard was "Orla." But he didn't think they'd be talking about Teagan's grandmother.

"As in the first unifier of Ireland and my gran's namesake?" Teagan asked breathlessly.

"Aye," Colm said. "Which is all the more reason to use her ideas against your challengers. The other leaders may have forgotten that one of the bravest leaders in Irish dragon-shifter history was female, but they'll soon remember."

Aaron couldn't help but say, "I know a fair bit of Irish history, but I've never heard of Orlaith."

Teagan shrugged. "She's a bit of a poorly kept secret. Most of the texts that mentioned her were burned a few hundred years ago, when males were trying to eradicate any knowledge of female leaders. Glenlough didn't agree, and whoever was in charge must've preserved the records."

Aaron waved toward Colm's documents. "So what's involved in this quest-like challenge?"

"Quite a bit. But I think if we modify the rules and a group of us plan a new quest, it may work." Colm looked to Teagan. "Let's go over the old version and then you can either give your approval or not. However, you can't be part of the planning, Teagan. In this, you need to remain oblivious."

She bobbed her head. "I know. But I'm anxious to hear about this old quest first."

As Colm went over the full account, Aaron tried his best to keep his expression neutral. Some of the challenges, such as standing in the middle of a circle of burning logs to warm up a metal object to see a certain inscription, was bloody dangerous.

His dragon grunted. *Teagan is clever. She won't have a problem.*

I agree, but what do you think will happen if one of the other leaders gets himself killed in the process?

It won't be our problem.

I'm not so sure, dragon.

His beast fell silent and Aaron focused on Colm's words. If Teagan agreed to an old-fashioned quest and series of puzzles to solve, then Aaron might need to adjust his tactics for her training sessions. Beating the crap out of someone wouldn't be enough. No, he would need to think of ways to stretch her mind, too.

Chapter Thirteen

The next morning, Aaron completed his hundredth push-up and jumped to his feet. He'd hoped that the exercise would wake him up, but the long history lesson the night before was still taking its toll. Colm and Teagan had talked for hours, and in the end, Aaron had gone home to his own place to nab what sleep he could.

Slapping his cheeks, he headed toward his small kitchen. It was time for coffee.

Mentally poking his dragon, Aaron said, *Wake up.*

No. Too early.

Aaron prepared the coffee machine. *Stop being grumpy.*

We were supposed to have a night with Teagan. Instead, we listened to that male drone on about a long-forgotten quest. Of course I'm grumpy.

I was skeptical at first, but I think it's a good idea. Nothing like giving the other leaders a good challenge.

His beast yawned. *I'm sure they'll think of a way to use it against her.*

Since Grant McFarland is one of the judges, he won't put up with the gender bias bullshit. His mate is proof of his belief in giving females a chance to do anything.

Grant's mate, Faye MacKenzie, had once been head Protector of Lochguard until an injury had taken it from her. However, she now shared the responsibility with her mate.

His dragon grunted. *I suppose. I'm going back to sleep.*

As his beast curled up and ignored him, Aaron flicked on the coffee machine and leaned against the counter.

Before he could think of how to handle his next assignment mentoring some young dragon-shifter named Revelin Collins, someone knocked on the back door to his cottage. Frowning, he made his way to it and yanked it open.

Teagan stood there, dressed in a long, flowing dress that dipped to a low V, giving him a glimpse of the tops of her round breasts.

His dragon also took notice. *Bring her inside and strip her.*

Teagan's voice prevented him from replying. "Can I come in or are you just going to stare at my breasts all day?"

Aaron cleared his throat and stepped aside. "What did you want?"

She entered. "Someone's a bit tetchy."

Aaron closed the door and ran a hand through his hair. "I haven't had my coffee yet. Don't push me."

She tilted her head. "This isn't my cottage, you know. There are no exceptions here about ignoring my authority."

"I don't care," he muttered and turned back toward the kitchen.

His dragon growled. *What are you doing?*

I'm not ready to deal with her teasing right now.

And what about charm? She used the back door for a reason.

He stared at the coffee machine and willed it to finish brewing. Teagan leaned on the counter next to him. "What's wrong with you? You're quite grumpy this morning. Should I call the doctor?"

"I'm fine, bloody woman. I was up half the night listening to old stories. I don't have the energy for you right now."

She paused and he mentally cursed. He'd never been charming in the early morning hours, but Teagan didn't deserve his anger. "Look—"

She put up a hand. "Don't worry about it. You're nothing compared to my brother when he misses a meal. He's grumpier than anyone I've ever met then, although don't tell him I told you that."

He turned to face her. "Why are you here, Teagan?"

Running a finger down his bare bicep, she murmured, "You're a little sweaty."

He captured her hand. "Don't change the subject." He leaned closer to her face. "Why are you here?"

Her pupils flashed and Aaron's beast roared. *Kiss her. Don't wait.*

Teagan's voice was barely a whisper when she replied, "I haven't been able to concentrate all morning."

They may not be in her cottage, but fuck it. There was no way he could be alone with her and not touch her. He traced her jaw with a finger. "And why is that, love?"

Her eyes moved to his chest. As she caressed him with her eyes, blood shot straight to his cock. "I had looked forward all day to last night." She met his gaze again. "To say I was disappointed I had to work would be an understatement."

Aaron released her hand on his arm and placed a hand possessively on her hip. Rubbing in slow circles, he murmured, "And here I thought you had found a safer bloke to find your release with."

She frowned. "Colm? No, he's just an old friend and ally. Kissing him would be like kissing a brother."

Smiling slowly, Aaron pulled Teagan against his body. "Good answer."

She opened her mouth, but Aaron cut her off with a kiss. As she melted against him, he stroked the inside of her mouth and relished in the sweet taste that was Teagan.

If he wasn't careful, he might become addicted.

Not wanting to think on that, he moved his hands to her waist, took hold, and raised her to sit on the counter. After sucking on her bottom lip, he stepped a foot away from her. Teagan blinked. "What's going on? My time is short, Caruso. I don't have time for games."

"Aaron," he growled out.

"Fine, Aaron. Same question."

He took the hem of her long dress and slowly slid it up her thigh. "I need to make sure you're ready."

She watched the material as he inched it up her leg. Her husky voice asked, "Ready for what?"

Moving his hands further, he reached her inner thigh. Her skin was softer than anything he'd touched in a while.

Teagan's voice was weaker when she repeated, "Ready for what?"

"To take you on the counter."

Her cheeks flushed pink. "On the counter."

"Since most people don't use the back door, no one will know you're here, let alone can they watch unless they sit on top of the garden wall." He bunched her skirt around her waist and glanced down. With her legs spread, her beautiful, pink pussy was on display. "You're not wearing underwear. Is this a daily thing? Because if so, I'm constantly going to wish I was your clothes since they'll always be touching the most tender part of you."

He lightly ran a finger through her folds, and Teagan sucked in a breath before saying, "I thought it might speed up the process." She glanced down to his cock straining against his tracksuit bottoms. "I think it's time you show me yours."

As her hands moved to the top of his tracksuit pants, the last vestiges of Aaron's tiredness slipped away. It seemed Teagan was as good as coffee for waking him up in the morning.

Hell, for waking him up in all ways.

His dragon spoke up. *Another reason to see her every day. It'll be better for your heart.*

Stop thinking of my bloody heart. We have more important things to worry about.

Teagan's fingers dipped under his waistband and brushed the tip of his dick. Aaron clenched his fingers to keep from reaching out to her. Teagan deserved a chance to do what she wished with him, and he was anxious to see what the clever woman came up with, especially since she always seemed to blush when sex was concerned.

~~~

Teagan's previous sexual experiences had been secreted in a bedroom or maybe an isolated bit of forest.

Yet as she had her legs spread wide, exposing her center to the world with Aaron standing in front of her in the kitchen, she decided she liked taking her time and doing things differently. First on a chair and now on a counter. Maybe Aaron would even be open to sex in a lake. She'd always wondered what it'd feel like to do it while being surrounded by water.

Her dragon growled. *Think about that later. Get him naked. I want his cock inside us.*

Teagan ran her finger back and forth across the tip of Aaron's penis. Whenever she lightly used her nail, his pupils
~~~

flashed. She decided to see if she could read him as well as he'd read her two days before and use his cues to drive him wild.

Teagan slid her fingers down his hard length and encircled him. Aaron sucked in a breath and she smiled. "How about this?"

She squeezed him at the base and Aaron groaned. "Fuck, yes."

Not releasing the pressure of her grip, she pulled up and then down. Aaron placed his hands on the counter to either side of her hips as she repeated the motion, but he never severed eye contact.

She heard his thundering heartbeat and saw his flashing eyes. Strong, contrary Aaron Caruso was weak at the knees from her touch.

For all the control she had over her clan, Teagan had never felt as powerful as she did in that moment.

She increased her pace, but Aaron cursed and took her wrist to still her movements. His voice was low and gentle as he said, "As much as I'd love to come all over your hand, I want to be inside you, love."

As they stared into one another's eyes, Teagan wished she had more time to spend with the dragonman in front of her. He was turning out to be the opposite of what she'd thought. Strong, stubborn, and irritating, yes, but also gentle, caring, and willing to respect her position.

Her dragon whispered, *He would be a good fit.*

Teagan couldn't afford to think of the future beyond the next two weeks. That thought brought her crashing back to reality and she released Aaron's cock and withdrew her hand. "So what now?"

"Time to get naked." He guided her arm to his shoulder. She dug in her nails as he quickly took something out of his pocket and shucked his tracksuit pants.

Her eyes zeroed in at his long, hard penis curved against his belly.

She itched to touch him again and find exactly what drove him to moan.

Aaron ripped open a package and slowly slid a condom over his hard length. Teagan smiled. "Someone was prepared."

Once done, Aaron slid his fingers into her hair. "Let's just say I was thinking of ways to hunt you down before my balls turned even bluer."

She took a condom packet from her bra and held it up. "And here I thought I was doing the hunting."

Snorting, Aaron took the package and tossed it on the counter. "It just means I can have you again later."

Her heart skipped a beat at seeing him naked once more. "Later?"

He moved closer. "Once isn't going to be enough." He took hold of his cock and lightly ran it through her folds. Teagan gasped and barely caught his next words, "And I remember a deal for an entire night's worth of sex. It just means we'll have to space it out to fit your schedule." The bastard brushed her clit and Teagan lost her train of thought. Aaron chuckled and said, "We can discuss scheduling later."

"Do I get a say in this?"

Positioning his cock at her entrance, he murmured, "Tell me no now. It's your last chance to back out because once I start, I'm not going to want to stop."

If she were a perfect clan leader, Teagan would push him away and resist temptation.

Her dragon growled. *No one is bloody perfect. And if you never take a break, it will hurt everyone in the long run.*

She made her decision and dug in her nails. "Don't keep a lady waiting, Aaron."

With a growl, he kissed her and inched his cock inside her. She clenched her jaw at his fullness, but he kissed her and she opened her mouth. His tongue caressing hers soon made her forget about everything but how deep he reached. Maybe there was something about half-Italian dragon-shifters.

Once he was to the hilt, he broke the kiss. "Fuck, you're tight. I love how you hold onto me as if you won't ever let go."

A yearning she'd long buried deep, to have a partner at her side to help with the clan and eventually raising a family, broke free.

But she didn't want to ruin the moment. Aaron was only there for sex, nothing more. She would have to take what she could get.

Teagan wiggled her hips. "Move, Aaron. Make sitting on this hard, cold counter worth it."

He took her lips again before moving his hips. Each long, languid stroke made her cry out. Yet Aaron swallowed her cries, never breaking their kiss.

Not liking the distance between the rest of their bodies, she pulled him closer until she could wrap her legs around his waist. Aaron kept one hand in her hair and moved the other to the small of her back. He pulled her closer to the edge of the counter and increased the motion of his lower body.

The tension built, but it wasn't enough. She was about to end the kiss and let him know when Aaron ran his hand from her back to her belly and then lower. When a rough finger brushed her clit, she cried out. Aaron finally released her mouth and whispered, "Don't hold back on me, Teagan. Never hold back with me."

The words barely cleared her lust haze. However, when Aaron started a steady rhythm on her sensitive bundle of nerves, rubbing back and forth before circling the hard bud, she lost all train of thought. She was so close.

"Harder," she whispered.

Aaron pressed his thumb against her clit and pleasure shot through her body as lights danced in front of her eyes. Combined with Aaron's movements as she orgasmed, Teagan cried out louder than she ever had before with a male.

She'd barely come down from her high when Aaron stilled and growled as spasms racked his body. She knew the condom was necessary for many reasons, but she secretly wanted to feel him come inside her.

Quickly pushing aside that thought, Aaron finally slumped his shoulders, as if exhausted. Teagan leaned her head on Aaron's collarbone and wrapped her arms around his back. She still had her legs around his waist, and when Aaron engulfed her in his strong arms, she sighed.

In this moment, she didn't have to be strong, clever, and concerned with everyone else's well-being. She was merely a female in the embrace of a male, listening to his heartbeat and reveling in his spicy masculine scent.

The yearning that had been overpowered by lust returned in full force. What she wouldn't give for such closeness every day.

But she knew Aaron belonged with Stonefire, not with her.

For the first time, she wished he would stay.

His lovely deep voice interrupted her thoughts. "What are you thinking, love?"

~~~

Aaron should've stepped away as soon as he found his release. After all, he and Teagan weren't a couple and probably never could be.

But as he stood with Teagan in his arms and her wrapped around his body in more ways than one, he couldn't bring himself to do so.

His dragon spoke up. *And why is that?*

Don't.

Why? She is not her. *Give Teagan a chance.*

A part of him wanted to. *But what about our responsibilities back home?*

Teagan tightened her arms around him and Aaron focused back on her. He'd never seen her so quiet. "What are you thinking, love?"

She sighed. "Just that I want more of this."

"Sex on a counter?"

She glanced at him with narrowed eyes. "I'm trying to be serious, Aaron."

Lightly rubbing circles on her back, he answered, "Then tell me in detail what you mean by 'more of this.' I can keep a secret, you know."

She searched his gaze and he held his breath. Why he wanted her to confide in him, he had no idea.

Teagan finally let out a long sigh. "If I say sex with you, will you start cracking on about having a magical penis?"

He grinned. "Well, you did seem to enjoy it."

She rolled her eyes. "That's not the point."
~~~

"So you did like it." He roamed a hand up her back to fist her hair. "Maybe one of these times we can both be naked at the same time. Then I can really work my magic."

"I'm not sure when that'll be, though."

His dragon hummed. *See? She thinks of being with us again. It should be every night. Then we can take care of her always.*

Stop planning my bloody future.

He kissed the corner of her mouth. "Then surprise me. Even if I have to wake up early and go without coffee again, it'll be worth it if it means I get you naked in either of our beds."

She shook her head and her hair tickled his chest. "You say that now, but it could be this evening or days from now. I don't have the most predictable schedule right now."

Gently tugging her hair, he moved to kiss her jaw. "Anticipation is a heady thing, Teagan O'Shea. Maybe one day I can convince you of that."

As soon as the words were out, he wanted to curse. Aaron was only on Glenlough for a short amount of time. He had no right hinting of a future.

Especially when Teagan could lose everything if the clan found out about them.

He took her lips in one final, rough kiss before he stepped away and pulled out of her.

His dragon huffed. *Don't let her go.*

What the hell are you talking about? I can't walk around the clan with Teagan attached to my dick.

That's not what I mean.

He paused and simply said, *I know.*

Aaron took Teagan's waist and lifted her off the counter and back to the floor. She stumbled a second and crashed into his chest.

He held her tightly, more than aware he should push her away.

After a minute, Teagan's whispered, "I should go, Aaron. There's a lot to do."

He gave her one last squeeze before he released her. "Find me whenever you need me, Teagan."

He expected a snarky reply, but Teagan merely nodded. "I need to go."

She adjusted her dress and exited the back door.

Standing in silence, Aaron clenched his fingers and forced himself to turn away from the door. Teagan's wasn't his to go after.

Besides, he had assignments to do. Bram and all of Stonefire were counting on him. He wasn't letting anyone down because of a female ever again.

Chapter Fourteen

A loud crack next to her ear woke Teagan and she jumped to her feet. Scanning her office, she found her grandmother lowering her cane to the ground. "What are you doing here, Gran?" she demanded.

Orla looked to the crowded sofa and back to Teagan. "I could do with resting my old bones first."

Resisting the urge to roll her eyes, Teagan cleared one side of the sofa. It seemed everyone was a critic. "Hurry up before you fall over and hurt yourself."

Orla tsked as she maneuvered her bum onto the cushion. "Odd that you're giving health advice, granddaughter, when you're not taking care of your own."

Teagan smoothed her hair and sat back in her own chair. "I eat, I sleep, and I'm in perfect physical shape. Are you sure you're not losing your mind, Gran?"

"Oh, stop it, Teagan Marie O'Shea. You've lived in this office for the last three days. I think you need some help and so I'm here to offer my services."

Teagan sighed. "Gran, I appreciate the offer—"

"I won't fall asleep every five minutes. You, on the other hand, won't be able to defeat anyone if you remain cooped up in this room."

Teagan felt as if she were five years old again and having to explain herself. "The DDA has strict deadlines, which weren't helped by the fact that Clan Greenpeak waited until the last possible second to submit the names of their visiting judges." She patted a stack of papers. "Once I send these in today, I can have a proper sleep at home."

"Again, someone else can fill out paperwork." Teagan opened her mouth, but Orla beat her to it. "I understand proving yourself. After all, I was in your position. But unless you learn to delegate, you will work yourself to death, Teagan Marie. At least let me help you until the bloody challenge is complete and you send those males running home with their tails between their legs." Her voice softened. "I may be old, but I'm not useless."

For a brief second, Orla wasn't the former clan leader full of bite and a steely will. She was simply an elderly female with longing in her eyes.

Her dragon spoke up. *Let her help. She has no great-grandchildren, mate, or job to occupy her time. Give her a task. Gran has always hated being idle.*

Teagan sighed. "You can help, but with a few conditions." Orla raised an eyebrow and Teagan continued, "You have to promise not to change any of my decisions or issue orders in my absence. Even if I'm unconscious, the task falls to Killian first to take charge."

"I'm not used to following others, but if it gets me out of my damn cottage and gives me something to do beyond watching the grass grow, then I suppose I can try my best."

That was the closest thing to a promise her gran would give. "Right, then this pile needs to be filed—"

Orla waved a hand. "The DDA hasn't changed their filing process in fifty years. I'll double-check to make sure everything is filled out and ensure they send a confirmation receipt."

Teagan frowned. "Everything is as it should be, Gran."

"Look, you're sleep-deprived and overworked. There's nothing wrong with a quick check. I'm not trying to overstep my boundaries. I just want to make sure there's one less item for the other clans to use against you. Could you imagine if a missing letter on a name ended up canceling the challenge? The others would rally the support they need to attack and do who knows what. Glenlough may be strong, but we're not invincible."

Her beast sighed. *She's right. Let her help us. Maybe after a quick nap, we can go for a short flight. The exercise will maintain our strength. I also miss the sky.*

Me, too, dragon. Me, too.

Teagan stood. "I will take your help, Gran." She paused before adding, "Thank you."

"No need to be so formal. Now, hurry up and sneak out before someone comes knocking."

"If they do—"

"I'll take the message and redirect as much of it to Killian as possible."

Teagan looked around the room, wondering if she had forgotten anything important.

Orla thumped her cane on the ground. "I'll tidy up a bit as well. If I find anything that needs immediate attention, Killian will sort it out. Go, Teagan, before I smack your bum and chase you out. No matter how long you're leader, I will always be your grandmother first and foremost."

She smiled. "I love you, Gran."

"Aye, I know. Now go."

Teagan hesitated one more second before she plucked up her mobile phone and headed out the door. She took the back exit out of central command and stepped into the fresh air.

Since it was barely six in the morning, few people were awake and walking around. It was easy enough for Teagan to make her way without being questioned by curious or anxious clan members.

However, when she reached the fork in the path, she stopped. One way would take her back to her cottage, but the other way went to Aaron's.

Beyond him dropping off meals at her office, she hadn't seen or spoken to him for three days. She shouldn't yearn to hear his deep English voice, but it had occupied much of the dreams she'd had during her naps.

She wondered if he'd welcome her showing up at his door so early in the morning.

Her dragon sighed. *Just go. If he doesn't want to see us, then he's unworthy of our time in the first place.*

Tired as she was, Teagan didn't argue and took the fork toward Aaron's cottage. She reached the back wall of his garden, looked around, and scaled the wall. She stopped at the back door and took a deep inhalation before lightly rapping on the wood.

As the seconds ticked by, she debated leaving or not.

Just as she turned away, the door opened and a voice gravelly with sleep said, "It's early."

She looked over her shoulder. The sight of Aaron's hair sleep-mussed brought a smile to her face. "If you look this disheveled on your own, what would you look like if you had someone else in bed with you?"

Rubbing a hand down his face, Aaron replied, "If you think I'm going to be witty this early, you'll be waiting a long time."

He yawned, and she took advantage of his action to trail her gaze lower. His bare chest called to her, and his semi-erect cock punching against his boxers turned her mouth dry.

She wondered if he'd been dreaming of her.

Her dragon sighed. *Dreams don't matter when he's standing right in front of us.*

She ignored her beast. Keeping the want from her voice, she met his gaze and raised her brows. "Good morning to you, too. If I'm that much of a bother, I can just leave. I don't need you witty first thing, but a little welcoming would nice."

She took a step away, but Aaron's strong hand gripped hers and yanked her inside. She barely had the chance to squeak before he pulled her close and kissed her gently. "You know what I'm like without coffee in the morning. Not grunting every word is about my limit. Welcoming requires a little motivation."

She looped her arms around his neck. "I don't want to start a bad habit. I like to save my seductions for special occasions."

He brushed the hair from one of her cheeks and over her shoulder. "Don't take this the wrong way, but why are you here?"

As she stared into his lovely brown eyes, full of nothing but curiosity, she decided to be honest. "I've been ordered to rest, but when I came to the fork in the path, I was pulled here." She laid her head on his chest. "You help me forget about the world outside, and I need that right now."

Aaron merely stood there, rubbing her back in silence. Doubt yet again reared its ugly head. She had no right to put him in such a spot. After all, he'd stated their relationship was purely physical from the start.

Then he stepped back and released her. The hug was him just being nice.

She cleared her throat. "Don't worry, I'll go and leave you in peace. I shouldn't have come here."

Before she could bat an eyelash, Aaron scooped her up and lifted her against his chest. He grunted. "You're not going anywhere. You need to rest."

If anyone else had tried to pick her up in public, she would've slashed their arms and wrestled them to the ground.

Yet as Aaron carried her in his arms and walked toward his bedroom, she snuggled against his warm chest. His heat and steady beating heart lulled her to sleep.

Her beast spoke up. *He will watch over us. Sleep.*

Why do you trust him so much?

He is meant for us. He will stand by our side.

Aaron laid her down on the bed and climbed behind her. As he wrapped his arms around her middle, he kissed her ear. "Sleep, love."

With Aaron's heat at her back, Teagan closed her eyes, and the world went blissfully black.

~~~

Aaron listened to Teagan's even breaths and hugged her closer to his body.

He was in trouble.

When she'd shown up at his front door, barely able to stand upright with shadows under her eyes, anger had coursed through his body, followed by concern.

She was working too bloody hard.

He'd done his part to feed her, but since she wasn't his mate or even his girlfriend, he had no claim to force her to do anything else. He understood clan leaders had duties, but even
~~~

Bram back home would take a break every once in a while, more so after he mated Evie Marshall.

His dragon spoke up. *If you would pull your head out of your arse, then you'd see she should be ours. No one else takes care of her. We should be able to. Just imagine how much stronger she'd be with someone always at her back.*

He hugged Teagan a little closer to him. *It's not that simple.*

Maybe it is.

Not wanting to argue with his dragon, Aaron buried his face in the crook of Teagan's neck and closed his eyes. With her warm back against his front and her wild feminine scent filling his nose, he instantly fell asleep.

~~~

Aaron stood at the foot of a hill, scanning for Teagan. They were playing chase and it was his turn to find her.

He finally caught a glimpse of black hair waving in the wind at the top of the hill. He quietly inched his way up, determined to surprise her.

Lying on his belly, he crawled the last few feet until he could see Teagan sitting on the ground and leaning back on her hands, basking in the warm sunshine.

Something was wrong. She should've been waiting to attack him, not sitting out in the open with her eyes closed.

Opening her eyes, she looked straight at him and smiled. "Aaron. Come, I want to introduce you to my newest good friend."

Curious, he stood and walked toward Teagan. However, when he was nearly to her, the dark-haired, olive-toned form of Nerina appeared from out of nowhere. "What are you doing here?" he demanded.

Teagan stood and walked to Nerina. Teagan answered, "Nerina told me how useful you were to stir up jealousy. The male I truly wanted has
~~~

noticed." The blond-haired form of Colm crested the hill and swept Teagan off her feet. Teagan gazed up at him and said, "He's Irish and won't cause any problems when I mate him." She looked to Aaron. "It's time for you to go home."

Aaron took a step toward Teagan and Colm, but they vanished. He was left alone with Nerina.

She laughed. "You aren't worth the trouble. Go home and stay there. Why would any of us want an English dragon-shifter to tear apart our clans? If no one wants you on Stonefire, then maybe there's a reason."

Nerina snapped her fingers, and Aaron sailed through the air, over the Irish Sea, and landed at the gates of Stonefire. Bram stood in front of locked gates. His voice rang out. "You failed us, Aaron. You're no longer welcome on Stonefire. Leave and never return."

Aaron tried to shift, but his mind was silent.

His dragon was gone.

The gates to Stonefire grew taller and taller until Aaron stood alone inside a steel pen. A small window appeared, with his mother peering through. Disappointment shone in her eyes. "You'll be just like your father, useless and untrustworthy. You're the reason I've never had an easy life. Leave, and maybe I can finally be happy."

His mother shut the window. Aaron stood alone, his dead father's laugh echoing inside his new prison.

"Aaron."

Teagan's voice snapped him back to reality, and he opened his eyes to find her hovering over him. She searched his gaze. "Are you all right? You were muttering and are covered in sweat."

He rubbed a hand down his face. He couldn't remember the last time he'd had a nightmare. Most of them had stopped once his father had left all those years ago.

The question was whether he should tell Teagan the truth or not.

His dragon growled. *You should.*

Why? So she can think I'm weak? I've spent over half my life proving my worth to the clan. As Stonefire's representative, I can't give her a reason to question the alliance.

This isn't about the bloody alliance, and you know it. If you don't take down your walls for Teagan, then for who? It's not weak to admit faults. Maybe she is the one to help us finally leave this past behind and look toward the future.

Teagan's voice prevented Aaron from replying to his beast. "While it's nice you get along with your dragon, talk to me. What the bloody hell was going on? And don't bother saying nothing." She moved to straddle his stomach and extended a talon. "Do I really need to threaten you for the truth?"

His beast huffed. *Two against one.*

For once, Aaron didn't want to challenge her or his dragon. He sighed. "I had a bad dream."

Teagan raised an eyebrow. "And?"

"And what? People have bad dreams all of the time."

"Maybe, but not when I'm lying right next to them. I'd rather not have you sweating all over me every night if I can help it."

He paused and echoed, "Every night?"

"Don't change the subject. Just be honest. Otherwise, I'm leaving."

He didn't answer and hurt flashed in her eyes. She leaned to swing off the bed, but Aaron placed his hands on her hips to keep her in place. "Telling you will change things between us, Teagan. Are you sure you want that?"

She retracted her talon and brushed his cheek with a finger. "Considering I came here instead of my own cottage already means things have changed between us."

His dragon huffed. *Don't push her away, too.*

As he stared up into her beautiful green eyes, her black hair dancing around her face, he took a chance and leaped. "I'm sure you've read my file and know I spent some time in Italy." She nodded and he continued, "It was for my mother. Most of her family lives in Italy and she missed them. I didn't know if she was going to stay long-term or not, but regardless, I went with her to help her settle in. I was only going to stay a few months, but then I met a female named Nerina."

Teagan's jaw tightened, but she grunted and he continued, "She was pretty, loved to laugh, and always knew how to find a good time. After spending most of my childhood in isolation and controlled by my father, I thought a carefree and social female was what I wanted. In my mind, I thought Nerina was the key to that kind of future."

Teagan's eyes turned curious. "What happened?"

While Aaron didn't blink at facing a challenge on the battlefield, he glanced to the side to avoid seeing Teagan's pity. "She pretended to want me and only used me to stir jealousy in the male she truly wanted to catch." He paused and growled. "When I tried to remind her of the good times, she laughed in my face and said no Italian dragon-shifter in their right mind would want the trouble of having an English dragon as a mate. Besides, English dragon-shifters were cold and unfeeling. She would never saddle herself with that."

"Aaron," Teagan whispered.

Determined to finish, he kept his gaze averted. "If it had only been me, I would've given Nerina the finger and returned home with purpose. But my failure cost my mother, too. She defended me and called out some of the higher-ups in the Italian clan. As a result, we were kicked out and forced to return to Stonefire."

He paused. Telling her about his dream could ruin his chances with Teagan. She wouldn't want a weak male.

And yet, if he didn't carry on, he would most assuredly push her away forever.

That's not what either of us wants, his dragon growled.

Aaron was tired of lying to both his beast and himself. *No.*

No matter how much he wanted to reach out and take Teagan's hand, he instead clenched his fingers into a fist and continued, "As for my dream, in it, Nerina was a friend of yours, and you agreed English mates aren't worth the trouble. I was also just a plaything, to make the male you truly wanted jealous and eager to be by your side." He finally looked back to Teagan, relieved not to see pity but anger there. He could handle that. "Let's just say I have trust issues. You already have a full plate. Are you sure I'm worth the extra trouble? I might even cost you your position, Teagan. Maybe I should go home early and only return to help with guarding the judges."

He waited for Teagan's reply, which would quite possibly determine his future as well.

~~~

As Aaron told Teagan about his time in Italy, it took everything she had not to bolt from the room, shift, and fly straight to the Italian clan's gates to kick Nerina's arse.

No doubt the female had preyed on the lingering effects of Aaron's childhood and his desire for acceptance. If his father
~~~

wasn't already dead, Teagan would've had to fly to America to kick his arse, too.

She could only imagine the strength it took to survive the British Army and be a bloody good Protector without ever revealing his true self and fears.

He may not be a clan leader, but Aaron probably understood her nearly as well as if he had been. Both of them essentially lived double lives—strong in public, but vulnerable and lonely in private.

Maybe he was meant to be the male who stood at her side to challenge tradition after all.

Pushing aside that thought, she focused back on Aaron. She spat out, "Nerina is a bitch."

Aaron's brows drew together. "What?"

"You heard me. If your mother had family there, then Nerina probably heard about what your father did to you both. Verbal abuse leaves scars like any other type of abuse, even if they aren't visible. Nerina used that knowledge to her advantage, not caring if it destroyed families, let alone lives or happiness."

He searched her gaze. "Considering you've never met the female, you're doing a lot of assuming."

Teagan waved a hand. "She's not worth my time. She used you, and that's enough to cement my opinion of her. If I ever meet her, she'll learn a lesson or two." She leaned down until she could lay her forehead against his. "And if you try to leave now, I will catch you and tie you to this bed. I need you, Aaron, and not just for a bit of fun." She hesitated, but decided he deserved truth as well. "Apart from my family, you're the only one I can relax and be myself around. Not only that, you respect my position." The corner of her mouth ticked up. "Well, at least in public."

He moved an arm so he could gently hold the back of her neck. "So, you want me to stay? I can tell you now that it'll cause strife and division. I'm not Irish, remember. Between the British and Irish DDA offices, not to mention our clans, it's going to be a fight."

"Fuck what others think. I already have males with ego issues threatening to attack me. Besides, once the clan sees your dedication to the clan and me, they'll come around. They've already seen you win over my grandmother, and that counts for a lot around here."

"Well, Orla did ask me to look out for you. She'd better be on my side."

For a split second, Teagan wondered if she'd made a mistake. "Is that why you've been feeding me and put me to bed earlier today? Just because my gran asked you to?"

He growled and tightened his grip on her neck. "Of course not. You need someone to tell you to breathe and take a step back, even if for only a few minutes. Maybe it was to humor her at first, but now, whenever I see you about to fall over from exhaustion, and yet someone still approaches you, I want to intercede and tell them to call on you later." He gently squeezed her neck. "Will you give me that right, Teagan O'Shea? I want to be your male."

Her heart pounded faster as an image of her and Aaron leading the clan together flashed into her mind, followed by one of them much older with them teaching their daughter to fight. As the little green-eyed girl pinned Aaron and grinned, her black hair flowing in the breeze, Teagan's heart swelled with pride.

She had no idea how it would play out, but she wanted those glimpses of the future.

She whispered, "I want you to stay."

His hand moved from her neck to fist her hair. "And be your male?"

She nodded. "And be my male."

"Good." He raised his head to kiss her gently. "Don't break my heart, love, and I'll do my bloody best to be the male you deserve. Although I have conditions."

She sat up and Aaron released his grip on her hair. She rolled her eyes. "Of course you do."

"I'm serious. I can't leave my mother unprotected. And you'll have to convince Bram to give my mother and me up. You can't afford to make Stonefire an enemy."

Tracing his jaw, she asked, "Why don't you ask your mother what she wants? Believe me, I understand wanting to protect someone, but sometimes people need freedom to find happiness. Your mother should know she has a choice."

"I'll ask her, but I'll always worry."

"That is part of the reason I want you as my own. Underneath the muscles and morning crankiness, there is a caring, kind male who isn't blinded by ego and insecurities about his manliness."

He grunted. "I hope you're not going to share that with your clan and ruin my reputation."

Tapping her chin, she answered, "Well, we'll see. I guess it depends on if you piss me off or not."

His muscles tensed to move, but she allowed him to flip her onto her back and pin her wrists above her head. His voice was husky as he said, "Arguments can be fun. After all, making up is the best part."

Lifting her hips, she rubbed against his erection. "I know we're not making up now, but maybe we should practice for the future. I like to be prepared."

He nipped her jaw. "Just as long as there is a future." He kissed the corner of her mouth. "And to ensure you're in charge for it, I'm going to help you prepare for the trials using every dirty trick I can think of. No more going easy on you."

As Aaron moved to her earlobe and worried her flesh, she let out a moan. "Trials?" He blew on her wet flesh and she shivered. "How am I supposed to concentrate on anything when you do that?"

He nipped her ear. "It's my secret weapon against you." Moving to her neck, he gently bit her and eased the sting with his tongue. "But for now, it's my duty to help you relax."

"Your duty, aye?" Arching her back, her hard nipples brushed against Aaron's chest. "Then you'd better demonstrate your skills so I can determine if you're qualified for the task on a regular basis."

Aaron took her lips in a rough kiss, his tongue sweeping into her mouth and claiming her tongue. Each stroke heated her body and made her ache between her thighs.

The male knew how to claim.

When he broke the kiss, he whispered, "How was that?"

"Fair."

He narrowed his eyes, extended a talon, and sliced through her top and bra. Pushing aside the material, he took one of her nipples into his mouth and suckled.

Teagan moaned and tried to rub against him for friction, but he moved his lower body out of reach. She let out a cry. "Aaron."

He released her tight point and met her gaze. The heat and desire in his eyes sent even more wetness between her legs. "Stay still or I'll extend my torture even longer." He licked her other nipple. "After all, I need to prove my skills are worthy of a clan leader."

She opened her mouth to say he'd more than passed the test, but he tortured her nipple with slow caresses and gentle bites. Her entire body burned with yearning, wanting to feel Aaron inside her again.

Fisting his hair, she gently tugged until he raised his head. "I think it's time you prove yourself with your cock."

"As long as I can flip you over and take you from behind, I'm up to the task."

"Stop talking and start doing."

He released her wrists and turned her onto her stomach. His warm hands caressed her ribs and moved to her arse cheeks. As he slowly rubbed her skin, Teagan melted into the mattress. "I want a massage later."

Aaron kissed her shoulder, and his breath danced against her skin as he said, "You'll have to earn it first."

"What?"

One of his hands slid down and lightly brushed her opening. "I'm going to make you come hard and then hand over control to you. If you make me scream your name, I'll do whatever you wish."

She glanced over her shoulder. "That sounds like a challenge."

Plunging a finger inside her, Aaron chuckled at her intake of breath. "The day I stop challenging you is the day I die."

Before she could comment on his serious remark, Aaron removed his finger and opened a condom package. She watched as he rolled it down his cock. "I love that you think of me."

He finished and raised her hips. "I won't take your future away from you, Teagan. When the day comes that you want a child, ask, and I'll be ready. I can be patient."

His words chiseled away at her defenses. She was starting to believe he would be content to be her equal and not force her to be someone she wasn't.

Aaron's eyes flashed. As soon as she had the chance, she needed to get to know his dragon better, too.

Her dragon spoke up. *Maybe later I can be in control.*

We'll see, love. I don't know how much time we have before I'm called away.

If I have anything to say about it, we have the rest of our lives.

She wanted to agree, but there was still so much uncertainty in her life.

Aaron's husky voice interrupted her thoughts. "I think of you often, but right now, I want to do this." He positioned his cock at her entrance. "Can you take what I give, love?"

Teagan nodded and he thrust into her. Taking hold of her hips, Aaron moved in quick, hard thrusts, each movement hitting her in just the right spot.

As the pressure built, she focused on the sensation of Aaron filling her to near bursting. No delicate motions for her male.

He increased his pace and soon she cried out his name as pleasure coursed through her body.

Aaron roared as he stilled and found his own release.

Teagan watched as the cords of his neck relaxed, and he slumped over her back. He gently kissed her neck and whispered, "I don't think you screamed my name loud enough. I'm going to make you come once more before you get a go."

She opened her mouth to argue, but Aaron pulled out and flipped Teagan to her back. He settled his head between her thighs and went to work. Each lick and nibble on her already sensitive, throbbing flesh quickly pushed her over the edge.

She lost count of how many times she yelled Aaron's name before she finally elicited a roar from him with her own mouth.

Chapter Fifteen

Much later the same day, Aaron lay on the bed and watched Teagan as she returned from the door with a bag in her hand. She waggled a finger at him. "If I ever have to call my mother again to bring me clothes because you destroyed mine, you're going to be the one answering the door."

He grinned. "It won't bother me. Although I'm not sure you want your mother seeing my jewels."

She picked up a shoe from the ground and hurled it at him. Aaron moved out of the way.

Teagan glared. He tried his best not to laugh as she growled out, "At this rate, the entire clan will see your penis before the week's out."

He lazily stroked his semihard cock, and her eyes followed the motion. "They can look, but it's only for you, love."

His dragon spoke up. *Why are we lying here? Take her again. She is ours and laid claim on us.*

She has duties, as do I.

One more hour shouldn't matter.

Teagan's voice prevented him from replying. "As much as I want to shout 'Prove it,' I can't. Today is my weekly appointments with disgruntled clan members. I can't afford to irritate anyone right now by canceling."

Aaron released his dick and rolled off the bed. Closing the distance between them, he kissed her and murmured, "If there's any way I can help, tell me." She hesitated and he pushed. "I mean it, Teagan. The sooner this is done, the sooner I can set a puzzle to exercise your brain and maybe even wrestle you in dragon form. Tell me what you need me to do."

"You aren't going to like it," she said slowly.

"Try me."

She tilted her head. "Well, if you could find out the reason for each visit, in detail, as they wait their turn, it would dramatically reduce the amount of time it takes to handle each person. They tend to ramble, you see, or shout. With you, they might be less comfortable and just give the pertinent details."

The corner of his mouth ticked up. "So I should use my scary Protector frowns and growls to whip them into shape."

Teagan smiled. "That might help." She laid a hand on his chest and idly ran her fingers back and forth through his chest hair. "You don't mind? I know it's not exactly the best use of your skills, but it would help me out quite a bit."

"If I offer to help, I mean it, no matter what it is. You need to understand that now. I won't have you doubting me or wondering if you'll scare me off. Provided you don't cut off my balls, I'm staying."

Amusement danced in her eyes. "Is that a challenge to see what I can come up with and see if you stay?"

He growled. "It's not a joke. I'm staying, Teagan. And my top priority is taking care of you so that you have the strength to take care of everyone else."

Teagan's face softened. All he wanted to do was kiss her, but he somehow resisted. He needed to hear her response.

She finally cleared her throat. "Thank you."

He ran a hand down her back to cup her arse through the fabric of his shirt she wore. "Stop being so formal." He lightly slapped her bum. "I think once I've made you scream my name, all pretenses are off."

She swatted his chest. "Aaron."

He nuzzled her cheek. "I'm going to have to work hard to make you stop blushing." He lowered his voice as he pulled her closer. "After all, no one needs to know what happens between us when we're alone. You don't want the clan members pointing and whispering because your cheeks turn pink whenever you see me."

Pushing against his chest, Teagan leaned back. "And you can train me for that later. Right now, I need to shower and change. My first appointment is with Renny Walsh, and if I'm late, he will complain for ages about it to anyone who'll listen."

Aaron kissed her once more before releasing her. "Then to save time, let's shower together."

She searched his gaze. "No funny business."

"I promise no sex, but if you think I'm going to keep my hands off your wet body, then you're in for a surprise."

She smiled. "Oh, you might have a few surprises coming your way as well."

Teagan took his hand and led him into the bathroom.

It was hard to believe the sexy, clever leader of Clan Glenlough wanted him. But as she looked at him with a devilish glint in her eyes, he quickly pushed aside any doubts and joined her in the shower. It was going to take death to pry him from her side. She may not know it, but Teagan O'Shea would be his—she was his future.

~~~

Teagan's head began to pound when her first appointment, Renny Walsh, asked her point-blank if she was sleeping with the English dragon-shifter.
~~~

She managed to keep a smile pasted to her face as she answered, "Your appointment is for airing grievances, not talking about my personal life. You resisted telling Aaron your purpose for coming here, and I still allowed you to keep the appointment. But if you don't have anything for me to hear and rule on, then you should probably go."

The male's silver brows came together. "If you're sleeping with him, then I have the right to know. Him being here will put my life in danger."

She shouldn't encourage him, but she couldn't help but ask, "How so?"

"You might accept Stonefire as an ally, but memories are long. We were enemies once. Some won't forget that."

"And we were allies once, too."

"Hatred of enemies always lasts longer," Renny stated.

She shrugged. "I have no control over that. I'm working on making new memories with Stonefire. The world is changing, and it's becoming harder and harder to face the human world alone. My hope is that Stonefire is just the first. The more clans we have with us, the easier it'll be to keep our lands and ensure the well-being of everyone in the clan."

He waved a hand. "I care nothing about other clans. Glenlough is all that matters."

She folded her hands in front of her, drawing on every bit of patience she possessed. "Are you insinuating that I don't care about Glenlough, Renny? If so, you're on dangerous territory."

"It's not the caring I'm concerned about. Rumors will fly soon, Teagan, and weaken your support for the upcoming challenge. You need to be honest with the clan about your relationship with the male to curb the rumors. You know the consequences for taking a mate. The challenge may not be necessary at all if you step down."

Her dragon huffed. *Maybe revealing our relationship with Aaron will help with dismantling the old way of thinking and put* Renny's *ridiculous suggestion to rest.*

I agree, but the timing needs to be right, which isn't now.

Teagan focused back on the older dragonman. "I am honest and open about most things—more than the average clan member for certain. For example, would you answer a question about sleeping with someone? I've heard rumors about you as well, Renny. Maybe we should talk about your dalliance with a human widow living just outside Letterkenny."

He blinked. "How do you know about that?"

"It's my business to know. Killian checked out her background and cleared her. Otherwise, I would've talked to you much sooner." Teagan leaned forward. "So, I repeat my question: would you want the clan to know about your private life? Because it can easily be arranged, if it's that important to know about mine. Dallying with a human female may not be illegal, but it's frowned upon, especially by the Irish DDA. You'd either have to mate her or break up with her."

Renny narrowed his eyes. "What I do with Colleen isn't the same thing at all. The English dragon-shifter could be a spy, merely using you for information. Does the DDA even know he's here?"

Teagan raised her brows. "The Stonefire dragon-shifters are here to help us all. If you report them, then you dash any hope of forming an alliance with Northcastle. As I recall, you have cousins there. Wouldn't you like to see them again?"

Renny didn't answer, but Teagan knew from chatter that Renny banged on about missing one cousin in particular.

She continued, "Now, I've heard your grievance and will note it down in the records. Aaron is not a spy and whenever I choose to mate, it will be my decision, and I'll share it with the clan. For now, our only priority is preventing attacks from other dragon clans."

Renny muttered, "A male in charge would stop that, too."

Teagan raised an eyebrow. "I assure you that despite what history may want you to believe, having a penis doesn't grant magical powers. Now I think it's time for you to leave. Others are waiting their turn."

The elderly male slowly rose to his feet. "Don't say I didn't warn you, Teagan. The English bring nothing but trouble. You'll see."

As soon as Renny closed the door, Teagan let out a sigh and spoke to her dragon. *If he's this way now, I can only imagine what Renny will be like if Aaron and I mate, but I refuse to step down.*

I'm glad you're seeing things my way and accepting Aaron as our own.

Few trained soldiers would lower themselves to acting as a receptionist. I think he's proved his dedication. He's at least earned a chance.

You're still afraid he'll run away.

She hesitated but finally said, *Maybe. Standing by my side for a few days is one thing, but long-term it may eat away at his feelings for me.*

Between his past and yours, I'm surprised you two have managed to let down any walls.

Don't start, dragon. I have to be careful.

A text message beeped on her phone, garnering Teagan's attention. It was from Aaron, about her next appointment: *Some bloke called Hugh. Refused to talk with me. Arsehole.*

She snorted. Hugh was indeed an arsehole, although she wondered what had happened to her original appointment for the day. Hugh's name hadn't been on the list.

A knock on the door ceased her wonderings. The tall, balding form of Hugh Burns waltzed in.

Teagan steepled her fingers in front of her. "I don't have you on the schedule. Why are you here?"

"Donna gave me her spot."

Donna Mullins had been scheduled for this time. Teagan would have to seek out the female later and see if she'd been coerced in any way to abandon her appointment.

Her former rival to lead the clan sat down in the chair in front of her desk. "And what do you want, Hugh?"

Hugh waved a hand toward the door. "I had to see it for myself. You've all but cut off the English male's balls."

Teagan had suffered years of Hugh's taunts, so it was easy to keep her expression neutral. "What is your grievance, Hugh? Others are waiting their turn."

"My grievance is inviting Padraig and Orin to our clan for a bloody challenge. An outsider has no place ruling here."

Orin Daly was the leader of Clan Greenpeak in Killarney, and Padraig O'Leary was in charge of Clan Wildheath not far from Dublin.

"It's happened many times over the centuries, Hugh. Glenlough has done a fairly good job of finding our leaders internally, but most of the other Irish clans haven't."

Hugh grunted. "Just because it's happened before doesn't mean I have to accept it. We have plenty of strong candidates here."

"I acknowledge your opinion, but since I won the leadership challenge nearly five years ago, this is my decision by right. And while I know you don't think I can win, I'm out to prove otherwise. The clan will be updated as things unfold," she stated.

"You won't win, you know. Your being clan leader is a result of luck."

Teagan had suffered Hugh's bullshit over the years, but she was done dancing around. "You can leave, Hugh. If you continue to stir up trouble, Killian will pay you a visit."

"Hiding behind a male, I see. Without us males to assist, you would've destroyed the clan long ago."

She didn't miss a beat. "All members of a clan are important, and even the arseholes play their roles. So of course I need the males to help; otherwise, there wouldn't be any babies."

He sneered. "Being witty won't help you win. You've invited strangers onto our land without our consent. I could challenge you because of it."

Raising her brows, it took everything she had not to laugh. Hugh had gained several stone and a flabby middle over the last five years. "You want to challenge me and lose a second time? Fine, then join the contest with the other leaders. Unless you're too afraid of losing to me again?"

Hugh smiled slowly. "I heard the challenge will be different this time. Having a former leader's coaching won't help you this round. I will be there and I'll win the leadership. Once I do, I'll be reporting your deeds to the DDA's office. Then I won't ever have to deal with you again."

Her dragon growled. *Are you sure we can't wrestle with him now and put him out of the running? I can't take much more of his smugness despite his obvious flaws. While we all have flaws, he is blind to them.*

No, dragon. We can't afford to injure ourselves dealing with him.

Her beast huffed and fell silent.

Teagan gave her best glare and thread every bit of dominance she possessed into her voice as she said, "Then you know if you continue to harass me, you could be disqualified and it'll squash your dreams early. Now get out before I literally kick your arse out of my office. We're done talking."

He stood. "When I'm leader, you'll be tried for your crimes, Teagan O'Shea. Remember that."

Hugh waltzed out of her office, leaving the door wide open behind him.

A beat later, Aaron popped his head into the doorway and raised his brows in question. She gave a small shake of her head to indicate they would discuss it later. She merely said, "Send me the details of the next person and send them in a few minutes later."

With a bob of his head, Aaron closed the door.

In the spare minute of solitude, Teagan rubbed her forehead. *Hugh is going to be a pain in my arse.*

Perhaps. But if he loses to you and the other leaders, any claim he thinks he has will vanish.

The other leaders might take offense at including him.

You never said it was for other clan leaders only. That is their assumption, and thus their problem.

Teagan sighed. *Well, there's nothing to do now. This is the only way to silence Hugh for good.*

Gran would teach him a lesson, if we asked.

She snorted. *I wish. Maybe I'll use that as a punishment if he ever breaks one of the clan laws.*

Before her dragon could reply, her next appointment entered. As Teagan listened to the rest of her clan members for the day, solving the majority of the problems, her tension eased. While she would have Killian root out any troublemakers, the majority seemed unconcerned with Teagan's actions regarding both Aaron and the leadership challenge.

She only hoped it stayed that way.

~~~

When Aaron showed out the final appointment of the day, he locked the front door to Teagan's secondary office suite and rushed to where she sat behind her desk. Without asking, he moved to her side and leaned down to kiss her gently.
~~~

He pulled away, and she made a content noise in her throat. "A female could get used to that every day."

"My lips are rather powerful. They can cure most anything when it comes to you." She gave a playful shove and Aaron took her hand in his. "I'm just glad you don't have a frown permanently etched between your brows. Some of the grievances were rather petty. Is a tree growing into someone else's garden that much of an inconvenience?"

She shrugged and interlaced her fingers with his. "Sometimes people just need to vent. If it helps their mental health, then so be it."

"A clan psychologist would be better suited. Or maybe a gardener," he drawled.

She raised her brows. "Are you volunteering to cut trees for the clan?"

He winked. "I could be fairly vicious with a chainsaw in my hands. But in all honesty, there are probably deeper issues at work. I'm too stubborn to visit a psychologist, but others could use the help."

"We don't have one, and given the instability at the moment, I doubt anyone would want to take on my clan's problems. Besides, I don't mind listening to them. It's nice connecting with people, on some level at least."

"Because you're usually isolated from them."

She stared at their hands, and it took everything Aaron had not to pull her close. He had a feeling she wouldn't tell him anything if he did.

She talked to their hands. "It's odd in a way. I know everyone and most of their situations, yet I don't truly know them, if that makes sense. I can't go to every birthday party or invite them over for dinner."

"You can't afford for them to think of you as merely a friend."

She met his gaze again. "Exactly."

He did yank her up and pull her close. Cupping her cheek, he murmured, "I'm going to be there for you when you finish for the day, not to mention celebrate everything that should be celebrated. You'll never be alone."

She played with the hair at the nape of his neck. "Just don't hide things from me and be yourself. That's all I ask."

His dragon spoke up. *See? I told you she is perfect for us.*

Ignoring his beast, he focused on Teagan. "I'll try, but as you know, males are tough to crack."

She rolled her eyes. "And that is an excuse I don't believe for a second."

He stroked her cheek with his thumb. "Is that so?"

She smiled. "Let's just say that if you stop being honest with me, you will be sleeping outside in the rain before you can blink."

"I hate the bloody rain," he growled.

She grinned. "Exactly."

"Then do I get to mete out the same punishment if you hide from me?"

She shrugged. "Rain doesn't bother me. I do have a few weaknesses, but you'll have to figure them out yourself."

He lightly slapped her arse. "I think you should tell me one."

She moved a hand to the scar near the corner of his mouth and traced it. "This scar ruins your perfect stubble." She looked up. "How did you get it?"

He grimaced. "My father."

Teagan's eyes turned fierce. "The more I hear of him, the more I hate the male."

He shrugged. "He's gone and doesn't matter. You're much more important."

The anger faded a fraction from her eyes. "Pretty words won't distract me from finding out the whole truth. Just tell me, Aaron."

He raised his brows. "Someone's a bit demanding."

She growled. "Fuck, yes. If you want all of me, then this is part of the deal."

With the fire in her eyes and flush on her cheeks, Aaron wanted her all the more. "He threw a book at my head. The corner caused a scar."

Since they were the same height, Teagan merely leaned over and kissed the small scar. "Thank you for telling me."

"Don't go getting all bloody formal on me, O'Shea."

"I can easily say you're a bastard instead if that'll make you feel better."

He pulled her tighter against his body. "Cheeky wench."

She flashed her teeth before saying, "You'd be bored if I weren't."

As they stared into each other's eyes, Aaron finally chuckled. "Damn you, you're right." He kissed her quickly. "I only wish you didn't have to go talk with Killian in the next few minutes or I'd take you home and show you how far from bored I am."

"Then take a few minutes to kiss me and give me a preview. It'll help me unwind."

Without another word, Aaron took Teagan's lips and devoured her mouth slowly. As she melted against his chest, his heart skipped a beat. And not just because a sexy, capable female was leaning against him. No, for the first time in a long time, he was happy.

More than that, he trusted Teagan. Not to mention that imagining a future without her in it would be bleak. He didn't want to go back to hiding behind fake smiles and winks just to get through the day.

His dragon spoke up. *You know what that feeling is.*

No, not yet. It's too soon.

Coward.

After a few minutes, Teagan finally pulled away, and she cupped his cheek. "I would say thank you, but you don't like formalities." She leaned over to his ear and whispered, "So just know that merely kissing you gets me wet for you, Aaron. Think of that until you see me tonight."

His beast roared. *She is gaining confidence. I like it. Can we have her soon?*

Later, dragon.

He took her hand and guided it to his crotch. He murmured, "I'll be thinking of you the whole time. I won't even find release by my own hand. I'll save it all for you."

Her pupils flashed and Aaron grinned. "I also say we should let out our dragons for the second round. It should make things interesting and may shut them up a bit."

His beast growled. *That's not very nice.*

Aye, but it's true.

She nodded and opened her mouth, but her mobile phone beeped. She sighed. "That would be Killian."

He reluctantly released her. "Go, but just remember frisky Aaron will be waiting for you at home."

Teagan moved a hand to between his thighs and cupped his balls. His cock became even harder as she played with them. "Then I think we'd both better hurry up and finish our tasks so I can meet frisky Aaron properly."

Taking her lips in a rough kiss, Aaron tweaked her nipple, and she moaned into his mouth.

What he wouldn't give to bend her over the desk and take her quickly.

His beast growled. *Why wait?*

Ignoring his dragon, Aaron broke the kiss and murmured, "You need to go, love. My nobility has limits."

Teagan gave him one more kiss before moving to her desk. Collecting her things, she said, "Thank goodness because mine is being tested to the limits."

She winked and dashed out of the room. Aaron stared at the closed door.

Fuck anyone who tried to take his female away from him. Teagan could handle herself, but he would always be her ally. He needed to find other ways to support her. Her well-being meant everything to him.

His dragon spoke up. *And I know why, even if you're too chicken to admit it.*

The last time I used the "L" word, it was too soon. I won't make the same mistake.

Teagan is different. How many times do I have to say it?

For now, let's treasure what moments we have with her. There won't be many until the leader trials are over.

His dragon huffed. *Fine. Just remember to let me out and claim her, too. Otherwise I may have to let slip what you won't say.*

Bloody dragon. When his beast remained silent, Aaron mentally sighed. *I promise you'll have a chance.*

Good. Then your secret is safe with me for the moment.

He didn't like the "for the moment" bit of his dragon's reply, but he would take it.

In the present, ensuring Teagan had a future as Glenlough's leader was all that mattered.

CHAPTER SIXTEEN

Ten days later, Teagan rolled onto her side and snuggled into Aaron's warm body. His strong arms instantly went around her, and his gravelly voice filled the room in a poor Irish accent. "Top of the morning to you."

Teagan sighed and pinched his skin. "I told you to stop that. I'm not a cartoon leprechaun."

"Then maybe you should show me your pot of gold at the end of the rainbow."

She opened her mouth, but his finger danced between her thighs and she sucked in a breath. Aaron chuckled. "It looks like I found it."

Hitching a leg over his hip, she answered, "Maybe I should cut off access until you stop with the horrible Irish accents and leprechaun jokes."

He lightly pushed a finger inside her entrance, which was already wet and swollen. "You wouldn't last a day."

Aaron removed his finger, positioned his cock, and thrust inside. Not for the first time, Teagan was glad she'd been on birth control long enough to feel every inch of him. "Do you really want to throw down that challenge?"

He moved his hips in gentle strokes. "What I want to do is distract you."

As he pressed against her clit, Teagan moaned. "One day, sex isn't going to work as a distraction, Aaron Caruso."

Increasing the friction against her sensitive nub, he murmured, "You say that every time."

She kissed him and focused on matching his rhythm with her hips. It wasn't long before she cried out and pleasure coursed through her body. Aaron stilled and held her close as he came shortly after.

Teagan laid her head on his chest and listened to his heartbeat. She treasured the morning ritual of teasing and sex. In a short time, Aaron had become an essential part of her life.

She'd find out later in the day if she would be lucky enough to keep him.

Her beast spoke up. *Of course we will. Don't doubt we will win.*

I don't want to, but I have a sense that something bad is about to happen.

Weren't you just castigating Aaron for superstitions?

It's not the same thing.

Aaron's deep voice rumbled in his chest. "Are you nervous?"

With anyone else, Teagan would have to be strong. But not with Aaron. "A little. I know I've done all I can to prepare for the leadership challenge, but all it takes is one person violating the rules and killing me to end it."

Aaron placed a finger under her chin and forced her to look up at him. "Observers and judges will be watching at various stations in the area. Also, doctors from several clans will be at the ready. Killian won't let any of the participants die."

She nodded. "I know. If anyone can keep us all alive, it's Killian. It's just that things have been a little too quiet recently, and that makes me worry."

Aaron growled. "Nothing will happen to you, Teagan. If I have to dive down and take a bullet to protect you, I will. I love you."

She paused and asked slowly, "You love me?"

Aaron sighed. "Yes, Teagan, I love you. Don't sound so surprised."

Considering Aaron had supported her every day during the last two weeks, even when she had wanted nothing more than to spar and get out pent-up frustration, she shouldn't question him.

Her dragon roared. *You love him, too. Why is it so hard to say?*

Because it starts yet another battle, and he might grow tired of fighting.

Aaron's voice cut through her thoughts. "Talk to me, not your dragon. Do you doubt my words?" He cupped her cheek and continued before she could reply, "I love how you care for your clan, how you're willing to take up a fight for anyone's happiness, and your selflessness. But just because you care for your people doesn't mean you can't take time for yourself. I won't force the words out of you, but just know I'll be here for you when you finally do say them. I love you, Teagan O'Shea, and you're worth waiting for."

Teagan stared into the brown eyes of the male who had supported her more than any other person unrelated to her ever had in the past. And all without trying to wrestle away her power or force her into having a family before she was ready.

He might not be her true mate, but Aaron Caruso was quite simply her perfect fit.

She opened her mouth to tell him so when her phone rang.

Aaron plucked it up and handed it to her. The caller ID said Killian. She answered, "Killian?"

Her brother answered, "Yes, it's me. Orin Daly and his accompanying clan members are at the front gates."

Teagan had invited the other leaders to stay on Glenlough, but they'd all declined and instead opted to arrive on the day of the challenge. Formality dictated they arrive via the gates instead of the landing areas. "Take him to the main meeting room inside the great hall and I'll be there as soon as I can."

She clicked off the phone and turned toward Aaron. He nodded and murmured, "I guess it's showtime."

Touching his cheek, she leaned over and kissed him. "It's time to see how the rest of our future plays out."

"I believe in you, Teagan. Show the others what you're truly capable of, even without a penis."

She shook her head before rolling out of bed. "Considering how vulnerable it makes you lot, I'm not sure why it's such an asset to have."

Aaron grinned. "Males like having something to play with, so they come up with reasons as to why it's so important."

Snorting, she gathered up her clothes. "That sounds about right." She sobered. "But I should get ready as quickly as possible. That means no sharing a shower today."

He bobbed his head. "Good idea. Now, hurry up. Males also don't like to be kept waiting. Remember that."

She flipped him off before heading to the bathroom.

As she prepared for the most important day of her life, her thoughts kept returning to Aaron's words. *I love you, Teagan O'Shea, and you're worth waiting for.*

Her dragon huffed. *You should've told him.*

There's too much to do, and I don't want it to seem forced. I'll tell him after my victory.

You had better. I'm growing impatient. I want the entire clan to keep their paws off him.

She mentally sighed. *I'm fairly certain they already know.*

Maybe, but until we declare it in front of the clan and show them we're not going anywhere, I'm going to keep harping on about it to you.

Just save it until after the challenge is over, aye? We need to work together.

Her dragon grunted. *In that, I agree. Let's get ready and kick some arse.*

~~~

Aaron stood at the edge of the rear landing area and watched as Faye MacKenzie's blue dragon and Grant McFarland's green dragon touched down. As soon as they were on solid ground, Grant spread his wings in front of Faye. When he lowered them, she stood in her human form, wearing a simple dress.

Grant shifted and soon stood naked next to her in his human form. Aaron approached them and said, "I've seen Faye shift before, McFarland."

Faye rolled her eyes. "Don't get him started. He tried to prevent me from coming at all, but that didn't end well."

Grant grunted. "You're pregnant. You don't need any unnecessary stress."

"Me staying home and twiddling my thumbs is far more stressful," she stated.

Grant frowned. "You only think it's more stressful because you'll be bored."

Faye shook her head. "Let's not have this argument again. We're here, and that can't be changed." She looked to Aaron. "And I can't wait to meet Teagan O'Shea. It'll be nice to have another female ally in a male-dominated role."
~~~

Aaron raised an eyebrow. "Nikki is a Protector, same as you."

Nikki Gray was a young female Protector for Stonefire.

Faye waved a hand in dismissal. "And quite pregnant. Otherwise, I'd have invited her along for support. Nikki and I both have to deal with grumpy, overprotective males whilst still kicking arse."

Grant sighed. "You do realize I'm standing right here?"

Faye patted his chest. "And I love you, overprotectiveness and all." She looked back to Aaron. "Will we have a chance to meet Teagan before the trials?"

Aaron shook his head. "No. She has to play clan leader and be civil to the bastards who think she's weak first. The challenge will start in two hours. My job is to bring you to central command and fill you in on your duties." He motioned with his head. "We should probably get going. Although I'd suggest Grant put on some clothes so the unattached females don't throw themselves at him." Aaron winked. "After all, non-Irish dragonmen are becoming popular here."

Faye searched his gaze. "Yes, about that. Is it true about you shacking up with the leader?"

"It's not shacking up."

Faye grinned. "I knew it. I swear Bram plans these things to extend his reach. First Arabella coming to Lochguard and now you to Glenlough. I wonder where he's going to set his sights on next?"

Arabella MacLeod was originally from Stonefire and had mated the Scottish clan leader the year before.

Aaron sighed. "Not even Bram is that powerful or omniscient to plan such things." He noticed Grant had tossed on a kilt. "Let's go. The sooner you're debriefed, the sooner we can put you in position."

Aaron started walking and the others followed. Grant spoke up. "Are they finally going to tell us what the challenge is? I can't bloody judge something I don't understand."

"Yes," Aaron answered. "It's been kept a secret from most everyone. The judges will all review the plan and voice any objections. If there's perceived bias, then the challenge will be delayed as the judges hash out changes."

Faye asked, "Are the other judges already here? I've never met anyone from the French clans before."

"They should be," Aaron said. "Clan PerleForet is being guarded by one of the other Protectors. You already know the Snowridge pair sent to participate as judges since we all met during the exhibition in Scotland. They sent Wren and Eira."

Aaron, Faye, Grant, and several other Protectors had served together to protect artists from their respective clans as they participated in an art exhibition that had toured around Scotland. The event had been a sort of outreach between humans and dragon-shifters.

Faye smiled at Grant. "I was busy keeping my mate from killing everyone with a glance, so I didn't get as many opportunities to talk with the Snowridge Protectors."

Grant growled. "You spent too much time talking with the bloke from Northcastle."

Faye shrugged. "We needed to learn about the Northern Irish clan."

Aaron jumped in. "You may want to keep from mentioning that clan for the time being. Tensions are high here between the two clans."

"Oops, sorry. I didn't know," Faye replied. "I still say we should have a huge party and invite all the clans of the UK and Ireland. With some alcohol and closely watched fight sessions, we'd all get along before too long."

Grant motioned in front of them. "Let's finish this first, love, and then we can worry about uniting everyone."

Faye beamed. "I'm going to hold you to that later."

As Aaron watched the pair flirt and argue, he didn't doubt their love for each other. He wondered if he'd have the same with Teagan. Even if she lost, which he didn't think would happen, he wasn't giving up on her.

His beast spoke up. *Can we start yet? I want this to be over so we can focus on Teagan.*

Soon, dragon. It'll start soon.

They reached central command, and Aaron guided the Scottish dragons inside. He only hoped the challenge was approved by all the judges. He was bloody tired of waiting for this day to end.

~~~

Teagan pasted a smile on her face and walked into the conference room where Orin Daly and Padraig O'Leary sat waiting. While Hugh was participating in the challenge, the meeting was for clan leaders only.

The two males looked at her. Orin, from Greenpeak in Killarney, was first to speak up. "Making us wait to assert your authority isn't going to intimidate us, girl. Keep that in mind."

He'd called her "girl" on purpose, but Teagan wasn't going to rise to the bait. "Believe it or not, I'm not going to drop everything and neglect my clan just to please you."
~~~

The older of the two males, Padraig from Wildheath, frowned. "I hope you were releasing my captive clan member as promised."

"Oh, he'll be released once the trials are over."

So he couldn't cheat was left unsaid. The bastard hadn't cracked during his stay on Glenlough.

Teagan continued, "All of your appointed judges are being debriefed as we speak. Once they approve the set of challenges, we'll begin. This is your last chance to back out and call it off."

Orin raised an eyebrow. "Getting cold feet, are you?"

"No, I look forward to it," Teagan said without missing a beat.

Orin shook his head. "This isn't going to end well for you. It's not arrogance to say males are stronger. It's pure fact. Males are leaders. It's always been that way and it always will be. To defy tradition and logic is to put your own people in danger. Even when you had so-called female leaders, you always hid behind a male. It proves you're not a good fit for the job. After all, a true leader can lead on his own."

Her dragon growled. *I'm ready for him now.*

Believe me, so am I. His arrogance will be his downfall.

She replied to Orin, "Times have changed, gentlemen. In this day and age, it takes more than brawn to keep a clan safe. Besides, females have been clever for centuries. We were afraid of being killed in times past for speaking our minds, but no longer." She looked at each male in turn. "However, for the time being, our individual opinions don't matter." She opened a folder on the table and took out two documents. She handed them to each leader. "These are legally binding statements. You agree that if I win, you acknowledge my right to be leader and won't attack on those grounds. If you do attack, the DDA will punish you accordingly."

Padraig muttered, "Hiding behind the DDA is weak."

"Sign, or forfeit and leave. It's that simple."

"I look forward to winning and sending my eldest son to take over your clan. I may even change the clan's name since Glenlough sounds bloody stupid to me," Orin stated.

Her dragon spoke up. *As if Greenpeak is any better.*

Pick your battles, dragon.

Teagan motioned toward the papers. "If you're so cocky, then sign the papers. You'll have nothing to lose if you win."

She didn't back down from the glares of the two males. They may not like that Teagan had come prepared, but that was their problem. With the Irish DDA on her side, she could maintain some semblance of peace if she won. Only a fool wouldn't use every tool available.

Her dragon huffed. *There's no 'if' about us winning.*

Cockiness is a sure path to failure.

There's a balance between cockiness and confidence. We need that because if we don't win, then a future with Aaron is uncertain.

Even if we're banished, I'd still want him.

Let's not allow it to come to that.

Once the two males finished reading and signing the papers, Teagan collected them. "With that done, you can relax here until the judges make their decisions." She moved to the door, opened it, and motioned for the person waiting in the hall to enter.

Orla Kelly made her way inside and plopped down on a chair. She eyed the two leaders. "Even though I have a few more gray hairs than you two, make sure not to underestimate me." She pointed a finger at Padraig. "Your father once tried to kiss me against my will. He earned a scar on his neck for that transgression."

Padraig raised his brows. "That was you?"

"Aye, it was." She extended a talon. "So no funny business."

Teagan bit back a smile at the bewilderment in Padraig's expression. She spoke to her gran, "If you need anything, Brenna is waiting in the hall."

Orla leaned forward, never taking her gaze from Orin and Padraig. "That's right, laddies. Females were sent to be your guards. And don't think for a second we're going to cower and run away."

Orin shook his head. "This just proves further how much Glenlough needs structure. The females are out of control."

Orla took a small rock from one of her pockets and tossed it at Orin. It bounced off the top of his head. "That was just a small one. I have bigger ones waiting for your true arsehole self to come out."

Teagan paused to see if Orin would lose control, but the male merely shrugged. "I'm not about to hurt an old female. But I do look forward to locking you up once I'm in charge."

As her gran grunted and reached for another rock, Teagan decided she had things in hand. "An escort will come if the challenge is approved and we're ready to begin."

She exited the room and stopped next to Brenna. Even though the conference room was mostly soundproofed, she whispered, "Keep an ear out and maybe check on her every once in a while. She's throwing rocks at them, and I'm not sure how long they'll resist throwing them back."

Brenna nodded. "Orla can usually take care of herself, but I'll check on her in a few minutes."

Teagan touched the Protector's arm and walked down the hall. It was time to check in with Killian and wait. What happened next was in the hands of the judges.

CHAPTER SEVENTEEN

An hour later, Teagan stood outside the clan's front gates with Orin, Padraig, and Hugh standing in a line to her side. All of Glenlough and the visitors waited on the sidelines.

The judges had approved the challenge. And to their credit, Orin and Padraig hadn't thrown a tantrum about Hugh, probably because the male wasn't in the best shape of his life.

While she wanted nothing more than to shift, jump into the sky, and begin, Colm, as main organizer of the challenges, needed to speak and officially start the event. Only then would the judges hand out the first clue.

Puzzles weren't part of modern-day clan leader trials, but Teagan looked forward to it. In some ways, mental acuity was more important than ever in the present.

Her dragon huffed. *I like the physical tests in the old way. My strength is important.*

Of course it is. But I almost think it will sting their pride more if we beat them this way.

I don't care how we do it, but we just need to win.

Before she could reply, a gong sounded and everyone quieted down as Colm took his place on a small raised dais. After another few beats, he spoke. "Orin Daly, Padraig O'Leary, and Hugh Burns have formally filed challenges against Glenlough's current leader, Teagan O'Shea. To erase any doubts and to prevent war, Glenlough has decided to host a leadership challenge. However, this particular event will follow the challenges of old. Each participant will receive the first clue and must solve it and the subsequent ones in a certain order to find the hidden treasure at the end. To prevent cheating, each participant has a different set of clues, meaning the resulting treasures will be different. If any participant thinks to merely wait and steal another's find, the judges will know. It is one of the ways for a person to be disqualified.

"Two others include killing or maiming an opponent. It should go without saying it's forbidden, but I'm stating it for clarity. Observers have been stationed in key areas to ensure violence doesn't occur. Any dragon who violates these rules will not only be disqualified, but will also stand trial on Glenlough once someone wins the challenge.

"Lastly, if any outside help is detected, the person in question will forfeit. This is a test of an individual's skills alone." Colm paused to look at them each in turn. "If the participants understand these stipulations, say aye."

"Aye," Teagan and the others answered.

Colm nodded. "There is no time limit to solve your set of clues. However, you must remain in the field and not take shelter or find food at any establishment or private residence. No other human or dragon-shifter is allowed to assist you, unless you are gravely injured and your life is in jeopardy. The puzzles will test your mental acuity, but you also must prove your survival skills." Colm motioned to a group of people Teagan decided must be the judges since their faces were similar to the photographs she had received earlier. "Judges move into position to hand over the first clue."

As the four individuals walked toward them, Teagan searched and found Aaron off to the side. He smiled and nodded at her.

Her dragon spoke up. *He believes in us.*

A female dragon-shifter with curly brown hair stopped in front of Teagan. It was Faye MacKenzie.

Even though they'd never been formally introduced, Faye smiled and the warmth reached her eyes. Teagan instantly knew she'd get along with the Scottish female.

We just have to win first, her dragon stated.

Colm's voice filled the air again. "One final note—the humans have been barred from entering Glenveagh National Park and the surrounding areas for the duration of this contest. Anyone you see in the field is an observer or judge. They aren't to be harmed." He paused. Teagan and the others nodded. Colm added, "Right, then with everything laid out, it's time to begin. Judges, hand over the clues and retreat back to your original spots."

Faye handed over an envelope. The second it was in Teagan's hands, she ripped it open and read the slip of paper inside:

Germany, Austria, and Mexico treasure me. However, Ireland killed me, but I was resurrected. Find your own possible rebirth in the tallest tree near the Derryveagh Mountains.

Teagan reread the clue before she pondered the meaning.

Germany and Austria both had eagles in their coat of arms. She didn't know as much about Mexico, but there was a bird on the Mexican flag that resembled an eagle.

On top of that, eagles had been hunted to extinction in Ireland and were only reintroduced to County Donegal in 2001. In a way, that was a type of resurrection.

Her dragon spoke up. *Then let's find the nest in the tallest tree.*

I only hope it's a manmade one. I don't want to harm the eagles. There are too few of them.

If Colm planned it, it will be a fake one. Now let's go.

Teagan ran to a space big enough to shift, tore off her dress, and imagined her arm growing, her nose elongating into a snout, and wings sprouting from her back. Once she stood in her golden dragon form, she jumped into the sky and beat her wings.

One of the other competitors did the same a minute behind her, but Teagan focused on getting to the Derryveagh Mountains as quickly as possible. No doubt the next clue would be tougher, and she wanted to get started on it straight away.

~~~

Three hours later, Aaron stood next to Faye and Grant on the temporary viewing platform that had been constructed for the event. The challenges had been set up so that every participant would pass near one of the viewing platforms at least once. Well, if they solved the clues correctly at any rate.

However, no one had appeared near the northwest corner of Glenveagh National Park so far. The lack of activity made time move slower, especially since he wasn't allowed to do anything but watch or talk with the judges.

His dragon huffed. *Our luck, we won't have anyone come by for days. I don't want to camp that long.*

Someone has gotten soft.

Look at the gray skies. You hate the rain as much as I do.
~~~

Instead of doing what his dragon asked, Aaron glanced over to see Faye leaning against Grant's chest with Grant's arms wrapped around her. His hands were protectively covering her lower belly.

Seeing the pair at such ease with each other made him miss Teagan all the more. He was anxious to hold his own female again, without worrying about their future. When she won the challenge, they could finally stop snatching a kiss or hug here or there and be open about it.

He hated the secrets, but he hadn't lied earlier when he'd said that Teagan was worth waiting for. Even if the challenge took weeks, he'd manage.

His dragon spoke up. *This challenge won't take more than two days.*

He tapped his fingers against his thigh. *Even if that's true, that's still too bloody long.*

"Where is she?" Aaron muttered. "I had expected her to be on the fourth clue by now, which would bring her our way."

Grant spoke up. "Considering our first contender, Hugh Burns, hasn't shown up, you're being overly optimistic."

Aaron met Grant's gaze. "Hugh's a bastard and not as brilliant as he claims to be. In my opinion, he might not be able to solve the clue at all and will never come this way."

"Didn't he challenge Teagan before and lose?" Faye asked. Aaron nodded and she added, "Then maybe he has something sinister planned."

Aaron grunted. "If so, the other judges at their platforms and the Protectors flying overhead will catch him on it, and he'll be thrown out of the contest. Once he forfeits, Teagan will have the power to banish him, and it'll be one less thing for her to worry about."

Grant jumped in. "Banishment may not be the best solution. Look what happened on Lochguard."

The Scottish clan had asked the unsupportive members to leave. They had then formed a rogue band of dragon-shifters, which currently hid in Scotland. They often attacked and caused trouble.

Aaron shook his head. "I wouldn't worry about it just yet. Teagan is the one to make the decision when it comes to banishing a clan member, and I'm not sure if she'd want to push anyone away. Unlike Finn, she's been leader for almost five years, and there are only a handful of dissenters. Glenlough has had many female leaders in the past, including her grandmother. Speaking of which, Faye needs to meet her. She's full of fire."

Faye grinned. "That would be fantastic. While I'd never challenge Finn, maybe my daughter can lead the clan one day, and I could use all the pointers I can collect for her."

"So you'll be disappointed if we have a son?" Grant asked.

Faye rolled her eyes. "Oh, don't start that again. I'll love any child we have. But let's just say that I'm open to trying a few times to have a daughter. I'd like some balance in our cottage."

"You already have balance," Grant muttered. "I let you do what you wish with it."

She sighed. "Except for the ridiculous amounts of security."

"It's necessary," Grant stated.

As the pair continued to argue, Aaron gave them some privacy and scanned the skies yet again.

He tapped his fingers against the rail of the viewing platform. *Come on, Teagan. Where are you?*

His dragon answered, *She'll be here when she's ready. Have faith.*

Faye's voice calling his name caught his attention. He looked at her and she asked, "Does anyone on Glenlough know that you love her, including Teagan herself?"

Aaron blinked. "How in the bloody hell do you know that I love her?"

Grant glared at him for his tone, but Aaron ignored him to focus on Faye's reply. "Between the nonverbal exchange you two shared and how anxious you are right now with your flashing dragon eyes and constantly demanding to know where she is, it's not that difficult to put it together. But I'm guessing you're not true mates, aye?"

He could grunt and refuse to answer, but talking about it with the Scottish dragons wouldn't do anything to harm Teagan's reputation. He knew them well enough to know they could keep a secret, so he answered, "No, we're not true mates. But I say fuck fate. Teagan is mine, and no one is going to take her from me."

Grant grunted. "Be sure of your choice, Caruso, because if you try to change her, it won't end well."

Faye looked up and craned her neck to scowl at her mate. "So now you're giving advice you can barely follow yourself?"

Grant kissed her nose. "I try to follow it, but I'm not always successful. It's the effort that counts."

Faye sighed. "I'm not sure I agree." She looked back to Aaron. "But he's right. If you're hoping she'll give up her clan to live an easier life, it won't happen. I know Finn would rather die than hand it over, no matter how much stress it causes him and Arabella with three recent babies."

Finn and his mate, Arabella, had recently had triplets.

Aaron scowled. "Of course I'm not going to bloody change her. And before you ask, I have no interest in being in charge myself. Do you know how much paperwork clan leaders have to fill out? She can have the leadership and the hand cramps that go with it. I'm content to protect her and the others in the clan. Together we make a good team."

Faye smiled. "Good. It's a bit selfish, but you living here gives me the chance to visit. Who knows what a few strong, clever females can come up with when they get together?"

Grant scowled, but before he could say anything, a red dragon appeared in the distance. Given the timing and order of the clues, as well as the fact that Hugh was the only red dragon participating, it had to be him.

Aaron growled out, "That's the Glenlough bloke I told you about. The one who can't let it go—Hugh Burns."

The red dragon glided down and landed at the foot of a large hill nearby. Faye moved forward out of Grant's arms. "Finally, something to do. Let's see what this bastard is up to."

According to the clue, Hugh should be digging in the ground. However, he sat on his haunches, raised his face, and roared into the sky.

"Something's not right. There's virtually no way for him to interpret the clue and think it means to roar." Aaron tugged off his shirt and unbuttoned his trousers. "Just in case my hunch is correct, I'll standby below, ready to shift and investigate. I need you two here as witnesses in case Hugh decides to fabricate a story of me attacking him unprovoked or some such bullshit."

Grant took out his mobile phone. "If he does try to pull anything, I have Killian's number ready to go."

He was glad that he'd been assigned to the Lochguard pair. They had a history of working together, and he didn't have to suffer arguments when it came to sound actions.

Aaron finished stripping and was also grateful that Grant didn't make a fuss about Faye with a possible threat nearby. Even protective mates knew when to focus, especially when it came to Protectors.

Hugh roared again and Aaron scanned the sky. It was still empty. "I'm going down," he stated as he climbed down the ladder to the ground. He wouldn't shift unnecessarily, but he wanted to be ready.

After reaching the ground, he strained his ears. At first, nothing. But soon a faint buzzing became audible. It was too steady to be any insect he'd heard before. And even though he didn't know all of the fauna in this part of Ireland, he'd bet everything he had it was a machine.

Drones, his dragon said. *Hugh must be working with the Dragon Knights.*

Since the bloody Knights had used a drone to drug Aaron's mother and he'd nearly lost her, he kept an eye to the sky. But even after a minute, he still didn't see anything. *Where are they? I'm not going to rush into it just because of a buzzing sound.*

His dragon replied, *Maybe they're tiny. Anything is possible.*

Hugh roared again. He clearly wasn't following the orders of his clues.

Part of his duty was to question participants if they acted strangely to ensure they hadn't gone rogue, so Aaron ran straight for Hugh's dragon form. While he had no proof, Aaron had a feeling the male would easily get rid of the judges, and maybe even the other participants, to take over Glenlough if he had help.

Too bad Bram had been instructed to hold off sending the second Stonefire Protector, Sebastian, until after the leadership challenge was complete. Aaron would've liked the male at his back.

Still, he trusted Faye and Grant, so Aaron shifted into his green dragon form. Once finished, Hugh met his eyes before jumping into the sky. Aaron crouched down to follow when Faye's voice yelled with a hint of panic to her voice, "Grant!"

Torn between duties, Aaron finally looked back to the judges he was supposed to be guarding. Faye was crouched down and Grant lay on the floor of the platform.

Cursing, he ignored Hugh and raced to the raised structure. Quickly shifting back to his human form, he climbed the ladder. Once he reached the top, he saw Grant's motionless body and demanded, "What happened?"

To Faye's credit, she hadn't started crying. But her voice did crack as she answered, "Something that looked like a bird flew close and the next minute Grant was down." She lifted the small dart. "This was in his neck."

Aaron clenched his fingers. "Lochguard didn't have problems with the bloody drones, but Stonefire and Glenlough did. I bet it's the same fucking bunch causing havoc and Hugh is involved. If so, Grant needs the antidote as soon as possible. The dart is no doubt filled with the serum that causes inner dragons to go mad and lose control. Let me reach out to Killian."

Taking out his mobile phone, he dialed Killian. The rings continued until his voice mail picked up.

Ending the call, Aaron tried Brenna next, and she did pick up on the second ring. Before he could say a word, Brenna said, "Tell me no one has been attacked where you are."

"Grant was targeted and is unconscious. Faye found a small dart in his neck. I suspect it's related to the attacks that happened not too long ago on Stonefire and Glenlough. I need you to send Dr. O'Brien and a few Protectors here to help Grant, just to be safe."

Dr. Ronan O'Brien was Glenlough's head doctor. Aaron had first met him on Stonefire during a previous crisis.

Brenna cursed. "Then that makes up half the viewing platforms reporting an incident in the last few minutes."

Aaron asked, "Were they also drugged with a dart?"

"That's what we think," Brenna replied, "although details are sketchy at best. The Protectors are on the move to guard each viewing platform's occupants as we speak."

Aaron grunted. "Has Hugh been spotted at each of the locations, letting out a series of roars like he did here?"

"No," Brenna said. "But Padraig and Orin each arrived near an observation platform and roared instead of doing what their clue required."

Aaron growled. "Bloody bastards are probably working together. I hadn't expected that. Has anyone spotted Teagan?"

"No. She's near Glenveagh Castle, last I heard," Brenna answered. "We didn't put any observers there since the humans have security cameras all over the grounds and we didn't think anyone would be stupid enough to make a move there."

"Right, then I'm going to get Faye and Grant to the closest shelter and then look for Teagan myself. Since every participant knows about the security cameras at the castle, they'll wait for her to leave. She's bound to be a target. If I can get to her before she leaves the grounds, I can probably prevent her from being attacked. Given what she represents, the others might do more than drug her."

His dragon snarled. *No, we won't let that happen.*

Aaron ignored his beast to focus on Brenna's reply. "I would try to stop you, but Killian is missing, and I'm not sure who to trust anymore. Just make sure to keep checking in, Aaron. As much as you think it sometimes, you're not invincible."

Aaron grunted. "I will keep in touch. And the Snowridge Protectors should be trustworthy and kept in the loop. Kai vetted them whilst I was in Scotland."

Once Brenna gave her assent, Aaron hung up and looked to Faye. After he summed up his conversation with Brenna, he waved toward the hills in the distance. "There are some cave-like spaces just big enough for you and Grant to squeeze into nearby. If I mostly cover the entrance with rocks, you should be safe and still able to use your phone until help arrives."

Faye nodded. "And I'll make sure to reach out to Lochguard while we wait and update Finn. Do you want me to ring Stonefire, too, and do the same?"

"Yes," he answered. "I need to find Teagan and can't spare the time to answer Bram's questions. If all three of the challengers are in a plot together, she and I need to focus on solving that problem before it spins out of control, especially if Killian's been targeted, too." He glanced to Grant and back to her eyes. "He should be all right. Stonefire shared their antidote formulas with Lochguard and Glenlough as soon as they found them. Even if the serum has been mutated slightly, Glenlough's doctor should be able to figure it out. Ronan O'Brien was part of the original research team at the time."

Faye grunted. "Right, then first help me get Grant to safety. I can pick him up if I shift into a dragon, but I need you to watch my back in case anyone else comes."

Without another word, Aaron descended the ladder. The sooner he saw Faye and Grant to safety, the sooner he could find Teagan and figure out what the bloody hell was going on. He hadn't expected Orin, Padraig, and Hugh to work together to thwart Teagan. Their hatred of change must be bone-deep.

He also wondered if Hugh had been the one to leak the information to the other two and then reached out to them.

His dragon growled. *They will soon learn their lesson. The Irish DDA will intervene.*

I hope so, dragon, but I'm not thinking about that right now. Getting to Teagan is our top priority.

Then stop talking and shift.

As Aaron imagined his body changing shape, he only hoped he made it to Teagan in time. She could usually take care of herself, but mini-flying machines that shot darts and looked like birds would take anyone by surprise if they weren't looking for it.

Chapter Eighteen

Teagan stood at the edge of a pond, the wind gently blowing her dress about her body, and looked for anything that could be deemed an island. Since she was within the gardens of Glenveagh Castle, she knew finding her next clue wouldn't involve destroying property. That would anger the humans.

Her dragon huffed. *We probably have to wade into the pond.*

Since shifting inside the castle grounds was illegal, it meant Teagan would have to do it in her human form.

She surveyed the water again to figure out where to start. That was when a dragon's reflection passed over the smooth surface.

Looking up, she spotted a green dragon form she knew well—Aaron's.

"What the bloody hell is he doing here?"

Two weeks ago, she would've wondered if he doubted her abilities. But now that she knew him better, Aaron would only desert his post if it were important.

Fuck, has something happened?

Her dragon growled. *Let's find out.*

Teagan turned away from the pond and listened for any unusual noises.

The birds chirped, the wind rustled the leaves, and she heard a dragon roar in the distance. The roar wasn't one of pain, but rather a ferocious one used for battle or to express anger.

She'd heard a few roars over the last twenty minutes or so, but had assumed it was one of the others cursing about getting something wrong.

If only she had her phone so she could check in. But none of them had been allowed to carry one.

Her beast chimed in. *That's why we need to check in with Aaron to see if anything's wrong.*

Doing so would disqualify us.

Then the question is—how much do you trust Aaron? If he's here, I think it's because we need to talk to him about something important.

After a beat Teagan answered, *You're right.*

Aaron would never jeopardize her role unnecessarily.

Since no dragon could land near where she was because of the abundance of trees, Teagan ran down the path toward the beginning of the View Point trail. That was the nearest open space for Aaron's dragon to land.

She pushed herself harder, and the stone wall surrounding the grounds came into view. Less than a minute later, she exited the gate and saw Aaron's naked human form studying the skies. "Aaron," she shouted.

He turned toward her and replied, "Stay inside the grounds, Teagan. There are more places to hide near the castle."

While her curiosity burned, she stayed put as Aaron jogged to her position. He was less than a foot away when he cursed.

Before she could do more than open her mouth, he jumped and covered her body with his. He murmured, "Stay still for a few minutes," before his body went slack.

Her heart hammered inside her chest. *Something's wrong.*

Follow his instructions or it may compromise us both.

Only because she heard Aaron's heart beating, albeit slowly, did she remain still. After the longest few minutes of her life, she moved enough to peer out from Aaron's body. She listened and surveyed the area for any sign of trouble, but she didn't hear anything unusual. Not even a roaring dragon in the distance.

Satisfied the threat was gone, at least for the moment, she shimmied out from under Aaron's weight and quickly checked his body. Two tiny darts, one in his neck and the other in his side, caught her attention.

If she were a betting dragon, she'd say it was the same type of drug-filled dart that had been used on one of the children of her clan not too long ago. Aaron had jumped to take the second one meant for her.

Someone was messing with her leadership challenge.

She spotted the small pouch Aaron had tossed aside after landing. His mobile phone would no doubt be inside, but she couldn't chance going out into the open to retrieve it. After all, she was supposed to be unconscious and couldn't risk being spotted. Who knew what was going on back inside the clan's lands.

Her dragon growled. *Find another way.*

She ignored her dragon as an idea struck. While it may get her into trouble with the DDA, she needed to get inside the castle and call her clan from there.

Plucking the darts from Aaron's body, she carefully buried them in a safe spot and marked it with a series of rocks before gripping under his armpits. Mustering her strength, she dragged him further inside the gardens. While she couldn't drag him the entire way to the castle quickly, she needed to stash him somewhere relatively safe so that she could dash and make the call.

Another dragon roared in the distance and Teagan pushed her muscles to the limits. Once Aaron was inside a protected area of trees and underbrush, she turned and ran to the castle's main entrance. Pulling the dress over her head, she covered her fist and smashed through the glass on the door. She reached in and unlocked it.

A reception desk used for visitors sat to one side. Teagan made her way over and dialed the Protectors' central command. She only hoped they bloody well answered the phone despite her calling from a strange number.

The familiar voice of Lyall O'Dwyer answered the phone. "Who is this?"

"Lyall, it's Teagan. Aaron is unconscious. What the hell is going on?"

"Just a second," Lyall replied.

Teagan wanted to scream, but Brenna Rossi's voice came over the line. "Thank fuck you're all right."

"Aaron's not. He's been drugged. What's going on? Where's Killian?"

"No one can get a hold of him. As for what's going on, judges and Protectors are being attacked by what we think are stealth drones. At first, it was just those at the observation platforms, but now a few Protectors patrolling the area have also been hit. I suspect it's only a matter of time before they strike inside the clan's gates."

"What's been done?" Teagan asked.

Brenna didn't hesitate to answer, "Finn and Bram both know what's going on and are sending help. The Irish DDA hasn't bothered to return my calls."

"Fucking DDA. Right, well, we'll do without them until everything is sorted and we can toss the traitors into their hands. Keep everyone inside and reach out to one of our males named Kerrin Dunne. He might have a few things that can short-circuit any sort of electrical object within a certain radius. If no one heard the attacks coming, then I have a feeling we're dealing with a different type of drone."

"I agree, and I have already contacted Kerrin. Orla suggested him and he's setting things up. Orla also reached out to a few people she knows in Clan Seagate."

Clan Seagate was inside Connemara National Park and to the southwest of Glenlough. While not officially allies, their leader had voiced his displeasure of Orin's plan to attack Glenlough simply because they had a female leader.

It seemed it was a good thing her gran had never truly retired. "I'm going to bring Aaron inside Glenveagh Castle and then look for Hugh, Orin, and Padraig. Unless you have them in custody?"

"No."

"Right, then since the darts look to be too delicate to pierce a dragon's hide, as long as I remain in that form, I should be safe."

"Unless they have a different type of gun waiting to use on us in dragon form," Brenna stated.

Teagan didn't miss a beat. "It's a chance I'm willing to take. In the meantime, you still have Roarke Bell in custody, aye?"

"Yes," Brenna stated.

"Then question him again. Now that we can threaten a treason charge, he might open up."

"I'll see what we can do. But one last thing—Protectors are patrolling all over the area, so if you do capture one of the three, then signal to someone flying over you. Don't risk shifting to your human form and calling."

Teagan murmured her assent and hung up the phone. Time to get Aaron to safety and handle the arseholes who thought they could mess with her clan, and her male.

~~~

Fifteen minutes later, Teagan soared through the air. She'd chanced shifting inside the castle's grounds, doubting the DDA would punish her for stopping a possible dragon civil war.

Because if Teagan didn't stop Orin, Padraig, and Hugh, then no doubt others would join their cause to oust Teagan. Or, possibly join her side to fight back.

And all because she lacked a penis.

Some males took insecurity to an extreme.

Her beast growled. *We will take care of them.*

The difficult part will be in not killing them.

Maybe we can just rough them up a little? her beast asked eagerly.

How about we find them first and then go from there?

Since the sound of other dragons roaring had ceased, Teagan had to find the traitorous dragonmen the hard way, by searching every inch of her land and beyond.

As she flew over one of the observation platforms, she spotted Dr. Ronan O'Brien examining one of the French dragon-shifter judges lying unconscious. Two Protectors in dragon form mostly shielded the doctor and his charge with their wings, no doubt acting as a barrier from any more darts.

Since Orin's clan had invited the French judges, it seemed not even allies had been spared. She wondered what Orin's long-term game plan might be. At any rate, if she captured the bastard
~~~

and proved his guilt, she might be able to use his betrayal to form her own alliances.

Her dragon grunted. *Even without proof, it'll be useful.*

The DDA will require a confession. While I think it's too much of a coincidence that my three competitors all acted the same way and disappeared at the same time, we need more.

Then let's find them and show the males what we're really made of.

Beating her wings, Teagan flew higher until she had a better vantage point of Glenveagh National Park. Dragons were at each of the viewing platforms. Her three competitors had probably left the park by now if her assumptions were correct.

She just needed to decide which way to go. Since venturing into Northern Ireland could provoke both Clan Northcastle and the British DDA into action, the three males would have no choice but to go along the coast to skirt around the tip of Northern Ireland before they could head further inland to any of their clans. And since flying would be more noticeable, they would probably drive a car to hide their escape.

If spotting them wasn't hard enough, she needed to find the trio before they reached Donegal or she might lose them. The town wasn't huge, but there was enough traffic to blend in.

Teagan turned her body toward the south and beat her wings quickly. The area was largely unpopulated, and she soon spotted two cars driving in the same direction but at quite a distance apart. One was an SUV and the other was a small car used by most families in the area.

Her beast spoke up. *Dragons hate tiny cars. Not only are we too tall for that, but it's also easy for a dragon to attack it.*

They might have taken the small car to try to throw us off.

The SUV turned off the road a few minutes later toward the west. Since they hadn't reached the town of Donegal, the SUV probably wasn't heading south.

Her gut told her to follow the small car. *Let's see if I was right.*

Teagan slowly circled around to ensure there weren't any other cars nearby. She didn't need for an innocent to become a hostage for her enemies.

Not spotting anyone but the odd farmhouse here and there, she swooped down until she was nearly to the ground. At the last possible moment, she extended her rear talons and picked up the small car. Straining her muscles, she ascended about ten feet and used the wind currents to carry her further.

Her beast huffed. *I wish I knew it was them. Then we could drop the car from a great height.*

No. They need to be given a fair shot.

Stupid human ways.

Once Teagan reached a series of rolling hills and nothing but unoccupied land for a few miles in every direction, she gently placed the car on the ground and landed. Just as she touched down beside it, something fired from the window and a burning sensation exploded in her rear leg.

The pain threw her off balance, but she used her wings to right herself. A quick check told her that the cheating males had used some type of dragon gun and the ammunition had grazed her leg.

With a roar, she hit the car with her tail and it rolled. Once the car stopped, a red dragon burst from the car, sending metal shrapnel flying every which way. Once fully shifted, the beast hissed.

It was Hugh.

He jumped and charged at her. Teagan waited until the last second and swung her tail around to hit him out of the air. Hugh tumbled to the ground and Teagan jumped on top of him. He tried to bite her neck, but she leaned away and swiped her talons across his cheek.

With a growl, Hugh used his weight and larger size to roll them over. But before he could pin her, Teagan slashed his chest. Hugh cried out in pain and she punched his wound with her forelimb.

He gave a high-pitched roar. Teagan pinned him by the throat and quickly scanned for a boulder to use. In the split second she looked away, he freed an arm and swiped at her throat. Pain exploded as she felt something warm trickle down her hide.

Focusing on merely getting out of the situation alive, she stuck to her plan and found a boulder. Clutching it in her paw, she smacked Hugh on the head hard enough to render him unconscious but not kill him.

Panting, Teagan turned toward the car. She quickly limped to the wreck and ignored the jarring pain each movement sent up her leg and across her throat.

Once she reached the car, she sighed. A piece of twisted metal protruded from Orin's chest, and he stared glassy-eyed into oblivion; probably a result of Hugh's sudden shift. As for Padraig, he had a gaping hole in his chest; it looked as if he had shot himself by accident when the car had been rolling. Both were dead.

Her beast growled. *Good. They deserved it.*

Maybe so, but the aftermath is going to be one huge headache.

I don't care about that. We need to contact the clan and check on Aaron and the others.

In the ruckus, she'd temporarily forgotten about Aaron. *He's strong and will do fine. He's too stubborn to die.*

Still, I want to see him and make sure. Hopefully Killian has returned, too.

She spotted a phone on the floor of the car. *I just need to call the others to check and update them on what's happened. I'm going to have to shift and risk it.*

Is that wise? We heal faster in dragon form.

Teagan wrenched off the side mirror from the car and lifted it. While the gash on her neck would need stitches, Hugh had missed the artery by a few inches. *As long as I'm quick and apply pressure, I should be okay.*

I don't like it, but it's the only option. Even I'll admit we're too weak to fly. And if we're hit again, then who knows what will happen to the clan.

As if I don't know that, dragon, Teagan replied dryly.

Teagan imagined her wings melding into her back, her limbs morphing back into arms and legs, and her snout shrinking into a nose and face. The shift caused a sudden surge of pain and made her leg throb more than her throat, but she gritted her teeth, applied pressure to the gash on her neck, and ignored the pain as best she could.

She did glance down at her leg to take a closer look and ensure she wasn't going to die. The deep gouge with burned edges was going to need medical attention for sure, but the wound wasn't fatal; the most important thing was that the bleeding had stopped.

Hurry and make the call, her beast said.

Focusing her attention on the car, she lifted and tugged the handle, but nothing happened. Eyeing the mostly broken window, she tore off a piece of fabric from Orin's shirt, careful to leave the cleanest bits to use as a bandage around her neck. She wrapped her hand and broke the remaining glass until she could safely lean into the car and pick up the phone.

With the prize in her possession, she tucked it between her knees so that she could also tear off a length from Orin's sleeve. She tied it tightly around her throat, just enough to stop the bleeding but not enough to choke her. She'd never been so grateful for Killian's field medic training sessions in her life.

Keeping her back to the wreckage and crouching down, it ensured nothing should be able to shoot her from behind. She wrenched off a hubcap to cover the top of her head. She then dialed central command's number, and Brenna answered. "Yes?"

"This is Teagan. I don't have a lot of time, but Orin and Padraig are dead, and Hugh is unconscious. I need backup as soon as possible." She eyed Hugh's dragon form. "As well as a car, a shot to force him into his human form, and restraints for Hugh."

"What about the DDA? Do they know?"

Teagan was grateful for Brenna not wasting her time. "I'll handle it right after I hang up with you. Is there anything I need to know about before I go? Is Aaron okay?"

"They found him inside the castle and he's still unconscious. Dr. O'Brien is still working on an antidote for the mutated serum but is confident he can find it soon. The two doctors from Stonefire who found the original cure, Trahern Lewis and Emily Davies, are on their way here as well."

"And Killian?"

Brenna sighed. "He hasn't reached out. We're still looking."

She pushed away the twinge in her heart for her brother. "Killian will show up, I'm sure of it. I'll give you my location and then wait here." Teagan gave the directions and landmarks of her position before continuing, "If there are any medical personnel to spare, maybe have one come, too. One of the bastards shot me and another slashed me with his talons. It hurts like hell."

"I'd ask if you're okay, but you'd probably just brush it off as a scratch, even if your entrails were hanging out."

Teagan snorted. "I'm still conscious. I'll call you again if I need you."

Hanging up, she took a deep breath and dialed the DDA liaison officer's number. She had to report the event while adrenaline was keeping her going.

When the woman picked up, Teagan kept her voice calm as she stated, "This is Teagan O'Shea from Clan Glenlough. I'd like to report an incident."

Chapter Nineteen

Brenna Rossi finished ordering some Protectors to go to Teagan's aid, hung up the phone, and looked to Orla at her side. "I'm not sure what else we can do right now but wait."

The old dragonwoman banged her cane against the ground. "Sometimes, that's all you can do. Sit down before you fall down, child."

Taking advantage of the few moments of quiet, Brenna gulped down her coffee and sat down. She said to her dragon, *I wish Killian was here.*

Why? As much as I'd like to fuck him, there are more important things to worry about right now.

Glad to see you have your priorities straight, dragon.

Her beast huffed. *Oh, if he doesn't show up soon, then we're going to find him.*

No—

Don't even try to stop me. Besides, it's not just for scratching my itch. Glenlough needs him, too.

And they should, no, will *find him. If he's hurt, he'll find a way to reach out to his clan. He lives and breathes Glenlough.*

Her dragon grunted. *Maybe. But he's a stubborn arse who thinks his sole existence is to protect and nothing more. At some point, he needs to loosen up a bit.*

Right, and you're the one to do it?

But of course. I've done a fairly good job with you, after all.

Orla's voice saved Brenna from trying to rationalize and argue with her dragon. "You're doing well for one so young, Brenna Rossi."

Brenna blinked. "Um, thank you?"

Orla frowned. "Own your accomplishments, child. Modesty won't get you to where you want to be. I can see you being head Protector or clan leader in your own right someday."

"I refuse to believe Killian won't come back."

"I never said you'd earn those roles here, or even straight away." Orla studied her a second before stating, "I do think you fancy my grandson, am I right?"

Her cheeks flushed. "That's not important. He's a good Protector and your own blood. You should care a bit more about his well-being instead of interrogating me about something unimportant."

Orla clicked her tongue. "Killian can take care of himself in these matters. However, he's not so skilled in recognizing good potential mates. That's why he needs me. Otherwise, he'll never find one. He needs a little guidance."

Brenna should let the matter drop, but she asked, "What are you talking about?"

Orla smiled. "You'll see, child. You'll see. If it's the last thing I do on this earth, I will see both my grandchildren mated and happy."

"Stop being silly, Orla. You'll outlive us all."

Orla shrugged. "I won't live forever, nor do I want to. But I can ensure my immortality through the continuation of my line. I rather hope both Killian and Teagan end up with offspring like me, personality-wise. That would keep them on their toes."

Her beast spoke up. *Listen to her. Just because Killian is much older doesn't matter.*

It matters to him. He sees us as a child.

Her dragon growled. *We're twenty-one and have served two years in the British Army. Most middle-aged humans couldn't stomach what we've been through.*

Even putting the age issues aside, I'm not ready to settle down. Staying on Glenlough has inspired me. I want to do more than I've ever dreamed of before.

You can do it all. I, on the other hand, don't care for celibacy.

Lyall rushed over. Brenna mentally sighed in relief and focused on the Protector. "What is it?"

"Kerrin is ready," the older male replied. "Should he proceed?"

Kerrin Dunne was an electrical engineer and Glenlough's best amateur inventor.

She stood and picked up the headset that patched through to Kerrin. "Kerrin, give me a minute to get everyone ready before we start."

"Just give the word, Brenna. I'll flip the switch as soon as you do," Kerrin answered.

She looked to Lyall. "Is all of the vital equipment protected and the necessary shields placed around central command?" He nodded.

That meant if everything went according to plan, Kerrin's device wouldn't affect the protected electronics.

Brenna switched the frequency to one that would broadcast to the entire clan as well as to the observation platforms. "Jabberwocky."

That was the current code word used for any clan emergency and signaled to everyone that something was about to happen. While it changed every few weeks, Brenna rather liked it. However, if she were in charge, she would have certain words for certain types of emergencies. She'd bring up the idea to Killian once he showed his face again.

She connected again with Kerrin. "Okay. Flip the switch in sixty seconds. Once it's done, send out your volunteers to scour the area for downed machines."

"Understood."

Kerrin's device would emit an electromagnetic pulse, or EMP, that should knock out any electronic device within a certain radius. He and his team had set them up at strategic locations around the clan and surrounding areas. The hope was that they could knock some of the machines—they didn't yet know if they were drones—out of the sky and study them. Arabella MacLeod, on Lochguard, was waiting to try and hack the operating system and information of one of them, too, if Kerrin's plan succeeded.

Crossing her fingers, she counted to sixty and waited for news from Kerrin. As the minutes ticked by, she wondered if something had gone wrong. Then a call came in on the main line and she answered it. "Yes?"

"This is Kerrin. It worked, although with a much smaller range than I had anticipated. I'll have to tweak a few things later. Still, we're going out to search now."

"Update me every five minutes or with every find you come across," Brenna said. "There may be enemies hiding in the forests. Be careful and don't be afraid to signal a Protector for help. You have your set of flares, right? Since their mobile phones probably won't work."

"Yes, I have everything. You'll hear from me soon."

He hung up and Brenna let out a sigh of relief. She looked to Orla. "Kerrin said it was mostly a success. It seems the shields placed around central command worked, too. He and his teams are looking for any downed foreign objects now."

Orla tilted her head. "Let's hope they find one of those bloody things. If this Arabella can trace back locations, then we can take care of the pests."

"Arabella said it was only maybe possible, depending on the sophistication of the hardware. It's also not an exact science," Brenna pointed out.

Orla waved a hand in dismissal. "No matter. These drone-whatever things can't be cheap. If we confiscate a few and can set them back for a while, that's good enough for now." She pointed at Brenna. "Now, go eat something. You've been working nonstop and need the rest."

"I can't possibly—"

"Don't argue with me, child. I won't keel over in the next twenty minutes. I can keep an eye and ear on what's going on. If there's any change, I'll send someone to fetch you."

Her dragon spoke up. *We can trust Orla. Make sure to take care of us, too. Glenlough needs us, and if you want to stay, we need to prove ourselves vital to them.*

Too tired to argue, Brenna waved goodbye to Orla and trekked toward the storage area stocked with instant meals for Protectors on duty.

Orla was right, she needed the energy. The day was long from over and just because she hadn't been born on Glenlough didn't mean she didn't care fiercely for the clan. Besides, if she couldn't help keep it in one piece, she would be sent back to Stonefire. And as much as she loved her home, Brenna had several reasons for staying with Glenlough, both for herself and for achieving her desired future.

She couldn't afford to fail them.

~~~

Teagan clicked off her phone and closed her eyes.

The DDA wasn't happy.

Not just because two dragon-shifters were dead or that she'd had a public brawl with Hugh in dragon form, but the law dictated that the DDA would contact the other clans to report the deaths of their leaders.

Considering that the DDA preferred to stay out of clan politics, they were now going to be more involved than they had been in decades.

Her beast growled. *It's their job. They don't deserve our worry.*

Maybe not, but I'm more afraid of war.

I doubt it will come to that. Orin and Padraig betrayed us. That won't sit well with most dragon-shifters.

"Most" being the key word.

The car driving Teagan back to Glenlough slowed down as the front gates opened. Because of the drugs she'd received, her pain was only a dull ache in both her leg and her neck. And thanks to the nurse who'd patched her up, Teagan was still conscious, which was quite a feat considering her blood loss.

Not for the first time she was glad dragon-shifters healed faster than humans.

Her dragon chimed in. *If we had stayed in dragon form, we'd be even closer to being healed.*

As much as you want to ride on the back of a lorry in dragon form, that would've drawn too much attention and taken too much time. Not to mention it would've made us a huge target.
~~~

With the three males taken care of and the darts probably not working on dragon hide, we would've been fine. At any rate, you can't complain about the pain and had better stay awake until we see both Aaron and Killian.

At the mention of the two most important males in her life, emotion gathered in her throat. She was optimistic, but also a realist. If anything happened to either Aaron or Killian, she would be strong for the clan, but then cry her heart out in private. She couldn't afford to let anything make her appear weak, especially in the current climate.

Needing a distraction and time to compose herself, Teagan focused outside the car window. As they cruised down the road, she noted that the streets and footpaths were empty. At least there wasn't chaos inside her own clan.

Communication had been sparse since Teagan had contacted Brenna earlier, but Teagan had confidence that Brenna and Orla had implemented the security protocols and had things in hand.

Speaking of which, she tried dialing central command to check on things. Her calls hadn't been going through during the drive because of something the clan had tried, probably to do with Kerrin. When Brenna finally answered, Teagan mentally sighed in relief. "Teagan?"

"Yes, it's me. I'm sure you saw that the car I'm in has arrived, but I wanted to let you know that I'm going to the surgery first and then I'll make my way over."

"We can come to you," Brenna answered. "Not only are you injured, but I'm sure you want to spend time with Aaron, too."

Yes, Aaron. We need to hold him close, her dragon said.

Not until we have the time. There is much to do, and regardless of my own desires, it has to be done.

Teagan answered Brenna, "I'll check in on Aaron whilst I'm there being examined, but until Dr. O'Brien tweaks the antidote, there's little I can do for him. It's more important to be brought up to date. Make sure to have a briefing ready for me when I arrive."

"Of course." Brenna paused and then added, "Just know that the clan has your back more than ever, Teagan. People keep calling in to ask how to help or to see if you're okay, and in overwhelming numbers." She lowered her voice. "Based on what I've witnessed, I'm fairly sure they'd support Aaron staying, too. His actions today are already well-known within the clan. Risking himself to save you is bloody heroic."

"And I'm sure he'll remind me every chance he gets when we're in private," Teagan muttered.

Brenna snorted. "I'm sure he will. But I've known Aaron most of my life. He'd do it again without batting an eyelash. It's just who he is, which is a brilliant male to have at your side."

Teagan opened her mouth to say she knew that already, but Orla's voice came over the line. "Ignore the hero poppycock. You and Aaron being together is the worst-kept secret on Glenlough. No one cares that he's English. Well, most don't, at any rate. I suspect a few are jealous of your catch."

Teagan sighed. "Gran, please. I don't have time for this."

Orla replied, "Just get yourself checked out and then check on your male. If anything changes, Brenna and I will let you know. Brenna's quite the capable lass. If Killian ever decides to show his face again, he might have a rival for his position."

A small part of Teagan was worried about Killian still being missing, but she trusted her brother to find a way home. She'd talk to some of the Protectors once she had a chance, as a precaution.

Her dragon spoke up. *Killian would want us to focus on the clan first, so we should.*

I know what he'd bloody want, but he's family. I'll give him a few more hours, but then I'm going to act on my worry and see if I can send some Protectors to search for him.

Brenna's voice came back over the line, which prevented her dragon from arguing. "The adrenaline in your body is long gone by now, Teagan. See the doctor and take care of you and your male. We need both of you well. This is long from over. I think Glenlough has been added to the target list of at least the Dragon Knights, along with Stonefire and Lochguard. Not to mention already being targeted previously by the dragon hunters. We need you healthy."

The line went dead and Teagan sighed before saying to her dragon, *It didn't take long to go from doing everything myself to having several strong-willed helpers.*

Good. Maybe we'll be able to do more than fill out paperwork or listen to arguments from now on. I want to fly more often.

We'll see, dragon. We'll see.

The car rolled into the back entrance of the surgery. As soon as the vehicle stopped, she opened the door and slowly inched toward the edge of the seat. Before she could reach it, Arlanna, one of Glenlough's nurses, frowned at her before the other female's gaze zeroed in on Teagan's crudely bandaged thigh and then on her neck. "Don't even think of standing on that leg or opening the wound on your neck again. You need to take it easy." She snapped her fingers and a wheelchair appeared. "Come and sit here."

Since each movement sent a stab of pain racing up her leg, not to mention the constant burning at her throat, Teagan complied. Once she was in the chair, Arlanna pushed her into the surgery. "For security purposes, you and Aaron will be sharing a room."

Teagan doubted it had anything to do with security, but she wasn't going to complain.

As Arlanna made her way down the corridor, each passing second made Teagan's heart thump faster. With the main threats to her clan taken care of, she wanted to see Aaron.

And not just because he'd taken a dart for her or risked his life to warn her of the threat. No, she needed to see his rising and falling chest as well as feel his rough hand in hers.

Through all the shit coming her way, her gut told her he would support her, not to mention ensure she didn't pull her hair out or give herself a heart attack from too much stress.

And selfish as it may be, she yearned for just a few seconds of his touch to ground her. After a few minutes with her male, Teagan would be ready to face anything and everything left to tackle.

Her dragon growled. *And to think you chickened out in telling him we love him.*

Teagan didn't hesitate in answering, *The second he wakes up, I'm telling him.*

Good, because if you go on about him not wanting to fight some more or getting tired of us being in charge, then I may just have to take control and claim him as our mate myself until you see clearly.

No need for dramatics. I love Aaron and want him to stay, no matter the cost.

Good.

Arlanna finally wheeled her into one of the rooms. Her eyes instantly zeroed in on Aaron.

He lay unconscious on a bed.

It was strange to see her male motionless and looking helpless. And all of it was because he had sacrificed himself to protect her. She wasn't about to say it was purely her fault since Aaron knew full well what he'd been doing, but it was her responsibility to ensure he woke up again.

The nurse stopped at Aaron's side and said, "Take a moment with him. I'll fetch the necessary supplies."

Arlanna left.

Teagan took Aaron's hand. She traced his knuckles and strong fingers. There was so much she had yet to feel and experience from his hands. So many years of pleasure and closeness.

Even when his digits were gnarled with gray hair on his knuckles because of old age, she wanted the chance to touch them whenever she wanted and remember every memory.

Bloody hell, how she wanted him. No, it was more than that. She loved him more than she'd loved anyone else before.

She finally threaded her fingers through his and gently squeezed. "You'd better wake up so I can punch you for your sacrifice and then kiss you to show how much I love you." She lowered her voice. "I need you, Aaron. Please don't leave me. If Killian doesn't return…" She trailed off to squeeze her eyelids closed. She couldn't afford to cry. If it were just her and Aaron, she wouldn't hesitate. But the clan was counting on her.

Taking a deep breath, she opened her eyes and raised their clasped hands to her cheek. The warmth of his skin helped her muscles relax a fraction.

She was content to watch Aaron's breathing and take comfort in his familiar scent and heat. He was alive, after all, and that was the most important factor.

Just as her eyelids kept drooping, Arlanna returned.

She pushed aside her sleepiness. However, Teagan didn't drop Aaron's hand and make excuses. She merely looked to Arlanna. The nurse nodded and said, "Any male who is willing to protect you is worth keeping around."

"I agree."

Arlanna held up her supplies. "I need to clean you up properly. We can't risk either wound festering or who knows what else. The doctor is also going to take a look and run some tests. If you're lucky, whatever grazed you wasn't covered in some unknown chemical."

Teagan kissed Aaron's hand and gently laid it back on the bed. "Let's hope not. Either way, whoever controlled the drones will now be a target of the Irish government as well."

"Bastards. But whatever happens, you'll find a way to keep us safe. I'm sure of it."

Teagan smiled at Arlanna. The nurse's gaze was warm and trusting. Between her people and Aaron, she could face the future.

How she ever thought she was alone, she didn't know.

She watched Aaron's face as Arlanna worked on cleaning her leg and neck wounds, the stings barely noticeable compared to the pain earlier.

With dreams of a happy future and a trusted male at her side, Teagan was more determined than ever to fight for her clan. Meeting with the DDA wasn't going to be pleasant, but she would make them understand the threat and try to convince them to help. If the Dragon Knights were involved, or any other enemy, she was going to need to work together with as many allies as possible. Otherwise, there might not be a Clan Glenlough for much longer. Not even Teagan could stop attacks on all sides.

Now all she needed to do was allow herself time to heal. Then she could tackle all of it, with a little help from those she trusted.

And Killian had better be one of them. Because if he was still missing when she was mostly healed, she was going to track down her brother and kill him herself.

CHAPTER TWENTY

Brenna peered down at the tiny machine that couldn't be much bigger than a robin. "How many of these did you find?"

Kerrin replied, "Four. Two were at the southern end of the park. I think they were heading toward Teagan's position, where she confronted those dragons."

"Can I touch it?" she asked.

Kerrin nodded. "Any remaining darts have been removed, and there's nothing harmful coating its surface. We checked."

She gingerly lifted the fifteen-centimeter-long—about half a foot—object. It was thicker at one end than the other and had wings to either side. The surface was painted in the guise of a bird with brown feathers.

Kerrin's voice filled the room. "It's quite sophisticated and expensive to make. Whoever did this has money to spare."

She looked up. "Have your volunteers keep searching for any others. We can't afford to let any of these be retrieved and stolen back."

"Of course. I'm also working on a temporary solution to keep them from flying inside the clan's lands. While I might be able to rig a sort of electrical barrier triggered by a motion sensor, the trick will be in ensuring a young dragon or an innocent bird isn't fried in the process."

Orla sat at her side and snorted. "Yes, fried dragon-shifter would be a bad thing." She motioned toward the door. "I know you want to go back to your work, Kerr. Leave this with us for now and go on."

With a nod, Kerrin exited the small room.

Brenna looked to Orla. "Teagan should be doing this, not me."

"Teagan's neck wound is worse than expected and shows signs of infection. Even with a dragon-shifter's ability to heal quickly, it could endanger her health if she doesn't rest. Besides, we can handle it for now. Maybe Killian will show his arse again. Then he can take over."

Despite Orla's light tone, Brenna had seen more than a few worried looks on the older female's face over the course of the day. Killian would never stay silent so long. Everyone in central command was starting to think he'd been taken prisoner.

Or worse.

Her dragon spoke up. *You don't know that for certain. Besides, once Teagan is better, maybe we can go searching. I'm quite good at finding things that are lost.*

A light flashed on the computer, signaling a video conference request. She quickly said to her dragon, *We'll discuss this later.* Brenna moved closer to the screen, checked the name, and hit Accept. "Do you have any information for us, Arabella?"

Arabella MacLeod of Lochguard's upper body appeared on the screen. The scar on her face and healed burn on her neck contrasted with the sleeping baby against her shoulder. "Keep your voice down, Brenna. I'm not risking this one waking up. Declan can nearly shatter glass with his cries. I'm convinced he's part banshee and not a dragon-shifter at all."

Since Brenna and Arabella were both originally from Stonefire, she wasn't fazed by the female's tone or casual remarks. Brenna asked more quietly, "So? Did you find anything?"

"I'm still trying to break the encryption," Arabella said. "However, I was able to determine the range of the thing. Someone had to be within a mile to control it."

Brenna cursed. "Which means they were inside or near the clan's lands."

Arabella nodded and gently patted her son's back. "At this point, I can't tell if it's the same design and programming as the devices that previously attacked Stonefire and Glenlough. As soon as I find out, I'll let you know. I have some of Lochguard's best and trusted IT people working on this with me."

The baby dressed in bright green dinosaurs squirmed against Arabella's shoulder, and she cuddled the tiny one closer. Despite everything going on, Brenna smiled. "It's nice to see you happy, Ara."

Arabella's face softened as she stared at her child. "Me, too." She looked back at Brenna. "Talk to you soon."

The screen went blank.

Orla spoke up. "The world will soon be ruled by females, and about time, too."

Brenna frowned. "I think we should all rule together, on equal footing."

"Equal in some ways, but a few more females in power would be nice. And preferably before I die."

"Your list of things to happen before you die is growing fairly long, Orla." A knock on the door prevented the older female from replying. Brenna shouted, "Come in."

Lyall appeared in the doorway, concern plain in his eyes. "We found Killian."

Brenna closed the distance between them. "What's happened?"

The older male sighed. "One of the volunteers found him unconscious in the woods surrounding Glenlough."

Orla stood. "Where is he now?"

Lyall answered, "He's in one of the conference rooms. Awake, but… different."

Brenna's stomach twisted. "Different how?"

"It's quicker for you to see than for me to try to explain. Come, I'll take you to him."

Her dragon huffed. *I don't like this.*

Me, either. But Killian is alive, which is the most important factor.

As they walked, Orla's cane thumping along with them, Brenna asked, "Does Teagan know you found her brother?"

Lyall shook his head. "The doctor thinks it's best to let her rest a bit longer, until her slight fever breaks. However, if Orla thinks we need to defy the doctor's orders, I will. But given everything Teagan's gone through today, I thought I would go to you two first."

Orla replied, "Good. I'm the best judge of whether stressing my injured granddaughter is worth it or not, especially considering that the DDA will be visiting tomorrow and she needs her strength for that."

"You would think that the DDA would wait until she's healthy again," Brenna muttered.

Orla shook her head. "You may be a good Protector, Brenna, but there is much for you to learn about dealing with the Irish government, or any government for that matter. To them we're pests and, at best, second-class citizens."

Lyall stopped in front of a conference room door. Ignoring Orla's opinion, he said, "Just prepare yourself and keep in mind he's not the Killian we know."

Once she nodded, Lyall entered the room. Brenna took a deep breath and followed the dragonman inside.

Killian sat in a chair at the far side of the conference room, his wrists cuffed and attached to long chains secured on the floor.

The restraints weren't a good sign.

Looking closer, she noticed Killian's dark hair was disheveled and his torso was bare, but otherwise he looked fairly normal. If he had injuries, they were somewhere she couldn't see.

And yet, as Killian silently looked at her with furrowed brows and confusion in his gaze, her gut sensed something was off. Brenna took a step toward him and said, "Killian? Are you okay?"

He studied her for a second before demanding, "Who are you? Are you the one who's going to release me? I've been waiting for the bloody leader to meet with me."

Her heart stopped a second. It couldn't be true. Killian had to be joking.

Maybe if she humored him, he'd tell her the truth. She touched her chest and said, "I'm Brenna."

"Who?" Killian demanded.

Orla moved to her side and leaned forward. "What's wrong with you, Killian? You've worked with Brenna for months. And I bloody well hope you remember me."

Killian crossed his arms over his chest, the chains jingling in the process. "Should I? And what's wrong is that strangers are keeping me locked in this room against my will."

Orla leaned forward. "Killian O'Shea, I'm your grandmother. Stop playing games."

He stood up, stretching his chains to the limit, and that was when Brenna noticed the tattoo on his arm had been lasered off. The flesh was still tender and slightly pink where the former design had been, but there was no longer ink there.

On high alert, Brenna watched his pupils. However, they never once flashed.

Something was very wrong.

She jumped in. "Does your inner dragon remember anything?"

"Dragon? What the fuck are you talking about? I don't have any bloody inner dragon. All I know is that I woke up surrounded by strangers and now everyone keeps asking me questions and saying I should know who the fuck they are."

Her beast spoke up. *And yet he remembers how to talk and retained basic knowledge of how the world works.*

Brenna decided that if she was to learn anything, she needed to treat Killian as a stranger found on Glenlough's land. Maybe he'd respond better to that approach.

She placed a hand on her hip and stood to her full height. "Before I can provide answers, my doctor needs to examine you. We can do this the easy way where you cooperate, or we can do this the hard way, where we drug you unconscious. Which will it be?"

Killian studied her gaze a second before replying, "If I cooperate, will you remove the restraints?"

She shrugged a shoulder. "Let's see how you do first."

"That's better than an outright denial," Killian muttered. "But if anyone tries to cut me open during the process, I'm going to punch them hard enough to break bones."

She should nod and walk away, but she couldn't help but say, "I'd like to see you try. I'm going to be there as they examine you and trust me, I know a few things about knocking a male down."

Killian grunted noncommittally. "Maybe, maybe not. I'll just have to be a good boy so you'll take off my bloody restraints. Then we can have a proper match.

Her dragon chimed in. *He's more talkative than before.*

Is it wrong that I like the change?

But then her eyes fell on Killian's missing tattoo, and guilt flooded her body. No matter if she already liked the new version of Killian better, she would never be selfish enough to wish he stayed that way. Teagan and Orla had trusted Brenna and provided opportunities she'd never dreamed of. The least she could do was do her bloody best to restore Killian to his former self.

She finally spoke again. "Just sit down for now. I'll call the doctor."

Brenna took out her mobile phone and dialed Dr. O'Brien. Between him and the Stonefire pair of scientists arriving at any moment, she only hoped they could pinpoint what had been done to Killian and reverse it.

Because there was no bloody way she would accept that Killian's memory and dragon were gone forever. After all, a doctor back on Stonefire—Dr. Cassidy Jackson—had lost her dragon and found it again.

Her dragon asked, *And what if he never has it again? What then?*

Afraid of speaking the truth, Brenna focused on the phone. Dr. O'Brien picked up and she went to work.

~~~
~~~

Teagan awoke to someone poking her shoulder and saying her name. Even though her eyelids were heavy and moving a finger took an enormous amount of effort, she slowly forced them open. Brenna's brown hair and green eyes came into focus. "Brenna?"

Brenna grimaced. "Sorry to wake you, Teagan. The doctor says you need to rest, but we have a problem."

Fully awake, Teagan registered the slight sweat on her body and that moving took some effort. The combination of fever and pain medication made her slow. She finally sat up and said, "Tell me what's wrong." She darted a glance over to Aaron's bed, but he was still there. The machines connected to him beeped the same as before.

Brenna shook her head. "It's not Aaron. It's Killian. He doesn't remember who he is or even that he's a bloody dragon-shifter."

Teagan blinked, now fully awake. "What the fuck are you talking about?"

Brenna filled in the details before saying, "He's sitting with your mother as we speak. Orla is hoping it may help with restoring his memory."

Teagan ignored the heaviness in her heart. A life with her brother never recognizing her would be unthinkable. Killian had had her back from the moment Teagan had stated she wanted to be clan leader.

Her dragon chimed in. *We'll try any avenue. There has to be a way to bring him back.*

Brenna's voice prevented her from replying. "Dr. O'Brien just finished with Killian, taking blood samples. He's going to analyze them and see if he can find anything unusual. However, there's someone I know firsthand who lost and found their dragon—Dr. Sid back on Stonefire. She may or may not be able to help us. However, I didn't want to reach out to her until you gave permission. This is, after all, a clan matter."

Teagan vaguely recalled the story of Dr. Sid Jackson and how finding her true mate had brought her dragon back after more than twenty years of silence.

However, Teagan had no bloody idea if Killian had ever found his true mate or even knew who she was. Teagan couldn't rely on the same tactic. She wasn't one for waiting around, for one. And she wouldn't stud out her brother to try and find his true mate.

Taking a deep breath, she forced herself to focus on fixing the problem. She'd take any help Stonefire provided. "Let Ronan do his tests, and then I'll reach out to Stonefire. Bram will want to send someone and I'd rather wait to have more visitors until after I deal with the DDA. I don't need them having a surprise inspection and finding people that shouldn't be here."

"Of course," Brenna replied. "Do you want Killian brought here? He's in restraints for the moment, so he should be safe to move."

Teagan shook her head and instantly regretted how her neck stung. "No. Moving him increases the risk of him trying to escape. Even if his inner dragon is silent, he's strong and can overpower most of the Protectors in human form. Not to mention that if he retained the knowledge of how to break out of handcuffs, he could slip away once I'm asleep again. As soon as I'm strong enough, I'll visit him. But make sure every Protector is on high alert. Also, they need to keep his memory loss quiet for the time being. We don't need a panic right now."

Brenna didn't miss a beat. "They've already been ordered to keep it confidential. Also, Killian never mentioned a second-in-command. Does he have one? I should probably hand over the reins to him or her now that things have calmed down a bit."

"He's had trouble finding a good fit. However, after all you've done today, I think you should stay in command for now."

"Until Killian is himself again," Brenna added quickly.

"I'm not good with false hope, Brenna. I will do everything in my power to bring back my brother to his original self, but there is a chance it can't be reversed. If it comes to that, then I'll reevaluate the situation. Does that sound fair?" Brenna bobbed her head and Teagan continued, "What about the Stonefire scientists? Arlanna mentioned them whilst cleaning my wound. Are they here yet?"

"They landed ten minutes ago and are being briefed by Dr. Guinness." Sullivan Guinness was Glenlough's junior doctor. Brenna studied her a second. "I should go get Arlanna so she can check on you. You're still pale and probably weak from the fever."

"I'm fine," Teagan barked.

Brenna raised her brows. "You're not. And don't even think of getting up until you're cleared. As temporary head Protector, I have the power to strap you to the bed and keep you there until the doctor clears your health."

Brenna stood tall. It took everything Teagan had to not smile at the young dragonwoman's posture.

Her beast spoke up. *She's still young, remember.*

Perhaps, but she's definitely coming into her own.

"I wouldn't dream of it." Teagan motioned toward the door with a hand. "Fetch the nurse and go back to aiding my family. Killian is going to need all the help he can get."

Brenna's pupils flickered, but the young female was gone before Teagan could say anything else.

Her dragon spoke up. *If anyone can help Killian, it's her.*

Are you not telling me something, dragon?

No. They aren't true mates; Killian's came and went years ago. But never underestimate a female soldier out to prove herself.

Teagan slid back down onto her back, too tired to interrogate her dragon's remark about Killian's true mate coming and going. *I don't care who helps him as long as Killian gets his memories back.*

And if he doesn't, at least we'll still have Aaron.

Teagan turned her head toward Aaron's bed. *His chances are better than Killian's, but not guaranteed.*

He'll survive. Just wait and see.

The longer she stared, the heavier Teagan's eyes grew. After memorizing Aaron's sleeping face, she allowed them to flutter closed.

With Killian's predicament, her male had bloody well wake up. She needed him more than ever.

CHAPTER TWENTY-ONE

Electricity raced through Aaron's body. His eyes popped open and he sat up with a gasp. "What the fuck?"

Everything was blurry for a second, but as his heart rate calmed down and the room came into focus, he met the brown, bespectacled eyes of Dr. Trahern Lewis, the Welsh dragon-shifter who had recently moved to Stonefire.

Trahern adjusted his glasses. "Who are you and where was your last location?"

Aaron slowly looked around the room. A curtain created a concealed space that included his bed, Trahern, Dr. Emily Davies, and Dr. Ronan O'Brien.

One very important person was missing. "Where's Teagan?" he demanded.

Dr. O'Brien looked to the other doctors. "He at least remembers her."

Aaron growled. "I'm right here. Where the fuck is Teagan?" He tried to move his feet, but they were restrained. "And why the bloody hell am I tied to a bed?"

Trahern's calm voice answered, "Because we were afraid of you going rogue. You were shot with a compound similar to what your mother received."

Aaron finally noted his silent dragon. His beast was curled up asleep in the back of his mind. No amount of mental poking would move him. "My dragon is still asleep."

"Yes," Emily answered. "Given what's happened recently, we wanted to ensure you remembered who you are before allowing him to wake up." The human female leaned forward. "Speaking of which, you still haven't told us your name."

He growled. "I'm Aaron Caruso, and the last thing I remember is trying to warn Teagan and then jumping to protect her." He threaded every bit of dominance in his voice he could muster. "So I ask again: Where is she?"

Dr. O'Brien motioned toward the curtain. "She's on the other side, asleep."

Aaron tossed off his blanket and leaned toward the restraint. However, since his dragon was asleep, he couldn't extend a talon. He also wasn't flexible enough to bend over and reach the latches. He looked directly at Dr. O'Brien. "Take off these fucking things right now and let me see her."

Emily raised her eyebrows. "Swearing and yelling aren't going to make us move any faster, Aaron. You just received a healthy electrical shock. Your muscles need a minute to recover. I doubt you'd be able to walk just yet."

He clenched the sheets in his fingers. "Okay, then bring me up to speed on everything else. I've proved that my ears are working. Maybe start with why the hell you had to shock me?"

Trahern replied, "Because the latest antidote needed a healthy jolt to speed up delivery and its effectiveness."

Aaron frowned, but Emily spoke before he could respond. "What Trahern is trying to say is that waking you was made a priority. The shock gets the antidote into your system and spreading almost a day quicker than without."

"And Teagan?" Aaron asked. "Was she also hit?"

Emily shook her head. "She wasn't hit with the darts, but she had a neck injury that became infected. Her fever broke an hour ago, so she's out of danger. Still, combined with her leg wound, she needs the rest so she can heal."

Images of Teagan with a slit throat rushed into his mind. But then he remembered Emily saying Teagan was out of danger, so he took a deep breath and focused on the other problems he might be able to help with. He asked, "And what about Killian? I remember he was missing."

All three doctors glanced at each other.

Something was wrong. "Just bloody tell me. I'm awake and remember everything. With Teagan out of commission, I might be able to help."

Dr. O'Brien cleared his throat. "In this case, probably not." He paused a beat and added, "Killian has lost his memories of ever being a dragon-shifter or a Glenlough clan member."

Aaron wished his dragon was awake as he felt like roaring himself. "How about you start at the beginning?" O'Brien filled in the general details surrounding Teagan's attack and Killian. Once the doctor was finished, Aaron asked, "Then get me Brenna or Orla. As soon as my muscles work again properly, I want to check on Teagan and dive in to helping the clan."

Emily spoke up. "You'll be physically weak for a few days and will be kept under observation, which means you won't be able to 'dive in,' as you put it, with full force. But we'll let them know you're awake. It'll be up to Orla and Brenna as to whether they come or not."

He grunted. In most areas of his life, Aaron wasn't a patient dragonman. "And how about getting me a bloody phone? I want to talk with Bram."

Dr. O'Brien jumped in. "The Stonefire leader is aware of the situation, as is the Scottish one."

At the mention of the Scottish dragon-shifter, Aaron remembered something else. "And what about Grant McFarland? He was hit. Is he awake?"

"He's been given the antidote, but it'll be at least eighteen hours before he wakes up. And I doubt Ms. MacKenzie will leave his side to come to you," Dr. O'Brien replied.

Aaron ran a hand through his hair. "I hate sitting here, not being able to do anything. Just let Orla and Brenna know I'm awake." He chanced wiggling his toes. The sheet above them moved, although each motion sent pins and needles racing up his legs. "And at least draw aside the bloody curtain. I want to see Teagan for myself."

Without a word, Emily walked to the curtain and drew it aside to reveal Teagan lying on a bed.

While her face was a little paler than normal and he could make out circles under her eyes, her chest rose and fell in a steady rhythm. Then his gaze moved to the bandage around her neck.

Aaron's female had gone down fighting and won to live another day. Pride mixed with love surged through his body.

His dragon swished his tail as if in agreement, but didn't move from the back of his mind or make any sounds.

Dr. O'Brien's voice filled the room. "She's stable and should make a full recovery."

He itched to take her hand and bring it to his cheek. Seeing her and hearing she would be okay wasn't quite the same as feeling her warm skin against his and listening to her heart beat.

After drinking in the sight of her face for another second, he looked back to the trio of doctors. "And what about the bastards who betrayed us? You didn't tell me the specifics of Teagan's brawl with the three males."

"Orin and Padraig are dead. Hugh is in custody. The DDA should be arriving at any minute to collect him and question the clan about Teagan's actions."

He frowned. "Who is doing that?"

"It was supposed to be Teagan, but Orla forbid it. She'll handle it instead."

Holy fuck. "No, let me up and take me to Orla. Even if it's in a bloody wheelchair, someone needs to be there to do damage control. Orla may have been a great leader once, but she's prone to voicing her opinions in her old age. That may not end well."

O'Brien raised an eyebrow. "We'll see if I mention your words to Orla or not." Aaron opened his mouth, but the doctor beat him to it. "Regardless, Brenna is there. The pair of them can handle it. I sense Orla is grooming the Stonefire lass to be her protégé to one day become a clan leader, but of where, I have no idea."

Aaron might remember who he was, but it was starting to feel as if he'd landed in the middle of a different clan. "Since when is Brenna in charge of anything on Glenlough? You should've mentioned that earlier."

O'Brien replied, "Since everyone else with a higher rank was taken out of commission and none of her compatriots stepped up."

Just as he tried to think of another way to convince them to let him out of bed, Teagan's weak voice garnered his attention. "Do you always have to be so loud, Aaron? I'm trying to sleep."

~~~
~~~

At first, Teagan had thought she'd been dreaming as she listened to Aaron's voice. But when all the doctors joined in and talked about things she'd never think about on her own, she started to wonder if the voices were real.

It took longer than she wanted to force her eyes open since the fever had sapped most of her energy, but the instant she saw Aaron's scowling face, all she wanted to do was jump out of bed and run into his arms.

Her dragon spoke up. *He is alive and himself. That is all that matters. Be patient.*

Did the fever addle your brains? You're usually impatient when it comes to Aaron.

There is a lot going on. We must take care of the clan first.

She mentally sighed. *I know. But I want to at least feel Aaron's hand in mine before tackling the mountain of shite at our doorstep. No one would think less of us for wanting to touch our mate for a minute.*

Not waiting for her dragon to respond, she spoke, her voice weaker than she'd like. "Do you always have to be so loud, Aaron? I'm trying to sleep."

Aaron's brown eyes instantly met her. Relief and then loved filled his gaze. "Teagan. You're awake."

She tried her best to smile. "They can knock me down, but I'll just get right back up."

He never looked away from her as he growled, "Let me out of this bed."

Ronan O'Brien turned toward her. "We should wait another few minutes, Teagan, to ensure his muscles are relaxed and that there're no ill effects from the sped-up antidote process."

Teagan slowly sat up and tried not to grimace as pain shot up her leg. At least her throat barely hurt at all, meaning the sleep had done its job. "Then I'll get out of bed and go to him."

Ronan sighed. "People in love always do stupid things. I'm not sure why I bother." He pointed a forefinger at her. "You stay there. I'll help bring Aaron to you because if he keels over from a heart attack, the clan can survive. I can't say the same about you."

Aaron muttered a few choice words about what the Irish doctor could shove where.

Teagan looked back to Aaron and barely noticed the doctors undoing the straps around his legs. She said, "If you need help walking over here, take it. I'm not about to watch you fall over and break a bone or two."

The corner of Aaron's mouth ticked up. "If you were well, I might consider breaking a bone. Then you'd have to be nice to me and do the cooking."

She fought a smile and lost. "Don't even think about it. If you break your bones on purpose, I'll leave you to fend for yourself."

"And then you'll starve soon after that. If for nothing else, think of losing your personal chef. You want him back." He lowered his voice. "Also, don't forget what else I'm good at."

Ronan rolled his eyes, but Teagan barely noticed. She and Aaron grinned at each other, and for a split second, she forgot about everything but the male she loved. Aaron had a knack for making her problems temporarily melt away.

If she could help it, she was never letting him go.

Her dragon grunted. *I told you he won't run away from a challenge. He'll never tire of fighting at our side.*

Ignoring her beast, she watched as Aaron maneuvered off the bed with Ronan's help. Aaron had to lean on the doctor to make his way across the floor. Each step seemed to take a year.

She outstretched her hand. As Aaron finally took it, his warm touch erased most of her sleepiness. "Kiss me quickly,

Aaron, because there's much to do, but I want to make sure you're real first and that all of this isn't a dream."

Amusement danced in his eyes. "Someone is waxing poetically."

With a growl, she yanked him toward her. He tumbled and landed half on her body, careful not to touch her leg.

She expected him to yell, but instead, he just maneuvered himself until his lips touched hers.

Opening, she allowed his tongue to slide between her lips and explore her mouth. At his taste, she moaned. It couldn't have been that long since she'd last kissed him, but it felt like years.

Yes, she needed to keep him around. Then she could kiss him whenever she wanted.

Aaron finally broke the kiss. He whispered against her lips, "Also don't forget that I'm the best medicine."

"Good grief," Ronan muttered at the same time Teagan shook her head.

She said, "Save your charm for the DDA. We're going to talk to them."

Aaron frowned. "You must've still been asleep when O'Brien told me about Orla and Brenna handling that duty."

"As much as I appreciate their help, I should be the one to talk with the DDA. Any punishments they issue will be mine to suffer, not theirs. Not that I'm going to take the meeting lightly. I'm going to challenge them every step of the way. After all, their lack of involvement helped cultivate confidence in the other clans about taking me down."

Aaron whistled. "I can't wait to see this. Don't even think of trying to keep me away."

"Come sit at my side. A few of your glares will have them shaking in their boots."

Ronan spoke up again. "I strongly advise against this, Teagan. You're weak." She opened her mouth, but Ronan beat her to it. "Anyone who suffered your injuries and ensuing fever would be weak. Despite your recent idiotic behavior regarding the Stonefire male, you're a good leader. You've proved that over and over again. I'm on your side, but I don't want a relapse. There's always a chance your condition will weaken further and you could die."

Teagan replied, "My neck already feels better. Besides, I'll use a bloody wheelchair and you can push me there yourself, Ronan, to conserve energy. I won't compromise on this, though. I'm a witness to Padraig, Orin, and Hugh's betrayal. My word will carry weight, and you know it."

Teagan and Ronan stared at each other. The doctor finally threw his hands up in the air. "Fine. But all you're going to do is talk and then you're coming back here where I'll examine you. Then you'll rest. Understood?"

Since Ronan was the head doctor, he was one of the few who could order Teagan around when it came to her health. "Yes. Now, hurry. If the clock in the room is correct, the DDA should be here by now." She looked to Dr. Trahern Lewis. "You, call central command and tell them I'm coming. Ask for Orla and Brenna to sit this one out. Also, they need to delay the DDA as long as possible until I can get there."

The male merely blinked at her. Thankfully the other doctor from Stonefire, Emily, spoke up. "I'll do it. But then we need to get back to helping the others who were attacked."

Teagan nodded, and the Stonefire pair exited the room. Ronan pushed the nurse call button and moved to Teagan's bed. "Just a quick check before you go."

Aaron asked, "And me?"

Ronan looked at the monitors hooked up to Teagan as he answered Aaron, "Just don't die until you come back."

Teagan bit her lip to keep from laughing at the frown on Aaron's face. Eventually, she'd talk to Ronan about being a bit nicer to her male. But for the moment, she merely tapped her fingers against the bed, impatient to deal with the DDA. Only then could she move on to rebuilding her clan and carving out her own future.

Chapter Twenty-Two

As the nurse Arlanna wheeled her into place inside the conference room, Teagan looked to Lara and Trevina, the two human Irish DDA liaisons.

Since it was still illegal for a human female to mate a dragon-shifter male—Ireland lacked the freedoms or even the sacrifice program of the UK—the DDA almost always sent females to deal with the dragon clans. That way, no attachments would be formed or at least pursued, unless the DDA employees wanted to be imprisoned.

Her dragon huffed. *I don't know why it's okay for human males to mate a dragon-shifter but not a female in Ireland.*

Like with most things, men usually gain the right first unless there are special circumstances, such as with the British sacrifice program.

The British sacrifice program enlisted compatible human females to sign contracts and live with the dragon-shifters for six months. While there, the female attempted to conceive a child with an assigned dragon-shifter male; if successful, she stayed until the baby was born. In return for their participation, the female received a vial of dragon's blood that could cure many diseases, or they could sell it for money. Since the program had started in the 1980s in the UK, Ireland had been too busy with other domestic problems to follow suit.

Teagan had never thought much about the rights of human females to mate male dragon-shifters, but maybe it was another thing she should add to her list of things to do.

Her beast chimed in. *Let's take care of this first and then you can plan how to change Ireland for the better.*

Once Aaron took his seat next to her, Teagan focused back on the DDA liaisons. Since she'd dealt with Trevina before, she smiled at the human. "We never seem to meet under happy circumstances, do we?"

The human didn't smile. "There's no time for jokes or chitchat today, Teagan. Two dragon-shifters are dead, one is in custody, and pictures, as well as a short video, have leaked all over the Internet. The DDA is being stretched thin to prevent outright chaos, and my superiors want a scapegoat."

Teagan replied, "I was careful to check that the surroundings were empty. The only ones who could've leaked anything were the farmers in the vicinity."

"Aye, but that was all it took," Trevina stated. "The only good thing from it all is the video begins with the other party attacking you. We'll question"—she looked down at a file—"Hugh Burns later. For now, we need an official statement from you. Tell us what happened and I'll report it to my superior. Make it convincing or you might become the scapegoat and suffer the consequences."

Teagan raised her brows. "There shouldn't be any consequences for self-defense."

Trevina shrugged. "Perhaps. But you must understand that we need to ease the public's fears and ensure them that dragons won't come to terrorize their homes. As it is, our sources have reported talk of a possible dragon war. Is one brewing?"

Teagan sat taller in her chair. She wondered if she'd ever get to tell her story what with how Trevina kept jumping around from topic to topic. "Those who attacked me were upset at Glenlough having a female leader. The leaked pictures and video have another consequence—they should deter anyone else from challenging me for not being male. Between dragon-shifter turning against dragon-shifter, the resulting deaths, and garnering the DDA's notice, it should quell any more thoughts of war or conquest."

At least for the time being, not that Teagan was going to mention that.

The other human, Lara, finally spoke up. "Or will their deaths only encourage the foolish, macho ones to have a go and prove they're better?"

"Look, there will always be male arseholes who think they're better than females since history tends to teach males are superior in all ways, apart from childbirth. I'm sure you deal with it yourselves inside the DDA. You've never had a female DDA director in Ireland. Most of the higher-ups are male, too. Doesn't that just make you want to work harder and show them you can do a better job through your actions?" Teagan asked.

Trevina cleared her throat. "I'm all for equal rights, Teagan. But it's a bit different working through the ranks and gaining promotions. We don't turn into dragons and scare the bejesus out of others."

Her dragon growled. *Why do they always paint us as monsters?*

Because it's easier and it attracts more eyes.

As Teagan searched her brain for another approach, Aaron laid his hand on her thigh under the table and squeezed.

He believed in her.

Drawing on his support, Teagan said, "If there is another incident and more males come calling for a challenge, I will step down and hand myself over to you." She focused her gaze on Trevina. "You've worked with me for years, Vina. Whilst my word should be good enough, I will sign anything you like to satisfy the DDA, provided it's fair."

The two DDA employees glanced at each other. It was Lara who spoke first. "That may placate our bosses. However, there is one other requirement. Everyone who visited for the leadership trials and isn't officially part of Glenlough must return home as soon as possible. I understand some of them are ill and they will be given time to recover. But we'll check back over the next few weeks to ensure compliance. Any violation of visitors without our approval will also result in you giving up your position."

The first thought that entered Teagan's mind was that Aaron would have to go home to England.

Just picturing her cottage empty again, with no male harping on about her mess or cooking her dinner, made her heart heavy.

Her dragon growled. *They can't send him away. He's ours.*

Not officially. Putting aside that he may not want to take a mate, making it official will cause more problems.

The clan will stand by you. The only question is whether you want Aaron regardless of the consequences or not.

She glanced at Aaron. *I do.*

Then we will find a way. Get rid of the DDA first and then we can talk with him.

Aaron patting her thigh brought her back to the present. She spoke again. "As long as the rule about no visitors can be revisited in a month or two, I'll agree."

Trevina folded her hands in front of her. "You're not in much of a position to bargain, Teagan."

"I disagree. If you revisit the ruling, I will also reach out to the other Irish clans and work on establishing alliances. If some or all of us sign a treaty, that will make your jobs easier."

"We can possibly allow other Irish dragon-shifters to visit, especially since many members of Glenlough no doubt have relatives living in other parts of the country. If the higher-ups approve of it, then how about once you get at least one clan to sign the treaty, we'll revisit the rule about no visitors from other countries. I can't guarantee the new restriction will change even if you sign an alliance with every dragon clan in Ireland, but your actions will help sway members of the DDA into fighting for you."

Teagan knew that was the best offer she would get. She nodded. "Deal. Put it in writing. Once it's signed, I'll start reaching out to other clans, but not before. I'll also put my account in writing and have it witnessed. That should be easier for both sides when it comes to finding out the truth."

Trevina stood and Lara followed suit. The former picked up her paperwork and said, "We'll send the paperwork in the next few days. I expect your report before then." Trevina glanced to the bandage around Teagan's neck and back to her face. "Although, if your condition worsens, you have my direct line. Let me know and I'll ensure you have a few more days."

"Thank you, Vina."

Trevina waved a hand in dismissal. "Not even dragon-shifters are invincible. And to be honest, you're easier to work with than many others, so my offer isn't completely altruistic."

If Lara wasn't in the room, Teagan would press for even more time with Trevina to better understand the human female for future negotiations. However, Lara was newer and more ambitious; Teagan wouldn't do anything to risk Trevina's reputation for results with dragon-shifters by delaying their more important task of collecting Hugh.

Lara spoke up. "We just need to secure the prisoner and we'll return to Galway."

The Irish DDA's main headquarters was in Dublin, but Galway's branch handled Glenlough.

Teagan looked to Aaron. Even though all he'd done was touch her leg, his presence had helped her. Still, he deserved to do more. Maybe then Trevina would warm up to the idea of Aaron staying on Glenlough, even without a mating.

Her beast huffed. *Let's hope it doesn't come to that.*

She ignored her dragon and asked Aaron, "Will you take them?" Aaron bobbed his head and Teagan looked back to the human females. "I apologize for not taking you myself, but I'm also recovering from a fever in addition to my wounds. However, call me with any questions that may come up or anything you learn from Hugh."

Trevina raised a dark eyebrow. "He hasn't talked to you?"

"Not much. Now that I'm on the mend, I intend to do a full-scale investigation. You'll be one of the first to know what I find, Vina."

Aaron stood. He smiled at the women, his teeth flashing, and Teagan wanted to growl. She knew that smile. He was going to flirt with them.

Her dragon spoke up. *The DDA could do with a little charming. It means nothing to him.*

I know. Jealousy is unlike me. But we just got him back and I want to spend time with him.

We will, soon enough. And once he's officially our mate, jealousy will fade.

Teagan wasn't sure it would entirely go away, but it would help. After all, Aaron was a rare dragonman, willing to support a female and not be constantly insecure or try to take over her job. Him supporting her during the meeting had washed away any lingering doubts about him changing or growing tired of her being clan leader.

Her dragon snorted. *About time.*

A few seconds after Aaron had ushered the DDA females out, the nurse came into the room to wheel her back to the surgery.

However, despite telling Ronan she'd return right after her meeting, there was something she needed to do first. Teagan looked up at Arlanna. "My grandmother should be in my office. I need to see her."

To her credit, Arlanna changed course without a word and headed toward Teagan's office.

But Teagan wasn't anxious to see her gran. No, her ultimate goal was to see her brother.

~~~

Killian O'Shea, or at least that was the name people kept calling him, looked through the pages of photographs in front of him for the tenth time. He was supposed to know everyone he saw.

Yet they all were strangers. Not even the backdrops were familiar. Seeing himself in some of the photos only frustrated him more.
~~~

Pushing the binder away, he stood up and paced. Well, he paced as much as his chains allowed.

Waking up and not knowing his identity was one thing, but to have people constantly saying he should know so-and-so and forcing it down his throat was another. And he may not know exactly what kind of man he was, but he knew in his bones he wasn't the type to sit around and do nothing. Hell, the muscles and scars on his body alone spoke of an active and possibly dangerous lifestyle.

And yet, all the people who supposedly cared about him didn't seem to mention that fact, let alone allow him out to see the bloody sky again.

He heard the door open and he turned around. The young and somewhat pretty woman with short, dark hair and brown eyes named Brenna stood there. Since she was the only one to accept his amnesia and not keep pushing him to remember her, he was actually glad to see her. Interacting freely may give him a better understanding of himself.

Brenna put down a tray laden with scones, ham sandwiches, and tea and pushed it closer to him. She waved at the offerings. "I brought both sweet and savory. One should please your taste buds."

He frowned. "I'd like it a hell of a lot more if you took off my chains."

"I can't do that, Killian. You know that, so stop asking." She took a step closer but was still out of his reach. "Besides, you have a visitor."

"If it's another fucking person come to tell me how we grew up together or how our bloody dragons would fly together, I'm going to toss a chair at them."

She placed her hands on her hips. "Do that and you'll never go free. Use your common sense."

He growled. "Why can't everyone let me be?"

Brenna whispered, "Because you're too important."

Before he could reply to that, someone knocked on the door. Brenna opened it to reveal a dark-haired woman in a wheelchair. She had one of those tattoos on her bicep that everyone seemed to have.

Like the one that he'd seen on his own arm in one of the pictures, but it had apparently been lasered off his arm.

Not wanting to think about how that probably verified the stories he'd heard, he studied the new arrival. Unlike most of his visitors, her eyes were neutral and assessing him. She also radiated confidence and a posture that said not to fuck with her. The wheelchair didn't diminish her power one bit.

He had to admit he was curious to see what she said about him.

As silence stretched, he grunted. "I would ask who you are, but the answer won't mean anything to me. So, what do you want?"

Something flickered in the woman's eyes but quickly disappeared. She shrugged. "I just came to see how you're doing. You might want to be nice to me, though. I'm the person who says where you stay and also decides what happens to you."

He moved as far as his chains would allow, but the woman was out of reach by several meters. "Then tell me this: when can I go free?" He shook his chains. "I'm not an animal to be chained."

"It's for your own protection more than anything."

He growled. "Don't give me that bullshit reason. If I were a threat, you'd have killed me already. You also wouldn't be showing me pictures of your people. From what I gather, this is a type of close-knit community. Therefore, you must trust me."

"For someone who doesn't remember his former self, you're fairly perceptive," the female said. "I wasn't expecting that."

Not wanting to hear memories that meant nothing to him, he leaned forward. "Either tell me what's going to happen to me or get out. I'm in no mood for humor."

The woman studied him a second before saying, "Call me Teagan. And I'm going to move you to a secure cottage, complete with security and guards. You'll have free roam of the house, but if you try to escape, you'll be sedated or detained at any cost."

"If you're waiting for me to weep and thank you for the bread crumbs, it's not going to happen."

She raised her brows. "I didn't ask for anything, did I? Now, are you going to let me finish? Otherwise you can rot in here for a few more days. Then we'll see what mood you're in. I'm sure you'll be pretty fucking grateful then."

Well, it seemed he had another female to add to his list of not completely hating. Her honesty was better than pity or hope.

He motioned with his hand for her to continue and she said, "As for your release, even you should realize it's dangerous to let an amnesiac run around. My people will look after you until the doctor thinks you can survive on your own."

"I'm not a fucking child," he spat out.

"No, you're not. But what you may not realize is that you're a walking target, probably with a bounty on your head. I know you don't know why at the moment, but you'll find out in time. It'd be pointless and time-consuming to explain it now. If necessary, you'll be briefed when I give the word." Teagan looked to Brenna. "I'll leave you in charge of securing an empty cottage and devising its security. Once the basics are in place, find me. We need to talk."

Brenna frowned. "I don't like the sound of that, Teagan. What's going on?"

Teagan's eyes darted to him and back to Brenna. "Not here."

He clenched his fingers. More fucking secrets. How was he supposed to try to remember anything if no one told him anything important?

With a nod, Teagan wheeled herself out of the room. He looked to Brenna. "I guess that means I'm beholden to your whims."

The corner of her mouth ticked up. "I suppose so. Behave, and I won't move you to the old dungeons inside the great hall."

He fought the urge to tease her. The female's smile was infectious.

Instead, Killian grunted. "Just go. The sooner you have everything ready, the sooner I can leave this blasted room."

After another beat, Brenna left with a wave.

Killian sat back down at the table and flipped through the pages inside the binder again until he found the picture of the woman named Teagan. She stood in the picture, dressed in a flowing dress tied over one shoulder. Something was familiar about her, but he couldn't place it.

He closed the binder and tossed it against the far wall.

Chapter Twenty-Three

Teagan kept up her smiling face and tall posture until she stood from her wheelchair and walked into her hospital room. Aaron sat in a chair on the far side. The second the door clicked closed, she slumped against it and let out a strangled cry. "Killian has no idea who I am."

Aaron was in front of her in a split second and wrapped his arms around her. "He may not now, but you're not the type of person who gives up so easily. If there's a way to bring back his memories, you'll find it, love."

Snuggling into his chest, she closed her eyes and took comfort from Aaron's steady heartbeat. "I'm not giving up, but it's still not easy to admit. He's been my supporter from the very beginning and has become my trusted second." She pulled back to meet Aaron's gaze. "Even putting aside his skills as head Protector, he's my brother first. Imagine if your mother didn't recognize you and may never do so again."

He smoothed the hair back from her cheek. "I'm not brushing aside your pain, love. But you're tired and recovering from not only a dragon fight that resulted in a kill-or-be-killed situation, but also a fever that took its toll on your body. Get some sleep and you'll feel stronger. You may even wake up with a brilliant new idea."

She shook her head. "I can't take a nap. There's too much to do." Aaron opened his mouth, but she beat him to it. "And no, I can't hand it all off to someone else. For one, I need to talk about us."

He frowned. "That sounds like an ominous conversation."

"It is. You heard the DDA—all the non-Glenlough members must return home. That includes you, unless..."

He stroked her cheek. "Unless what? You've never held back your punches before, Teagan. Don't start now."

Her dragon spoke up. *It's okay. He will say yes.*

Teagan placed a hand on Aaron's jaw and rubbed her fingers against his short beard. "Do you want to be my mate, Aaron?"

He growled and pulled her closer against his body. "Of course I do, bloody woman. The only reason I haven't asked, apart from all hell breaking loose, is that you could lose your position if you take a mate. I didn't want to force you to choose and possibly hate me for the rest of your life."

She smiled. "I love you for many reasons, Aaron. Your consideration of feelings is one of them."

He grunted. "Don't let everyone know about it. I have a reputation to uphold." His gaze softened. "Although since it's only us, maybe you can tell me how you love me properly instead of only mentioning it in passing."

Teagan hadn't even noticed how the words had slipped out. But she didn't regret them one bit. Aaron had quickly become an essential part of not only her life, but the clan's as well. The clan may not know it yet, but Aaron would help her make their futures better.

Her dragon huffed. *Just tell him already. No need to rationalize or think about it.*

Cupping his cheek, she said, "I love you, Aaron Caruso, grumpy mornings and all."

With a growl, he took her lips in a quick, rough kiss. Each movement of his tongue or lips showed her how much he treasured her, too.

He pulled away far too soon, and his breath was hot against her lips as he whispered, "I love you, too, Teagan. And if I have to return to Stonefire and wait for you until we find a way where you can both be clan leader and take a mate, I'll do it. I've said it before, but you are worth the wait." He nuzzled her cheek. "Just tell me what you want, love. And I'll fight to make it a reality."

Tears prickled Teagan's eyes. "Oh, Aaron."

He leaned back to meet her gaze. As he strummed her cheek, he murmured, "Next time, I want to hear you say my name with more pleasure than pain."

She lightly hit his chest. "It's not pain, you fool. I'm happy. And maybe a little bit tired. But I should also make clear that it's not going to be easy becoming my mate. So I'm giving you one last chance to back out."

"Even if you gave me a thousand chances to back out, I won't. I only want you, Teagan O'Shea. Although I have a condition—you can't step down as leader for my sake. You can step down only if you want to do so for yourself. It has to be for your own reason and no one else's."

Teagan hooked her arms around his neck. "We'll find a way to make it work. I, for one, can't abandon the clan right now. But the mating will have to be soon. The DDA will be back within weeks to check and make sure the visitors all returned home."

He brushed her long hair over her shoulder. "I'm ready anytime you are. My final condition is that you get some sleep first."

"You and your conditions," she muttered. "You're just going to keep adding them, aren't you?"

He winked. "Well, I have learned from the best. If you can make the DDA agree to conditions, I have much to learn."

If she were a normal female in love and about to be mated, she would smile, kiss her male, and merely hold him close to enjoy the moment.

However, Teagan didn't have that luxury. "As much as I love you putting me at ease, we need to focus." He frowned and she added, "But know that in my mind, I'm snuggling against your chest as I fall asleep."

He raised his brows. "And in reality?"

She sighed. "I need to tell Brenna she can't stay. As much as I think of her as part of Glenlough now, she's technically from Stonefire. The DDA will force her to go. And considering how she stepped up and did so much for the clan, I need to tell her myself in person. Rumors will fly soon enough about the non-Irish leaving, and I don't want her to find out secondhand."

Aaron tightened his arms around her and pulled her against his chest. "We have a little time to think of a solution. Let's take a quick nap and then reach out to Bram. He might have an idea."

Teagan raised her head. "And if he doesn't?"

"Then Brenna either has to get mated or go home."

~~~

Brenna could count on her hand the number of times she'd cried in her adult life and she was on the verge of adding another finger to the tally.

Teagan had to send her back to Stonefire.
~~~

Her dragon spoke up. *It's not by choice, and you know it. She would probably make us temporary head Protector if she could.*

But she can't. And all because a few idiots attracted the attention of the Department of Dragon Affairs.

Her beast sent comforting thoughts. *We still have a week or two to come up with a plan. I'm not giving up hope and neither should you.*

I want to be optimistic, but I don't think it's going to help in this case. She approached the room Killian was in and added to her dragon, *We'll discuss this later. I need to escort Killian to the cells for the night.*

He's not going to be happy about it.

I can't help it. The cottage won't be secure until morning.

Brenna pushed her way inside the room to find Killian watching a TV program. He turned to look at her. "I hope you're here to take me to my new temporary home."

"I will tomorrow. I have escorts coming to take you to one of the holding cells."

Killian's eyes turned dark. "For all that people seem to bang on about how close we were, they seem eager to take away my freedoms."

Between the bad news of leaving and Killian's surly tone, something snapped inside Brenna and she walked up to Killian. "Look, we all have bad days. I'm about to lose the only place I ever felt I belonged to. You, at least, will have the option to leave if your memories never return and you understand the dangers. I may never come back."

He frowned. "You're leaving? Why?"

"You must've noticed my accent by now. I'm not from around here."

"I may not have my memories, but I can tell an annoying English one when I hear it."

She curled her fingers into a fist and her dragon warned, *Hitting him is a bad idea.*

Not heeding her beast, Brenna moved to punch Killian's jaw. However, he caught her fist, rose up, turned her around, and wrapped his free arm around her waist.

A small part of her was aware of the dangerous situation, but the heat of Killian's chest against her back made it hard to concentrate.

Her beast growled. *Don't let down your guard.*

Snapping out of her trance, Brenna kicked her heel into Killian's knee. He released her and yelled, "Fucking hell," as he fell back on his backside.

Brenna dashed to the far side of the room, out of Killian's reach. "I may be younger and female, but maybe next time you'll remember I can hold my own."

Killian rubbed his knee as he studied her from the floor. Each second his green eyes bore into hers, her heart rate kicked up.

He finally spoke again. "Why are you leaving?"

She blinked. "That's what you have to say to me?"

He growled. "Excuse me for showing some fucking concern, although I assure you it's not entirely selfless. You're the only one I can stand around here." He lowered his voice. "I don't want you to go."

She opened her mouth and promptly closed it. For months, she'd daydreamed of Killian wanting her to stay, pulling her close, and kissing the living daylights out of her.

Now when he lacked his memories and she was about to leave, he noticed her.

How bloody perfect.

Her beast spoke up. *It gives me an idea. Ask if he truly wants us to stay and just how far he'd go to do it.*

Why? she asked cautiously.

Just ask him.

Killian's voice interrupted her inner conversation. "I should be alarmed that your pupils just turned to slits, but I'm not. I have no idea why."

Brenna had been avoiding conversations about inner dragons. Killian clearly had lost his, and the last thing she wanted to do was bring him pain if he remembered who he was. At least until the doctors had some more time to run their tests and reach out to Dr. Sid on Stonefire to hopefully devise a treatment.

He deserves to know, her dragon said. *Besides, the more vital we become, the more likely he'll agree to my plan.*

Which is?

Not yet. Answer him.

Too tired to argue, she cleared her throat and said to Killian, "I am a dragon-shifter, which means a human and a dragon half share a brain, each with a distinct personality. When I talk with her, my pupils change."

"Isn't it annoying to have someone constantly in your head?"

"Usually not. It's like having a twin, but more intimate. We are one whole."

He scoffed. "That sounds ridiculous."

She shrugged. "It's how it works. But as much as I'd like to tell you more, we need to leave soon, and I have a few more questions for you before the other escorts arrive."

He crossed his arms over his chest. "Then ask them."

She hesitated and her beast roared. *Ask him already.*

Before she could change her mind, Brenna blurted out, "How far would you go to keep me here?"

"I'm not going to spout fancy words. That much I know about myself. But if there's something I can do to keep you around and as my main guard, I will most likely do it."

"Why?" she blurted.

He raised his brows. "Does it matter?"

No, it doesn't. Her dragon hummed. *Ask him to mate us.*

Brenna sputtered out loud. Ignoring Killian's look, she said to her beast, *I can't do that for many reasons, one of which being he has amnesia and that's taking advantage of him.*

I disagree. It's the only option. Once the Irish DDA calms down and allows foreigners to stay on Glenlough again, we can dissolve the mating. Easy peasy.

There's nothing easy about it.

It's your choice. Either do this or we go back to Stonefire, perhaps forever.

Killian's voice interrupted her conversation. "For someone who says we need to hurry, you're taking your bloody time telling me your plan."

Staring at Killian, she saw how the future could be happy or disastrous. If his memories returned, he might dismiss her. Apart from cooperation during missions, he always had before.

And yet if they never did, the amnesiac version of Killian might actually give her a chance.

To be honest, she had no idea which path she was rooting for. Not wanting him to remember everyone and get his dragon back would be selfish of her. And yet, she was growing to like the new version of Killian.

She wished there was another way for her to stay and avoid a conundrum, but this was her last card to play. "If you take me as your mate, I can stay in Ireland."

He didn't even blink an eye. "Mate? As in wife? I don't love you. Bloody hell, I don't even know you."

"I'm not asking for a true mating, which is similar to a human marriage, just a pretend one. I can remain your guard because we'll be expected to share a home. As soon as enough time has passed, we can dissolve it and lead our separate lives."

Killian remained silent. As the seconds ticked by, she wondered if he would give her an answer before the other escorts barged into the room.

She opened her mouth to prod him, but Killian spoke first. "I'll agree. But know upfront that I have no intention of making it a true mating, as you put it. We'll share a cottage, but don't expect romance. I'm not in a place to focus on anyone but myself."

A mixture of relief and sadness coursed through her body. Brenna hadn't thought much about matings since she was only twenty-one; however, a fake one to a man she'd long fancied but who had no memory of her wasn't exactly what she'd imagined.

Just do it, her beast growled. *Then we can stay.*

Taking a deep breath, Brenna answered before she lost her nerve. "Then it's a deal. I'll work out the details with Teagan as soon as possible. Unfortunately, you still have to spend the night in the cells."

The corner of his mouth ticked up and took her by surprise. "The threat of tying me up takes on a whole new meeting if we're to be mates."

"If you expect sex whenever you want, that's not part of the deal."

He slowly perused her body and heat followed his gaze. When he finally met her eyes again, she saw smugness. His voice was low as he murmured, "We'll see. A little sex might make the situation more authentic to everyone else. Can't have them thinking it's a sham and sending you away, now can we?"

She should be offended at his words, but her heart pounded faster and desire pooled between her legs.

Her beast hummed. *Yes, a little sex could be nice. But make him work for it.*

Her dragon's words snapped her out of her trance. "If you want anything, you have to earn it, Killian. Keep that in mind."

Amusement danced in his eyes and Brenna studied Killian's face. Who was this male and what had happened to him?

A knock on the door garnered her attention. She whispered quickly, "Keep this a secret for now, okay?" He nodded, and she let in the other Protectors.

As they put on a different set of restraints and then removed the first ones, she never took her gaze from Killian's.

Yes, she wanted to stay on Glenlough, but what the hell had she agreed to? She only hoped she wasn't in over her head.

CHAPTER TWENTY-FOUR

Two days later, Aaron stood with Teagan in one of the conference rooms inside central command. Orla, Brenna, Teagan's mother Caitlin, and Colm MacDermot were inside the room as well.

To prevent sabotage or backlash, he and Teagan were mating in private. Teagan had asked Colm to be a witness in case the DDA questioned the mating; a nonrelative's word would hold more weight. As Aaron caught Colm's eye from across the room, they nodded at each other.

His dragon spoke up. *See? I told you he's not a threat.*

Maybe not, but he had yet to prove himself before. His help with coordinating search and recovery teams after the attacks has more than earned him my respect.

Good, because we need to forge our own allies within the clan.

His dragon fell silent and Aaron looked back to Teagan. She smiled at him. Keeping the fact that she was his mate from the others would be bloody difficult. However, the most important thing was that the DDA would know about the mating as soon as possible, both in Ireland and the UK, and it would allow him to stay.

Once the clan was stable and the DDA wasn't breathing down their backs, he and Teagan would make a formal announcement.

He studied Teagan's face for any traces of regret, but only saw love. Still, as leader, Teagan was supposed to speak first. Yet she hadn't said a word in the last sixty seconds.

Aaron asked softly, "Are you having second thoughts?"

"Of course not," Teagan answered. "I was trying to think of any last-minute ideas so that Killian could attend, too. It feels wrong for my brother not to witness one of the most important days of my life."

Taking her hands in his, he squeezed. "I know, love. But you laid out all the risks with having him here. Not only could he use it as a chance to escape, but he might also share our secret before it's safe. If he regains his memories eventually, he'll forgive you."

"I hope so," she whispered. "And I'm sorry we couldn't have your mother here either. The DDA is watching us too closely to risk sneaking her onto the clan's lands."

Aaron gave a sad smile. "I'm sorry, too. But once things calm down a bit, we'll find a loophole for her to visit. An in-law should count for something."

Orla tapped her cane. "Yes, yes, it's a shame. Now, let's begin. We all have appointments to keep today."

His dragon huffed. *I feel bad for her late mate. He must've been a saint.*

Rather than answer his beast, he squeezed Teagan's hands again. She nodded and took a deep breath before saying, "Aaron Caruso, you are the best kind of male. You support me when needed, but also know when it's necessary to take charge. In addition to your strength and intelligence, you have a way of erasing my doubts and frustrations in a way no other male has done before. Your humor and cooking skills are just icing on the cake. In other words, I love you, Aaron Caruso, and I want you to stand by my side to not only be my mate, but to also help me lead the clan. Do you accept my mate claim?"

"I should ask you to keep listing my positive traits and convince me your love is genuine." She growled, and he laughed. "All right, all right. Of course I accept your bloody claim, woman."

He released one of her hands. Teagan picked up the plain silver arm cuff that would later be engraved with her name and slid it onto Aaron's tattoo-free bicep. "Then this band symbolizes my claim. I will engrave it later, so don't think of doing your own design in the meanwhile."

He winked. "We'll see how long it takes you to have it done. If it takes too long, I may need to put 'Teagan's brilliant lover' in the old language." She glared and he lightly brushed her cheek. "I look forward to what you come up with."

At his touch, she visibly relaxed. She opened her mouth, but Aaron spoke again before she could. He'd delayed long enough. "Teagan O'Shea, you're a bloody brilliant leader. You care about your people and literally put your life on the line to stand up for them. While I love your ability to lead, I also love your feisty humor and inner strength. Not to mention your cleverness and quick thinking. Oh, and of course, your sexy body." She rolled her eyes and he added, "I love the whole package, and I'm honored to lead the clan at your side. Whatever you need of me, I will do as long as it doesn't involve tying me naked to a pole in the middle of the night, out in the open for the clan to see in the morning."

She smiled wider. "That option will always be on the table."

"We'll see about that." He brought her hand to his lips and kissed the back of it. "I love you, Teagan O'Shea. Will you accept my mate claim?"

"I suppose."

His dragon roared. *That's not a good enough answer.*

Then Teagan grinned and added, "Of course I do. Now, hurry up."

Picking up the smaller, plain silver cuff, he slid it into place on her arm. His beast grunted. *I want our name there.*

In time.

Aaron pulled her up against his body and took her lips in a rough kiss. Not caring that her family was there, he took the kiss deeper. Teagan wrapped her arms around him and met him stroke for stroke. Only when she needed to come up for air did he pull away.

The sight of her kiss-bruised lips and shortness of breath instantly flashed a picture of her naked in their bed, awaiting his latest torture.

His beast spoke up again. *We should hurry. I'm sure we can make her scream our name at least once before the next clan matter arises. She is recovered and strong enough. She could use the exercise.*

Just as Aaron was about to whisper the suggestion to Teagan, Orla's voice cut through the happy moment. "Yes, yes, you'll take her to bed later. For now, you two need to hurry. Whelan Ferrell said he has important information for you. You need to go."

Whelan was one of Glenlough's intelligence analysts.

Teagan frowned. "When did Whelan have a chance to tell you anything?"

"Right before I came here," Orla answered. "But I wanted the mating done before Aaron changed his mind."

Aaron growled. "I wouldn't have changed my bloody mind."

Orla tilted her head. "Good. You've passed another test of mine, Aaron Caruso."

Aaron merely sighed. His new in-laws were never going to be easy.

Teagan jumped in. "What does he want to talk about, Gran?"

Orla leaned on her cane. "He's found the link between Hugh, the missing money, and the recent attacks. And before you ask, that's as much as I know. Whelan wanted to save the details for you."

Teagan cursed. "You should've told us as soon as possible, Gran."

Orla shrugged. "None of us have a time machine, so take off the silver cuffs and go see him."

Aaron's dragon roared. *I don't like keeping it a secret. She is our mate. The others need to know.*

And they will. But wait until things calm down a bit, aye?

I don't like always being patient, his dragon whined.

Then let's do a thorough job of cleaning house and we'll have many happy years to come.

His dragon merely grunted. Aaron traced the edge of Teagan's cuff. "This is important, love. As long as I know you're mine, that's what matters."

I don't agree, his beast stated.

Constructing a maze, Aaron tossed his dragon inside. He'd apologize later.

With a sigh, Teagan removed her arm cuff, and Aaron followed suit. Once the bands were back inside the black decorative box, Teagan handed it to her mother. "I'll entrust you with them until we can finally have them engraved." Orla opened her mouth, but Teagan shook her head. "Don't argue about being elder and the one who should look after them instead of Mum. I know you'd just end up engraving them your way. Besides, Aaron and I have pressing matters to attend to." She looked to Brenna. "We're going to have to delay your appointment with me, Brenna. Sorry."

Brenna stood taller. "I understand, but I need to talk with you soon, Teagan. I can't stress that enough."

"And we'll talk, I promise. After everything you've done for me and the clan lately, I owe you."

Aaron swore he heard Brenna muttered, "I hope you remember that," but no one else acknowledged it.

Impatient to find out what was going on so he could claim his mate properly in their own home, he tugged Teagan's hand and pulled her through the door. "Now, let's see this Whelan male and see if we can finally get the DDA's scrutiny off our back for a little while."

Teagan nodded. As they made their way down the hall and then another, she said, "Most of the victims from the attack should return home within the next week. Once they do, and Brenna as well, we'll have more freedom when it comes to fighting for a future we want."

He squeezed her hand in his and picked up his pace. As anxious as him, Teagan matched it without missing a beat.

~~~

Teagan waited for Whelan to sit in front of her desk before asking, "What do you have to report?" Whelan looked over her shoulder at Aaron, and she added, "Aaron has full clearance. Whatever you would say to me you can say in front of him."
~~~

The fifty-something male with gray hair and blue eyes took out a folder from his briefcase. Teagan took it from him and Whelan said, "Information came in today that made everything click." He waved toward the paper. "We already knew that funds had been trickling out of the clan's coffers for several months, thanks to Killian's discovery. It was difficult to trace since the transfer was made from a secret account to another international secret account."

Teagan frowned. "International?"

"Yes, this extends beyond Ireland," Whelan answered.

"Go on."

The older male clasped his hands in his lap. "As I was saying, tracing the final destination of the funds was difficult. However, Arabella MacLeod provided information she hacked from the bird drones. According to haphazardly deleted data, they all originated from a point near Belfast in Northern Ireland."

Since Clan Northcastle lived not far from Belfast, Teagan asked, "Northcastle?"

Whelan shook his head. "No, the coordinates are quite a distance from their lands. However, according to sources, it's the base of the growing Belfast dragon hunter gang."

The dragon hunters had caused a lot of chaos and damage to the British dragon clans, especially to Stonefire and Lochguard. Their attempts to set up camp in Ireland had failed thanks in part to Stonefire's help, but rumors said they had been successful in setting up a large group near Belfast in Northern Ireland. It seemed the rumors were true.

Aaron spoke up. "I thought the drones were the calling card of the Dragon Knights."

"They were originally, but it's entirely possible that the hunters bought or stole the technology," Whelan answered.

If that were true, Teagan's job as clan leader would become a lot more difficult.

Not wanting to dwell on a maybe situation she prodded, "And?"

Whelan continued, "The missing funds may have bounced around the world to hide their tracks, but they terminated at a local branch near their base."

"And where did they originate from? Did you find that out, too?" Teagan demanded.

"Aye, from Letterkenny."

Letterkenny was a town in Ireland not far from Glenlough. "Where in Letterkenny? Was it one of us?"

Whelan took a laptop from his briefcase, laid it on the desk, typed something and said, "To answer who did it, you need to see this."

He turned the screen to face her and Aaron and clicked Play.

A video played with no sound, but that wasn't important. What was relevant was the person sitting down at a desk with one of the bank staff, probably making a bank transfer. Teagan had seen a picture of the female not too long ago during one of her briefings with Killian, before the leadership challenge.

It was the human female her clan member Renny Walsh had been seeing, named Colleen.

Her dragon roared, but Teagan ignored her. "We need to talk to both the female and Renny."

"Already done. I didn't want to bother you without evidence," Whelan stated.

Aaron spoke up. "Then tell us what you found out."

Whelan didn't hesitate, despite the order coming from Aaron. "Renny's female was the one to leak the information to

Killarney. Renny had no idea—the widow had merely been using him for information. Someone in her family was killed by a rogue dragon fifty years ago. The family still holds a grudge and wanted revenge. When Renny ran into her in the countryside by chance, she seized on an idea."

Aaron whistled. "Talk about cock blindness."

Whelan ignored the remark and continued, "On top of that, Hugh wasn't invited to participate in the plan until later. Originally, it was made without him. But when word spread of him joining the challenge, Orin Daly seized on the additional distraction. Orin and Padraig only knew about Teagan's secret and had no idea the information was coming from the widow."

Teagan leaned forward. "And the money? Renny can barely operate his phone. There's no bloody way he could've embezzled from our accounts."

"No, he didn't do it," Whelan answered. "But the human female's nephew works with computers. In short, he had the skills necessary and helped out. The nephew and the widow figured that donating money to the Belfast dragon hunters would only increase their chances of bringing us down. Thanks to the widow's relationship with Renny, she learned about the time and place of the trials, which she shared with the dragon hunters. Orin and Padraig had no idea about the funds. And, well, the rest is history."

And to think the entire headache of the last week was because a family had held a grudge for over fifty years.

Her beast said, *It shouldn't surprise you. We'll just have to be careful from now on about which humans are allowed to see any of our clan members.*

To say the least. At this rate, we're going to have to change a lot of things.

Don't worry, we'll be fine.

Aaron's voice filled the room. "You said you spoke to them already, right? Where are they now?"

"Still in custody." Whelan looked at Teagan. "What do you want to do with them?"

She sighed. "I don't really have a choice but to turn them over to the DDA. Otherwise, the Belfast hunters will think it's okay to attack us again. However, if the Irish government is aware of their meddling, they'll reach out to both the British Parliament and the Northern Ireland Assembly. Hopefully it will put the Belfast hunters at the top of their watch lists." Whelan bobbed his head and Teagan added, "But maybe leave out the part about Arabella MacLeod's involvement and say one of our own techs hacked the bird drones. While it's not illegal for our clans to work together, I don't want to experience extra scrutiny if I don't have to."

"Of course," Whelan said. "Unless you have any other questions, I'll set things in motion."

Teagan smiled at the older dragonman. "You've done a brilliant job, Whelan. Thank you. You can go."

Once Teagan and Aaron were alone in her office again, Aaron laid his hands on her shoulders and squeezed gently. "I had no idea about anyone secretly seeing a human female." He looked around the room. "I'm going to have to disrupt your system to get caught up. Otherwise, I'm going to be next to useless to you."

She placed a hand over one of his. "For you, I might just consider tweaking my system. Anything to make it easier to have more help. If we aren't careful, things will spin out of control in Ireland. Not only that, we could have another war with Northcastle, too, if I don't smooth things between us soon.

Especially if the hunters drive them out of Northern Ireland. Then Northcastle will be looking for new territory."

"We won't let it come to that, love. I'm not afraid of hard work. I'll help you sort out the clan as quickly as possible."

She was about to tell Aaron how she loved him, but her phone beeped with a message. It was a reminder about her appointment with Brenna.

Aaron leaned down and kissed her cheek. "Go. I'll start working here."

She met his gaze. As expected, she didn't see anger or hurt, only understanding. "We'll have our celebratory night of hot sex as soon as I can manage it. I promise."

He winked. "It just gives me more time to plan what I want to do to you."

She turned and drew his head down for a kiss. Once she released his lips, she murmured, "Good. Because I might even let you tie me up, if you prove yourself useful."

He growled and she laughed.

Aaron pulled away and helped her to her feet. "Go, before the temptation to take you on the desk becomes too great."

As much as Teagan wanted to try his suggestion, she forced herself to walk to the door. "Reach out to me when you need me. I'll keep my meeting with Brenna as short as possible."

With a wave, she exited the room. It was time to have what could be her final meeting with Brenna before the English female had to go back to Stonefire.

At the thought, sadness flooded her body. The female was more than useful; Teagan felt a kindred spirit with regards to goals and proving one's self.

But Teagan pushed aside her own desires. There was nothing she could do but send the dragonwoman home.

Chapter Twenty-Five

Brenna paced the front room of Killian's secured cottage. In an effort to save time in case Teagan wanted to question Killian, Brenna had requested Teagan to meet her at his place to discuss her future.

While she understood Teagan was the leader, she was still late, and Brenna just wanted to get this conversation over with.

Killian appeared in the doorway between the front room and the dining room. "All pacing does is irritate the hell out of me. Sit down and wait."

Brenna turned on him. "I thought we established that neither one of us would be giving orders to the other. We only make requests."

He raised an eyebrow. "Then would you sit down, my lady? Before you wear a fucking hole in my carpet."

Her dragon growled. *Are you sure we can't wrestle him to the ground and teach him a lesson? He might've been stronger before, but he doesn't have his beast. We will win.*

No.

She closed the distance between them. "You should be nicer to me. After all, I'm the reason you aren't wearing restraints and are out of that jail cell."

"It may be a bit bigger, but this cottage is still a prison."

Just as she opened her mouth, someone knocked on the front door. She raised her chin and said, "We'll discuss this later, unless you're backing out?"

"No bloody way. You're probably my best chance at freedom."

She wanted to ask what the fuck he was talking about, but the knock grew more insistent, so she raced to the door. Opening it, Teagan stood there. Brenna stepped aside. "Come in."

Brenna half expected Killian to disappear and leave delivering the news to her, but when she and Teagan entered the front room, he sat sprawled in a chair. He gave a mock salute. "Clan leader."

Brenna watched Teagan's face closely. Having her brother play the arsehole couldn't be easy for her.

And yet, Teagan's expression never changed from neutral. She moved her gaze to Brenna. "What did you need to talk to me about? Should we go somewhere private?"

Brenna's heart rate kicked up as she moved to stand next to Killian's chair. She quickly glanced down, and he gave an almost imperceptible nod.

She had to be dreaming. There was no way that the amnesiac, moody version of Killian would encourage her.

Her beast huffed. *Forget about him for now. We need Teagan's permission.*

Clearing her throat, Brenna met Teagan's eyes again. "As you know, the Irish DDA has said all foreigners must leave the clan for the foreseeable future."

Teagan frowned. "I would reverse it if I could, Brenna, but you know I can't."

Her heart beat faster. Taking a deep breath, she nodded. "I'm aware. But I found a way to stay." She motioned toward Killian. "Killian has agreed to mate me."

Teagan blinked. "What?"

"It's true, great leader," Killian drawled. "Brenna is the only reason I haven't tried to escape yet. If you want me to stay in one place, you'll let us do the deed."

Teagan put out a hand. "Wait, did I miss something?"

Brenna answered, "You've had a lot on your plate or I would've told you sooner. But think about it—I could stay to help you fill in the gaps with the Protectors. And once the Irish DDA eases its restrictions, Killian and I can dissolve the mating. All we have to do is pretend it's real in the beginning and Killian's agreed to do that."

Yes, yes, her dragon said. *I still say sex will make it authentic.*

Hush for now. This is important.

Teagan looked at Brenna, then Killian, and back. "Let's say I agree. With a few exceptions, the clan must think it's a true mating and not a farce. Otherwise, the DDA may sniff around. That could end up getting all of us into trouble. Are you two really going to be able to keep up the ruse? While I trust you, Brenna, I don't know who Killian is anymore."

Killian placed a hand on Brenna's lower back. The heat of his palm raced through her body and ended between her thighs.

Her dragon growled. *It's just a touch. Calm down.*

Rubbing slow circles on her back, Killian said, "We can both play our parts." He looked up at her. "Can't we, darling?"

She cleared her throat and placed a hand on his shoulder. "Of course we can, *love.*" She looked back to Teagan. "So? Will you allow it?"

"This could end badly on so many levels."

Brenna forced herself to walk away from Killian. The loss of his warm hand made her dragon whimper, but she ignored her and closed the distance to Teagan. "Everything will be fine. It's just a temporary arrangement that benefits everyone. But we can't do it without your permission. We'll need you to vouch for us if the DDA questions the mating."

Teagan searched her gaze. "I owe you for your part in keeping the clan safe the other day. This would fulfill that favor. Do you really want to waste it on this?"

Brenna nodded. "Yes. I've never felt as much at home as I have on Glenlough. Not to mention I have much to learn from you and your grandmother. I can't do any of that if I go home to Stonefire. Besides, I'm young and not interested in finding a real mate for many years to come. So living with him"—she motioned toward Killian—"won't be a problem. Well, beyond dealing with his behavior."

To his credit, Killian didn't make a remark. For whatever reason, he wanted Teagan to agree.

For what seemed like the longest minute of Brenna's life, she merely stared at Teagan and waited.

When Glenlough's leader finally let out a sigh, hope bloomed in Brenna's chest. Teagan spoke up again. "Fine. But do it quickly. We'll use the mating ceremony and ensuing celebration to lift the clan's spirits. However—" She paused and stared daggers at Killian. "—you must convince the clan this is a true mating. At the first sign of doubt, I'll dissolve the mating myself and send Brenna back to Stonefire. That will include you trying to run away without her. Understood, Killian?"

Brenna watched Killian's face. For all that he'd lost his memories and his dragon, he was still bloody good at keeping all emotions from showing. He folded his hands over his stomach before answering, "I'm staying around for now. That's all I'll say for the moment."

Brenna frowned. "Killian."

He rolled his eyes. "Fine, I promise not to escape in the near future." He met her gaze. "Is that better, *darling*?"

"Yes, *love*."

The way they used endearments was the equivalent of calling each other bastards.

Her beast hummed. *Good. The tension will only make the sex hotter.*

I didn't agree to it yet.

You will.

Teagan clapped her hands. "Then it's time to put everything into motion. I want this done as soon as possible, just in case the DDA orders all healthy foreign visitors to leave straight away. Here's what needs to be done."

As Teagan rattled off a list of orders of what to do, Brenna tried to pay attention. She really did.

But Killian never took his gaze from her face. When he finally gave her body a slow once-over, her dragon spoke up. *Yummy. He will be fun to fuck and play with.*

He finally met her gaze again, and Brenna stopped breathing at the heat in his eyes.

Bloody hell. A female could get used to that look.

For the millionth time, Brenna hoped she hadn't gotten in over her head. The mating would be a fake, and she needed to remember that.

~~~
~~~

Later that evening, Aaron hugged Teagan's naked body tighter against his chest. It was strange to think he had gained a new home and mate in the same day after thinking he might never find a female to spend his life with.

His dragon spoke up. *We will never be alone again. The bad brought us to the good.*

Bloody hell, you and your philosophical statements.

His beast yawned. *They come to me after sex. So, get used to it, unless you're going to keep a separate bedroom from Teagan?*

Never.

That's what I thought.

His dragon dozed and Aaron contented himself with listening to Teagan breathing and treasuring her heat against his chest.

However, no matter how much he stroked her back, she didn't relax against him. He murmured, "Please tell me you still aren't thinking about Brenna and Killian. That would be weird seeing as we're both naked and smell of sex."

Teagan sighed. "No. But I am thinking about how it's wrong to hide our mating from the clan."

He placed a finger under her chin and gently forced her to look up at him. "I'm ready to share it with them whenever you are, love. But I'll leave it to you to best judge your people."

"They're your people, too, now, Aaron." She ran one of her hands back and forth against his chest hair. "Tell me what you think we should do."

His dragon peeked his head up. *I say state she's ours in the great hall as soon as possible. Too many males have started to look at her in a new light, as if she's now a delectable treat to devour.*

Aaron ignored his beast to answer Teagan. "As much as I want to shout it from the rooftops, I think we first need to quietly ensure there aren't any other potential traitors or accessories to treason living inside Glenlough. As it is, both Greenpeak and Wildheath are in the midst of a leadership crisis with Orin and Padraig both dead. Too much too soon could cause chaos."

She sighed. "I was thinking exactly the same thing."

He kissed her forehead. "We should have a few weeks before the DDA will start checking for any foreigners still on our land. As long as we announce our mating before then, we should be fine. That human female Trevina seemed to like you. Hopefully she'll give us a warning before more DDA staff visit Glenlough."

When Teagan remained quiet, Aaron's dragon snarled. *She is still worried and tense. We should fix it. A break will do her good.*

Without another word, Aaron rolled until Teagan was under him. He pinned her hands above her head and threaded his fingers through hers. "Teagan." When she met his gaze, he continued, "I love you and will never ask you to put the clan second. However, you deserve to relax for an hour. And for that hour, I'm going to make you forget about everything but my name. Afterward we can plan our next steps until the wee hours. Deal?"

She smiled. "I might start to regret giving you two hours of every day to do whatever you want, emergency excepting."

He rocked his hips against hers. "If you ever start to regret it, love, then I'm not doing my job."

Wrapping a leg around his waist, she whispered, "Then remind me why I hired you for this task."

With a growl, Aaron took her lips as he pushed his cock inside her. He moved his lower body and Teagan was soon moaning into his mouth and melting into the bed.

Yes, yes, she is ours, always and forever.

Aaron increased his rhythm, and soon Teagan broke their kiss to shout his name. Aaron followed suit and pleasure coursed through his body as he let go.

As they came down, he cuddled her close, content to hold his future in his arms and hope that everything worked out as it should. It'd taken many mistakes for him to find where he truly belonged, but now that he'd found it, he was never letting go.

EPILOGUE

Many Months Later

Teagan leaned against Aaron's side as she watched the clan eat, dance, and enjoy themselves below on the main floor. After everything that had happened over the last year, they could finally all breathe a sigh of relief.

What with betrayals, Killian's journey, and even Teagan remaining leader despite having a mate, there had been a lot of changes.

Her beast grunted. *All good ones.*

For the most part. Still, I look forward to years of boring paperwork and hand cramps.

Aaron's whisper interrupted her conversation with her dragon. "You're not overly tired, are you? As much as I want to think I'm irresistible and you can't keep your hands off me, your energy levels have been low lately."

She shook her head and placed a hand on her lower belly. "No. The baby is behaving for the moment and not making me ill."

"As he or she should. It is my child, after all."

She gave him a half-hearted smack. "Don't sound as if you did it all by yourself. The baby is mine as well."

He hugged her tighter against his side. "I sure hope so. Otherwise, I don't want to know what sort of alien came to visit you and put their alien baby inside your uterus."

"Aaron, stop being ridiculous."

He chuckled. "Okay, I'll restrain myself for now, even though that was an order and not a request." She gave him the double finger salute, and he added, "Well, what with the treaties under way and the threats vanquished for the foreseeable future, you're going to have a lot more time alone with me. I hope you're not changing your mind and getting tired of me so soon."

Raising her head, she looked up at her mate. "Don't even joke about that, Aaron. If you don't know how much I love you by now, then you never will."

He traced a finger down her cheek. "I think by now we love each other the same amount. Although, if you need some convincing, we could sneak away for an hour. My dragon and I can tag team to ensure you know how much we both treasure you."

She fought a smile and lost the battle. Aaron did spoil her. "As tempting as that is, we need to dance first or the clan will notice we're gone."

He raised his brows. "Surely in your condition you can make excuses."

She rolled her eyes. "Right, and give fodder for the rumor mills about how I can't handle a little dragon-shifter growing inside of me. No, we need to do the opposite." She leaned back and stood. Putting out an arm, she asked, "Will you dance with me, Aaron Caruso?"

Without hesitating, he rose and threaded his arm through hers. "Let's show everyone how it's done. But no bloody fancy Irish dancing."

She grinned. "You're getting better." He growled, and she laughed. "Okay, then we'll do the same as our first dance. You know that one pretty well. And since I have clothes on, you shouldn't be distracted."

His gaze zeroed in on her breasts, and Teagan's nipples tightened as he murmured, "There's plenty to distract me."

Taking a deep breath, she thought of DDA regulations and training exercises to keep her cheeks from flushing pink. After a lot of practice, she was finally getting the hang of keeping desire from showing plain on her face.

Her beast huffed. *I don't understand why you try to hide it.*

It's a human thing. That should be enough of an explanation.

Whatever. Just hurry up and dance so we can play with Aaron and his dragon. I have a few new ideas of how to tease him.

Her dragon fell silent as they walked past Orla talking with Aaron's mother and Teagan's mother. She waved to her mother-in-law. Molly Caruso and her own mother had become fast friends. Together, they sometimes even won against Orla.

She and Aaron soon reached the audio setup. Teagan asked for the song and guided Aaron to the dance floor. As the first notes filled the air, Teagan stared at her mate and couldn't stop smiling.

Between her mate, her future child, and her family, she had plenty of love. The clan only added more.

And together they would make it the best future they could.

Dear Reader:

Did you enjoy this story? Then please consider leaving a review. :)

Before you ask, yes, Brenna and Killian will have a book. :D However, before the release of *Craved by the Dragon* (their full-length story, out in March 2018) comes Kai and Jane's follow-up novella, *Finding the Dragon*, in October 2017. The events in their story happen at the same time as Brenna and Killian's book, but in England and Wales instead of Ireland. Kai's sister Delia will feature heavily and the story will help set up the future story arc on Snowridge. You can read more details in my Author's Note section toward the end of the backmatter.

To keep up-to-date on releases, please join my newsletter on my website (www.jessiedonovan.com).

Please turn the page for an excerpt from the first book in my science fiction romance series, *The Conquest*.

With Gratitude,
Jessie Donovan

The Conquest
(Kelderan Runic Warriors #1)

Leader of a human colony planet, Taryn Demara has much more on her plate than maintaining peace or ensuring her people have enough to eat. Due to a virus that affects male embryos in the womb, there is a shortage of men. For decades, her people have enticed ships to their planet and tricked the men into staying. However, a ship hasn't been spotted in eight years. So when the blip finally shows on the radar, Taryn is determined to conquer the newcomers at any cost to ensure her people's survival.

Prince Kason tro de Vallen needs to find a suitable planet for his people to colonize. The Kelderans are running out of options despite the fact one is staring them in the face—Planet Jasvar. Because a group of Kelderan scientists disappeared there a decade ago never to return, his people dismiss the planet as cursed. But Kason doesn't believe in curses and takes on the mission to explore the planet to prove it. As his ship approaches Jasvar, a distress signal chimes in and Kason takes a group down to the planet's surface to explore. What he didn't expect was for a band of females to try and capture him.

As Taryn and Kason measure up and try to outsmart each other, they soon realize they've found their match. The only question is whether they ignore the spark between them and focus on their respective people's survival or can they find a path where they both succeed?

Excerpt from *The Conquest*:

Chapter One

Taryn Demara stared at the faint blip on the decades-old radar. Each pulse of light made her heart race faster. *This is it.* Her people might have a chance to survive.

Using every bit of restraint she had, Taryn prevented her voice from sounding too eager as she asked, "Are you sure it's a spaceship?"

Evaine Benoit, her head of technology, nodded. "Our equipment is outdated, but by the size and movement, it has to be a ship."

Taryn's heart beat double-time as she met her friend's nearly black-eyed gaze. "How long do we have before they reach us?"

"If they maintain their current trajectory, I predict eighteen hours, give or take. It's more than enough time to get the planet ready."

"Right," Taryn said as she stood tall again. "Keep me updated on any changes. If the ship changes course, boost the distress signal."

Evaine raised her brows. "Are you sure? The device is on its last legs. Any boost in power could cause a malfunction. I'm not sure my team or I can fix it again if that happens."

She gripped her friend's shoulder. "After eight years of waiting, I'm willing to risk it. I need that ship to reach Jasvar and send a team down to our planet."

Otherwise, we're doomed was left unsaid.

Without another word, Taryn raced out of the aging technology command center and went in search of her best strategist. There was much to do and little time to do it.

Nodding at some of the other members of her settlement as she raced down the corridors carved into the mountainside, Taryn wondered what alien race was inside the ship on the radar. Over the past few hundred years, the various humanoid additions to the once human-only colony had added extra skin tones, from purple to blue to even a shimmery gold. Some races even had slight telepathic abilities that had been passed down to their offspring.

To be honest, Taryn didn't care what they looked like or what powers they possessed. As long as they were genetically compatible with her people, it meant Taryn and several other women might finally have a chance at a family. The "Jasvar Doom Virus" as they called it, killed off most male embryos in the womb, to the point only one male was born to every five females. Careful genealogical charts had been maintained to keep the gene pool healthy. However, few women were willing to share their partner with others, which meant the male population grew smaller by the year.

It didn't help that Jasvar had been set up as a low-technology colony, which meant they didn't have the tools necessary to perform the procedures in the old tales of women being impregnated without sex. The technique had been called in-something or other. Taryn couldn't remember the exact name from her great-grandmother's stories from her childhood.

Not that it was an option anyway. Jasvar's technology was a hodgepodge of original technology from the starter colonists and a few gadgets from their conquests and alien additions over the years. It was a miracle any of it still functioned.

Aiding the Dragon

The only way to prevent the extinction of her people was to capture and introduce alien males into their society. Whoever had come up with the idea of luring aliens to the planet's surface and developing the tools necessary to get them to stay had been brilliant. Too bad his or her name had been lost to history.

Regardless of who had come up with the idea, Taryn was damned if she would be the leader to fail the Jasvarian colony. Since the old technology used to put out the distress signals was failing, Taryn had a different sort of plan for the latest alien visitors.

She also wanted their large spaceship and all of its technology.

Of course, her grand plans would be all for nothing if she couldn't entice and trap the latest aliens first. To do that, she needed to confer with Nova Drakven, her head strategist.

Rounding the last corner, Taryn waltzed into Nova's office. The woman's pale blue face met hers. Raising her silver brows, she asked, "Is it true about the ship?"

With a nod, Taryn moved to stand in front of Nova's desk. "Yes. It should be here in about eighteen hours."

Nova reached for a file on her desk. "Good. Then I'll present the plan to the players, and we can wait on standby until we know for sure where the visiting shuttle lands."

Taryn shook her head and started pacing. "I need you to come up with a new plan, Nova."

"Why? I've tweaked what went wrong last time. We shouldn't have any problems."

"It's not that." Taryn stopped pacing and met her friend's gaze. "This time, we need to do more than entice a few males to stay. Our planet was originally slated to be a low-tech colony, but with the problems that arose, that's no longer an option. We need supplies and knowledge, which means negotiating with the mother ship for their people."

"Let me get this straight—you want to convince the vastly technologically advanced aliens that we are superior, their crew's lives are in danger, and that they need to pay a ransom to get them back?"

Taryn grinned. "See, you do understand me."

Nova sighed. "You have always been crazy and a little reckless."

"Not reckless, Nova. Just forward-thinking. You stage the play, think of a few ideas about how to get the ship, and I'll find a way to make it work."

"Always the super leader to the rescue. Although one day, your luck may run out, Taryn."

Nova and Taryn were nearly the same age, both in their early thirties, and had grown up together. Nova was her best friend and one of the few people Taryn was unafraid to speak her fears with. "As long as my luck lasts through this ordeal, I'm okay with that. I can't just sit and watch our people despairing if another year or ten pass before there's new blood. If we had a way to get a message to Earth, it would make everything easier. But, we don't have that capability."

Nova raised her brows. "Finding a way to contact Earth or the Earth Colony Alliance might be an easier goal than taking over a ship."

"The message would take years to get there and who knows if the ECA would even send a rescue ship to such a distant colony." Taryn shook her head. "I can't rely on chance alone. I'll send a message from the alien ship, but I also want the technology to save us in the near future, too. I much prefer being in control."

Nova snorted. "Sometimes a little too much in control, in my opinion."

"A leader letting loose doesn't exactly instill confidence," she drawled.

"Then promise me that once you save the planet, you let me show you some fun. No one should die before riding the sloping Veran waterfalls."

Taryn sighed and sank into the chair in front of Nova's desk. "Fine. But how about we focus on capturing the aliens first?"

Nova removed a sheaf of crude paper made from the purple wood of the local trees and took out an ink pot and golden feather. "I'll come up with a fool-proof capture plan, but I hope you keep me in the loop about what happens next."

"I will when it's time. I need to see who we're dealing with before making concrete plans."

Dipping her feather into the ink pot, Nova scratched a few notes on the purple paper. "Then let me get to work. The staging is mostly done already, but I need to think beyond that. Since we've never tried to capture a large ship before, it's going to take some time. I think someone captured a shuttle in the past, but we'll see if I can find the record."

"You always go on about how you love challenges."

"Don't remind me." She made a shooing motion toward the door. "And this is one of the few times I can tell my settlement leader to get lost and let me work."

Taryn stood. "If you need me, I'll be in the outside garden."

"Fine, fine. Just go. You're making it hard to concentrate." Nova looked up with a smile. "And you're also delaying my next project."

"Do I want to know?"

"It's called Operation Fun Times." Nova pointed her quill. "I sense you're going to land an alien this time. You're a talented individual, except when it comes to flirting. I'm going to help with that."

Shaking her head, Taryn muttered, "Have fun," and left her old-time friend to her own devices. Maybe someday Nova would understand that while Taryn missed the antics of their youth, she enjoyed taking care of her people more.

Still, she'd admit that it would be nice to finally have the chance to get a man of her own. Most of her family was gone, and like many of the women of her age group, Taryn would love the option to start one.

Not now, Demara. You won't have a chance unless you succeed in capturing the visitors.

With the play planning in motion, Taryn had one more important task to set up before she could also pore through the records and look for ideas.

As much as she wished for everything to go smoothly, it could take a turn and end up horribly wrong. In that case, she needed an out. Namely, she needed to erase memories. The trick would be conferring with her head medicine woman to find the balance between erasing memories and rendering the aliens brain-dead. As the early Jasvarians had discovered, the forgetful plant was both a blessing and a curse. Without it, they'd never have survived this long. However, in the wrong dose, it could turn someone into a vegetable and ruin their chances.

Don't worry. Matilda knows what she's doing. Picking up her pace, Taryn exited the mountain into the late-day sun. The faint purple and blue hues of the mountains and trees were an everyday sight to her, but she still found the colors beautiful. Her great-grandmother's tales had been full of green leaves and blue skies back on Earth. A part of Taryn wanted to see another world, but the leader in her would never abandon the people of Jasvar.

Looking to the pinkish sky, she only hoped the visitors fell for her tricks. Otherwise, Taryn might have to admit defeat and prepare her people for the worst.

~~~

Prince Kason tro el Vallen of the royal line of Vallen stared at his ship's main viewing screen. The blue, pink, and purple hues of the planet hid secrets Kason was determined to discover. After years of fighting his father's wishes and then the ensuing days of travel from Keldera to the unnamed planet, he was anxious to get started.

Aaric, his head pilot, stated, "Ten hours until we pull into orbit, your highness."

Kason disliked the title but had learned over time that to fight it was pointless. "Launch a probe to investigate."

"Yes, your highness."

As Aaric sent the request to the necessary staff, the silver-haired form of Ryven Xanna, Kason's best friend and the head warrior trainer on the ship, walked up to him. "We need to talk."

Kason nodded. Ryven would only ask to talk if it was important. "I can spare a few minutes. Aaric, you have the command."

The pair of them entered Kason's small office off the central command area. The instant the door slid shut, Ryven spoke up again. "Some of the men's markings are tinged yellow. They're nervous. No doubt thanks to the rumors of a monster on the planet's surface."
~~~

"There is no monster. There's a logical explanation as to why our team of scientists disappeared on Jasvar ten years ago."

"I agree with you, but logic doesn't always work with the lower-ranked officers and the common soldiers."

Kason clasped his hand behind his back. "You wouldn't ask to talk with me unless you have a solution. Tell me what it is, Ryv."

"I know it's not standard protocol for you to lead the first landing party, but if you go, it will instill courage in the others," Ryven answered.

Kason raised a dark-blue eyebrow. "Tell me you aren't among the nervous."

Ryven shrugged and pointed to one of the markings that peeked above his collar. "The dark blue color tells you all you need to know."

Dark blue signaled that a Kelderan was at peace and free of negative emotions.

"You are better at controlling your emotions than anyone I have ever met. You could be deathly afraid and would somehow keep your markings dark blue."

The corner of Ryven's mouth ticked up. "The trick has worked well for me over the years."

"We don't have time for reminiscing, Ryv. You're one of the few who speaks the truth to me. Don't change now."

"Honestly?" Ryven shrugged. "I'm not any more nervous or worried than any other mission. The unknown enemy just means we need to be cautious more than ever."

"Agreed. I will take the first landing party and leave Thorin in charge. Assemble your best warriors and send me a message when they're ready. I want to talk with them and instill bravery beforehand."

In a rare sign of emotion, Ryven gripped Kason's bicep. "Bravery is all well and fine, but if there is a monster we can't defeat, promise you'll pull back. Earning your father's praise isn't worth your life."

"I'm a little insulted at your implication. I wouldn't be a general in my own right if I lived by foolish displays of machismo."

Ryven studied him a second before adding, "Just because you're a general now doesn't mean you have to talk like one with me."

Kason remembered their childhood days, before they'd both been put on the path of a warrior. Kason and Ryven had pulled pranks on their siblings and had reveled in coming up with stupid competitions, such as who could reach the top of a rock face first in freezing temperatures or who could capture a poisonous shimmer fly with nothing but their fingers.

But neither of them were boys anymore. Displaying emotion changed the color of the rune-like markings on their bodies, which exposed weakness. Warriors couldn't afford to show any weakness. It was one of the reasons higher-ranked officers weren't allowed to take wives, not even if they found one of their potential destined brides; the females would become easy targets.

Not that Kason cared. A wife would do nothing to prove his worth as a soldier to his father, the king. On top of that, being a warrior was all Kason knew. Giving it up would take away his purpose.

Pushing aside thoughts of his father and his future, Kason motioned toward the door. "Go and select the best soldiers to assist with the landing party. I have my own preparations to see to."

"I'll go if you promise one thing."

"What?"

"You allow me to be part of the landing party."

Kason shook his head. "I can't. In the event of my death, I need you here."

"Thorin is your second and will assume command. Give me the honor of protecting you and the others during the mission."

Deep down, in the place where Kason locked up any emotion, a small flicker of indecision flashed. Ryven was more Kason's brother than his real-life brother, Keltor.

Yet to contain Ryven on the ship would be like a slap in the face; the honor of protecting a prince such as Kason was the highest form of trust to one of the Kelderan people.

Locking down his emotions, Kason followed his logical brain. "You may attend. But on-planet, you become a soldier. I can't treat you as my friend."

Ryven put out a hand and Kason shook it to seal their agreement. "I'm aware of protocol. I teach it day in and day out. But I will be the best damned soldier of the group. And if it comes to it, I will push you out of the way to protect your life."

Kason released his friend's hand. "I won't let it come to that."

"Good. When shall we rendezvous?"

Glancing at the small screen projecting an image of the multicolored planet, he answered, "Nine hours. That will give all of us a chance to sleep before performing the prebattle ritual. You can lead the men through their meditation and warm-up maneuvers after that."

Ryven nodded. "I'll see you then."

The trainer exited the room, and Kason turned toward his private viewing screen to study the planet rumored to host the most feared monster in the region. One that had supposedly taken hundreds of men's lives over the years. The story was always the same—a small contingent of men disappeared from any group that landed on the surface. No one remembered how they were captured or if they were even alive. Anytime a second party landed, a few more would be taken.

Over time, the planet had earned a reputation. Even the most adventure-seeking ruffians had stayed away.

However, Kason dismissed it as folklore. Whatever was on that planet, he wouldn't allow it to defeat him or his men. Kason would bring honor to his family with a victory. He also hoped to give his people the gift of a new planet. Keldera was overpopulated, and its resources were stretched beyond the limit. The Kelderans desperately needed a new colony and hadn't been able to locate one that was suitable. The planet on the view screen showed all the signs of being a near-perfect fit.

Even if the fiercest monster in existence resided on that planet, Kason wouldn't retreat from an enemy. Death was an accepted part of being a Kelderan soldier.

Want to read the rest?
The Conquest is available in paperback

For exclusive content and updates, sign up for my newsletter at:

http://www.jessiedonovan.com

Author's Note

Thanks for reading Aaron and Teagan's story. You may have noticed that while their book has a happy ending, there are still questions lingering about how they got there. I did this deliberately because *Aiding the Dragon* and *Craved by the Dragon* (Killian and Brenna's story) form a mini-story arc within the Stonefire series. The background story spans two books and Killian's story will pick up right after the end of Chapter 25 of this book. I'll be doing something similar on Snowridge, too, in the not-too-distant future. Why? Well, experiencing my world from other points of view helps extend the series and (hopefully) keeps it from going stale. It also gives you, the reader, a chance to experience other dragon clans without me creating new series. Lochguard will continue on its own, but I don't expect any of the other clans to get brand new series of their own. I only have so much time to write and I don't want to confuse the overall storyline too much. Besides, I like to write non-dragon books, too, and need time for that!

I hope you also noticed that this book was longer than almost all of my other books. (Only *Healed by the Dragon* is longer, and only by a few thousand words.) I finally let go and wrote as long as I wanted without stress. The reason? Next year (in 2018) I'm raising my prices by about USD $1 or local currency equivalent to allow me to write longer. Many shapeshifter romances are about half the length of mine and charge almost the same price. As you can imagine, a longer book takes more time to write, hence the rise. It will be the first increase since I started publishing in 2013 and I think it's reasonable. I hope you agree and continue to follow the series. :)

Whew, with all of that all of the way I have some people I need to thank for their help in getting this book out to the world:

- To Becky Johnson and her team at Hot Tree Editing—you all are amazing. Becky gets me and helps my stories shine.
- To Clarissa Yeo of Yocla Designs—you yet again designed a beautiful cover that captures my couple perfectly. I couldn't imagine my series without your magic.
- To Donna H., Alyson S., and Iliana G.—My three betas are amazing and provide valuable honesty. Not only that, they catch the little typos that slip through. All three of you are invaluable. <3

And as always, I thank you, the reader, for supporting my dragons this long. When I first published *Sacrificed to the Dragon* I had no idea I'd reach double digits with the series, but we'll be there with Kai and Jane's release in October! Thanks a million times from my heart for not only reading, but also spreading the word. Word-of-mouth is more powerful than you think.

My next release will be *Finding the Dragon* (Stonefire Dragons #10), out in October 2017. This will be Kai and Jane's follow-up novella, but it will also move the overall storyline forward. I hope you follow their story with me later this year.

Thanks again for reading.

About the Author

Jessie Donovan wrote her first story at age five, and after discovering *The Dragonriders of Pern* series by Anne McCaffrey in junior high, she realized people actually wanted to read stories like those floating around inside her head. From there on out, she was determined to tap into her over-active imagination and write a book someday.

After living abroad for five years and earning degrees in Japanese, Anthropology, and Secondary Education, she buckled down and finally wrote her first full-length book. While that story will never see the light of day, it laid the world-building groundwork of what would become her debut paranormal romance, *Blaze of Secrets*. In late 2014, she became a *New York Times* and *USA Today* bestseller.

Jessie loves to interact with readers, and when not reading or traipsing around some foreign country on a shoestring, she can often be found on Facebook. Check out her pages below:

http://www.facebook.com/JessieDonovanAuthor

And don't forget to sign-up for her newsletter to receive sneak peeks and inside information. You can sign-up on her website:

http:///www.jessiedonovan.com

Made in the USA
Coppell, TX
16 October 2021